burnt sugar

burnt sugar

avni doshi

The Overlook Press, New York

This edition first published in hardcover in 2021 by
The Overlook Press, an imprint of ABRAMS
195 Broadway, 9th floor
New York, NY 10007
www.overlookpress.com

Abrams books are available at special discounts when purchased in quantity
for premiums and promotions as well as fundraising or educational use.
Special editions can also be created to specification. For details,
contact specialsales@abramsbooks.com or the address above.

Library of Congress Control Number: 2020944988

Printed and bound in the United States

3 5 7 9 10 8 6 4 2
ISBN: 978-1-4197-5292-6
eISBN: 978-1-64700-226-8

ABRAMS The Art of Books
195 Broadway, New York, NY 10007
abramsbooks.com

For Nishi, Naren and Pushpa the Brave

Ma, ami tumar kachchey aamar porisoi diti diti biakul oya dʒai
Mother, I'm so tired, tired of introducing myself to you

Rehna Sultana, 'Mother'

I would be lying if I said my mother's misery has never given me pleasure.

I suffered at her hands as a child, and any pain she subsequently endured appeared to me to be a kind of redemption – a rebalancing of the universe, where the rational order of cause and effect aligned.

But now, I can't even the tally between us.

The reason is simple: my mother is forgetting, and there is nothing I can do about it. There is no way to make her remember the things she has done in the past, no way to baste her in guilt. I used to bring up instances of her cruelty, casually, over tea, and watch her face curve into a frown. Now, she mostly can't recall what I'm talking about; her eyes are distant with perpetual cheer. Anyone witnessing this will touch my hand and whisper: Enough now. She doesn't remember, poor thing.

The sympathy she elicits in others gives rise to something acrid in me.

I suspected something a year ago, when she began wandering around the house at night. Her maid, Kashta, would call me, frightened.

'Your mother is looking for plastic liners,' Kashta said on one occasion. 'In case you wet your bed.'

I held the phone away from my ear and searched the nightstand for my glasses. Beside me, my husband was still asleep and his earplugs glowed neon in the dark.

'She must be dreaming,' I said.

Kashta seemed unconvinced. 'I didn't know you used to wet your bed.'

I put the phone down and, for the rest of the night, was unable to sleep. Even in her madness, my mother had managed to humiliate me.

One day, the sweeper girl rang the bell at home and Ma didn't know who she was. There were other incidents – when she forgot how to pay the electricity bill and misplaced her car in the car park below her flat. That was six months ago.

Sometimes I feel I can see the end, when she is nothing more than a rotting vegetable. Forgetting how to speak, how to control her bladder, and eventually forgetting how to breathe. Human degeneration halts and sputters but doesn't reverse.

Dilip, my husband, suggests her memory may need occasional rehearsal. So I write stories from my mother's past on little scraps of paper and tuck them into corners around her flat. She finds them from time to time and calls me, laughing.

'I cannot believe that any child of mine could have such bad handwriting.'

On the day she forgot the name of the road she has lived on for two decades, Ma called me to say she had bought a pack of razors and wouldn't be afraid to use them if circumstances deteriorated further. Then she started to cry. Through the phone I could hear horns bleating, people shouting. The sounds of Pune's streets. She began to cough and lost her train of thought. I could practically smell the fumes of the auto-rickshaw she sat in, the dark smoke it pumped out, as though I were standing right next to her. For a moment, I felt bad. It must be the worst kind of suffering – cognizance of one's own collapse, the penance of watching as things slip away. On the other hand, I knew this was a lie. My mother would never spend so much. A pack of razors, when only one would do the trick? She always did have a penchant for displaying emotion in public. I decided the best way to handle the situation was a compromise of sorts: I told my mother not to be dramatic, but noted down the incident so I could look for any razors and dispose of them at a later date.

I've noted down many things about my mother: the hour she falls asleep at night, when her reading glasses slip down the greasy slide of her nose, or the number of Mazorin filos she eats for breakfast – I have been keeping track of these details. I know the skirted responsibilities, and where the surface of story has been buffed smooth.

Sometimes when I visit her, she asks me to phone friends who are long dead.

My mother was a woman who could memorize recipes she had only read once. She could recall variations of tea made in other people's homes. When she cooked, she reached out for bottles and masalas without glancing up.

Ma remembered the technique the Memon neighbours used to kill goats during Bakra Eid on the terrace above her parents' old apartment, much to the Jain landlord's horror, and how the wire-haired Muslim tailor once gave her a rusty basin to collect the blood in. She described the metallic taste for me, and how she had licked her red fingers.

'My first taste of non-veg,' she said. We were sitting along the water in Alandi. Pilgrims washed themselves and mourners submerged ashes. The murky river flowed imperceptibly, the colour of gangrene. Ma had wanted to get away from the house, from my grandmother, from talk about my father. It was an in-between time, after we had left the ashram and before they would send me away to boarding school. There was a truce between my mother and me for a moment, when I could still believe the worst was behind us. She didn't tell me where we were going in the dark, and I couldn't read the paper sign taped to the front of the bus we boarded. My stomach grunted, full of fear that we would disappear again on another one of my mother's whims, but we stayed near the river where the bus dropped us off, and as the sun came up, the light made rainbows in the pools of petrol that had collected on the surface of the water. Once the day became hot, we returned home. Nani and Nana were frantic, but Ma said we hadn't left the grounds of the compound where we lived. They believed her because they wanted to, though her story was unlikely since the compound where their building stood was not large enough to get lost in. Ma smiled as she spoke – she could lie easily.

It impressed me, that she was such a liar. For a time, I wanted to emulate this quality; it seemed like the one useful trait she had. My grandparents questioned the watchman but he could verify nothing – he was often sleeping on the job. And so we paused in this stalemate, as we so often would again, everyone standing by their falsehoods, certain that their own self-interest would prevail. I repeated my mother's story when I was questioned again later. I had not yet learned what dissent was. I was still docile as a dog.

Sometimes, I refer to Ma in the past tense even though she is still alive. This would hurt her if she could remember it long enough. Dilip is her favourite person at the moment. He is an ideal son-in-law. When they meet, there are no expectations clouding the air around them. He doesn't remember her as she was – he accepts her as she is, and is happy to reintroduce himself if she forgets his name.

I wish I could be that way, but the mother I remember appears and vanishes in front of me, a battery-operated doll whose mechanism is failing. The doll turns inanimate. The spell is broken. The child does not know what is real or what can be counted on. Maybe she never knew. The child cries.

I wish India allowed for assisted suicide like the Netherlands. Not just for the dignity of the patient, but for everyone involved.

I should be sad instead of angry.

Sometimes I cry when no one else is around – I am grieving, but it's too early to burn the body.

The clock on the wall of the doctor's office demands my attention. The hour hand is on one. The minute hand rests between eight and nine. The configuration remains this way for thirty minutes. The clock is a fading remnant of another time, broken down, never replaced.

The most diabolical part is the second hand, which, like a witching wand, is the only part of the clock that moves. Not only forwards but backwards too, back and forth at erratic times.

My stomach growls.

An audible sigh comes from the others waiting when the second hand stops moving altogether, but it is only playing dead for a moment until it starts up again. I resolve not to look at it, but the sound of the ticking echoes through the room.

I look at my mother. She dozes in her chair.

I feel the sound of the clock move through my body, altering my heart rate. It isn't a tick-tock. A tick-tock is omnipresent, a pulse, a breath, a word. A tick-tock contains biological resonance, something I can internalize and ignore. This is a tick-tick-tick, followed by a length of silence, and a tock-tick-tock.

Ma's mouth falls open, shapeless like a paper bag.

Through the wavy pane of glass I can see a group of peons gathered around a narrow desk, listening to a Test match commentary. They cheer, basking in the transmission of glory emanating from the speaker. The ticking changes again.

Inside the doctor's examination room, we face another kind of clock. This is one he draws on white paper, leaving out the numbers.

'Fill this in, Mrs Lamba,' he says to my mother.

She takes the mechanical pencil from his hand and starts at one. When she reaches fifteen, he stops her.

'Can you tell me the date today?'

Ma looks at me and back at the doctor. She lifts her shoulders in response, and one side moves higher than the other, somewhere between a shrug and a twitch. Every sign of her physical degradation feels repulsive. I look at the cream walls. The doctor's certifications hang lopsided.

'Or the year?'

My mother nods slowly.

'Start with the century before the year,' he says.

She opens her mouth and the ends of her lips point down like a fish. 'Nineteen . . .' she begins, and looks into the distance.

The doctor tilts his head. 'You mean twenty, I think.'

She agrees, and smiles at him as though she is proud of some accomplishment. The doctor and I look at each other for an answer.

He goes on to say that in special cases they take fluid from the spine, but he hasn't decided if Ma is a special case yet. Instead he does scans, draws blood, checks orifices and glands, and lays the map of her brain against a plate of light. He analyses shades and patterns, and looks for black holes. She has the brain of a young woman, he insists, a brain that does what it's supposed to do.

I ask what a brain is supposed to do. Fire neurons and crackle with electrical currents?

He narrows his eyes and doesn't answer. The muscles in his jaw give him a square head and a slight overbite.

'But my mother is forgetting,' I say.

'Yes, that's true,' he says, and I begin to discern a lisp. The doctor draws a picture on a fresh piece of paper, a fluffy cloud that is supposed to be a brain. He picks his pen up from the page too soon and the curved lines don't touch at the end, as though the cloud is leaking. 'We should expect cognitive decline that will manifest in memory loss and personality changes. It won't be too different to what we've already noticed.

'What you have already noticed,' he clarifies. 'It's unclear how much your mother is noticing.'

With a pencil, he highlights areas where synaptic function is declining, where the neurons are dying. The pristine white cloud begins to look crowded. Now the opening where he didn't complete the shape seems a blessing, a way to let some air in. The neocortex, the limbic system and the subcortical regions are mapped in messy strokes. I sit on my hands.

The hippocampus is the memory bank and, in this disease, the vaults are being emptied. Long-term memory cannot be formed, short-term memory vanishes into the ether. The present becomes a fragile thing which, moments later, seems to have never happened. As the hippocampus gets weaker, space may appear different, distorted.

'Has she ever had a major head injury that you know of? Has she ever, to your knowledge, had prolonged exposure to any toxins? Perhaps some heavy metals? Has anyone else in the family had any problem with memory before? And any problems with immunity? I'm sorry, but we have to ask about HIV and AIDS.'

The questions come out of his mouth before I have time to answer, and I realize that what I say matters little in the end. Due diligence will not change what we've shared in this office, and Ma's history will have no bearing on her diagnosis.

Inside the curves of the cloud, he draws an asterisk. Next to it, he writes 'amyloid plaque'. The plaques are protein formations that usually appear in the brains of Alzheimer's patients.

'Did you see one of these in the scan?' I ask.

'No,' he says. 'Not yet, at least. But your mother is forgetting.'

I tell him I don't understand how that can be, and in answer he lists some pharmaceutical drugs on the market. Donepezil is the most popular. He circles it three times.

'What are the side effects?'

'High blood pressure, headache, stomach problems, depression.' He looks up at the ceiling and squints, trying to remember more. In the drawing, the amyloid plaque doesn't look so bad. It's almost magical, a lone tangle of yarn. I say this out loud and regret it a moment later.

'Does she knit?' he asks.

'No. She hates anything that seems domestic. Except cooking. She's a wonderful cook.'

'Well, that won't help. Recipes are notoriously difficult to keep straight. Knitting, when it becomes muscle memory, can bypass parts of the brain.'

I shrug. 'I suppose I could try. She'll hate the idea.'

'Nothing about her is certain any more,' he says. 'She may be a whole different person tomorrow.'

On the way out, the doctor asks me if we are related to a Dr Vinay Lamba, someone senior in an important hospital in Bombay. I tell him we aren't, and he looks disappointed, sad for us. I wonder if inventing a relation could have helped.

'Does your mother live with someone, a husband or a son?' he says.

'No,' I say. 'She lives alone. Right now.'

'Don't bite your nails,' Ma says on the way home.

I put my right hand back on the steering wheel and try not to clench it, but my left hand moves automatically to my mouth.

'It isn't really the nail that I'm biting, it's the cuticle.'

Ma says she doesn't care for the difference and thinks it's a shame my fingers should look this way when I'm always doing so much with my hands. I stay quiet as she speaks for the rest of the journey, listening less to what she says than how she says it, the rhythm and hesitation in her voice when she doesn't say what she means, misspeaks, inserts a reprimand to cover for her own uncertainty. She apologizes, says I'm to blame for my mistakes, thanks me and sighs, massaging her temples. Her lips cave in where two teeth are missing at the side of her mouth, and she looks like she has eaten something bitter.

I ask my mother who she is speaking to, but she doesn't answer. I glance at the back seat, just in case.

In her flat, we drink tea with digestive biscuits because they're Ma's favourite and it's been a hard day. I tell Kashta to make a paste of honey and ginger for my tickling throat. My mother is wordless as I give these instructions.

'Add some fresh turmeric to that,' she says a moment later. 'Just a sliver the size of a baby's foreskin is enough.'

She presses her thumbnail against the tip of her middle finger when she says this, measuring the exact amount. Then she looks down into her teacup, stirring an elliptical in its firmament.

'Please don't talk about foreskin,' I say, breaking the biscuits into halves.

'What's there in a little foreskin? Don't be such a prude.' She remembers how to insult me well enough.

Her apartment is a quiet mess. I consolidate three shakers of salt into one. A collection of untouched newspapers sits on the four-seater dining table. Ma insists on keeping them, says she will get to them one day.

I turn over a small bag of mung beans from the market into a steel thali and begin separating the pulse from the stone. Kashta tries to pull the plate from me but I push her away. When I'm done, I begin separating the mung by shades – military green, taupe, beige. My mother looks at the discrete piles and shakes her head. I crack my knuckles and continue separating. I know it won't make a difference once they're all in the cooker, but I've started now and I can't stop, can't stop looking for differences, until they are all where they're meant to be, coded, surrounded by their own families.

Ma naps on the sofa, and for a moment I can imagine what she'll look like when she dies, when her face slackens and the air abandons her lungs. Around her are objects, papers, photo frames filled with faces she hasn't seen in years. Among these things her body looks lifeless and alone, and I wonder if performing for the world circulates something vital, if the pressure of an audience is what forces the blood to pump. It's easy to unravel when no one is watching.

My old room stands apart from the rest of the flat, like a graft of foreign skin. There is an order, a symmetry I have left behind – one she hasn't been able to undo. On the wall, in identical frames, are black-and-white sketches of faces I have hung five centimetres apart. The bed is made, and I run my hands over the sheets to remove the creases but they have been ironed into the fabric.

*

9

Since the last elections, Ma shouts at the television every time the new prime minister comes on. He wears his saffron mantle like the attribute of a Hindu deity – with stylized pleats always crumpled in the same place. He is the reason, she says, that she's never known real love.

I wake up to the darkness. My phone is lit with a dozen missed calls from Dilip. Lights flash from the living room. My mother must be watching muted but moving mouths on TV.

The sky is dark, but the industrial complex fifteen kilometres away gives us pink light as a prelude to the sun. Ma isn't on the sofa when I come out, and I don't see her at first, standing behind the sheer curtains with her body pressed against the window. The woven drapes, grey-and-white paisley, shroud her in part, leaving shadows on her body. Through the fabric, I see her dark birthmark, an oblong disc that interrupts her shoulder blade, a bullseye on her back. Her chest is still, as though she isn't breathing.

She is naked, and steps back to look at her reflection in the glass. She looks at mine, as it appears next to hers, then back and forth, as though she cannot tell the difference. Opposites often resemble each other.

I touch Ma's elbow and she flinches. Then she points to the TV screen, to the man she has silenced with the remote control.

'You're in it together,' she whispers.

'Ma.' I try to calm her, to pull her away from the glass, but she moves back, her eyes feral, and I'm not sure she recognizes my face. She recovers quickly, but that look is enough to take the air out of my lungs. For a moment she did not know who I am and for that moment I am no one.

I coax her back to bed and call the doctor. His voice is gruff. How did I get this number, he wants to know. Our call suddenly feels intimate, as though I have crossed a line. His wife must be beside him, disturbed from her sleep. I imagine what they wear to bed, how their clothes shift through the night. I feel a dampening between my legs.

'My mother didn't recognize me for a second,' I say.

'That can happen. You should familiarize yourself with how this will progress.' His tongue sounds large in his mouth, his voice betrays annoyance and I have the sensation of failing an exam.

I spend the day turning ideas over in my mind. Science has never interested me, but I open myself up to the deluge of jargon.

I look up the chemical composition of my mother's medicine, a series of elegant hexagons, and a molecule of hydrogen chloride hanging off like a tail. I unearth the animal studies, diagrams of rat brains that were opened to chart their activity. The little tablets she has to take inhibit cholinesterase, an enzyme that breaks down the neurotransmitter acetylcholine. This promotes activity that should improve symptoms of the disease's progression.

Acetylcholine build-up in the body can be toxic.

Acetylcholine is found in pesticides and in chemical-warfare agents, commonly called nerve gas.

A low dose of something can be a panacea. A high dose can be fatal.

I open another window. *Helicobacter pylori* causes stomach ulcers and cancer if it multiplies out of control, but when completely absent from the bodies of children, rates of asthma increase.

I wish moderation were a comfortable state.

The list of side effects is longer than the doctor suggested. I want to call him again but I'm afraid. My relationship with him is strained. Can it be called a relationship? I hold myself tightly against thinking too long on this.

There are chat groups dedicated to the demise of Donepezil, citing inefficacy, among other grievances. Krill oil is recommended across the board for brain health. There is something complete in the make-up of this minuscule crustacean, this creature that can move its body with legs that are nothing more than filaments. Krill is better than fish, and a diagram explains why: the brain prefers the phospholipid form krill oil takes.

I copy the structures and chemical formulae of the oil down on a writing pad, but my drawings diverge from the originals, looking more like krill than molecules. The exoskeleton is a delicate ethyl ester, and three fatty acids form its flailing limbs. As I try to continue with purchasing the oil, I receive a warning that the company are not responsible for Indian customs delays.

They remind me that the oil is photosensitive and will spoil at high temperatures.

My husband, Dilip, grew up in America and he breaks his rotis with two hands. I met him a couple of years ago, after he had moved to Pune for work. The move was a demotion, but he didn't mention that when he started chatting me up at the German Bakery on North Main Road. I wasn't expecting to see another person there, since it was a Sunday morning and no one goes to the café much since a bomb went off inside in 2010.

I settled in a red plastic chair with my laptop as he slid into the place next to me. He smiled. His teeth were straight white tiles. He asked me if I knew the Wi-Fi password and if he could buy me a coffee. I told him coffee made me jittery, sometimes gassy. He asked me what I was working on, and even though I didn't want to tell him about my drawings, I reasoned that artists couldn't be fearful about sharing secrets with strangers.

He inhaled as he listened and leaned forward. The red plastic chair strained under his weight and his knee closed into an acute angle. We stared at each other for a while and he asked me if I wanted to go out for a meal that weekend. I blinked at the word 'meal' before realizing he meant dinner. (I have picked up many of his speech patterns since then.)

He asked me if I knew any of the restaurants in the ashram lane.

'Yes, I spent some of my childhood living in the ashram. I know that area well,' I said.

The date was pleasant. We shared spaghetti, cooked and plated in little nests. Green leaves of basil were tucked into the edges, with roasted red and yellow cherry tomatoes in the centre, situated like unhatched eggs. The tall banyan trees threw shadows around the floodlit courtyard, and the faces of occupants were obscured. We had a table hidden in the corner, one that would have been perfect for a couple having an affair, so perfect they could have sent each other one-character communications – a number to denote the time – because the location could stay the same.

I said this out loud without editing myself and he found it amusing, creative even, and asked me if I liked to make up stories. 'Communicating as efficiently as possible has always interested me,' I said. I wanted to ask if we were on a date. I usually slept with men who were friends or whom I met through friends, and we remained something between friends and lovers, but there was never a full plate of food involved or the payment of a bill.

Dilip tells the story differently. Or maybe the story just sounds different in his voice, with its round vowels and chewed words. He describes the feeling he had when he saw me, says I looked like a bohemian artist, and remembers the shirt I was wearing had paint on it. This is a fabrication – I never wear the clothes I work in outside of my studio. And I'm not a painter.

Dilip is prone to exaggeration. He says his sister is beautiful when she is decidedly not. He calls a lot of people nice who don't deserve it. I assign this to his being both beautiful and nice. Dilip also talks about the millions of friends he has back home, but only four came to Pune for our wedding. Not that I minded. Our wedding lasted only two days, at my insistence, which his mother said was not long enough to travel for. His parents and sister came from the States with half a dozen of their other relatives. My grandmother said Gujaratis from America make a disappointing wedding procession.

In the lead-up, Dilip's mother gave her astrologer my date and time of birth to ensure my stars aligned with her son's. The truth is my mother lost my birth certificate years ago, during the time we were homeless, and because looking into the official birth record would have been a hassle, we invented something that seemed like a fair approximation.

'I know it was dark,' Ma said.

'That narrows it down to early in the morning or late at night,' I replied.

We told Dilip's mother I was born at 8.23 in the evening, 2023 hours in military time, deciding on the twenty-three because anything that ended in zero or five might seem made up. Four months before the wedding, Dilip's mother called me at home.

'The pandit spoke to me,' she said. 'He's very concerned.'

A birth chart had been made for me, a chart to represent the sky at the moment I was born. Mangal, the red planet, was found to be in a dangerous aspect, placed squarely in the house of marriage.

'You're a manglik, that's what they call people like you,' she said. The line was fuzzy, and I missed the rest of the accusation. She explained that if I married her son, my fiery energies could kill him. I remained silent for a while, wondering if this was their way out: had Dilip asked his mother to call and break our engagement? I could hear her breathing, opening and closing her moist lips close to the receiver. Maybe she expected an apology. I didn't offer one.

'Don't worry,' she said, when the length of silence had passed into uncomfortable. 'The pandit has a cure.'

The next day a pandit appeared at our door. He was not my mother-in-law's priest but a local ambassador chosen to set things right.

'What is this?' Ma said as we watched him place a woven mat on the floor of the flat.

'Too much of the planet Mars,' the pandit said. 'It's bad for her husband.'

'Superstitious nonsense.' Ma pulled a stick of incense from his hand and began waving it around his head.

The man continued his work, unperturbed. He arranged fruit in steel trays. Then flowers. Milk. There were saris and embroidered red cloth. He seated himself in front of an earthen pot and lit a fire with ghee, wood chips and newspaper.

The torpor of summer was upon us, and the inside of the flat felt like a pressure cooker. I sneezed and a ball of dark snot landed in my palm, thick and bloody like a tumour. I was sure this was a bad omen and wiped it on the skin under my tunic. The pandit layered red and orange fabrics on top of several wood blocks. He moved his hands quickly, making swastikas out of uncooked grains of rice, placing whole betel nuts here and there to represent the planets in the cosmos, anointing them with some benediction that escaped me.

I sat down in front of four bronze idols. They were no more than ten centimetres tall, swathed and garlanded.

'Today, this is your husband,' the pandit said.

I looked at the gods. Their faces were mostly the same, except Ganesh, whose tusk curved in a smile.

'What? All?'

'No, only this one. Vishnu.' The pandit smiled. 'He will absorb your bad energies by marrying you first, so your next husband doesn't suffer.'

Vishnu looked delicate, with an aquiline nose and a shortened chin.

'Do I have to do this?' I asked the holy man. 'Can't we just tell everyone I did it?'

The pandit didn't answer.

The ceremony was long, longer than my wedding to Dilip would be a few months later, and full of chanting. I circled the fire, holding the small deity in my arms, watching his motionless face. A simple mangalsutra was placed around my neck and a crimson line of sindoor in my parting, to symbolize I was a married woman. After the ceremony, the necklace was ripped off and the red paste smeared across my forehead.

'Married and divorced,' the pandit said. I looked in the mirror. There was an imprint that the hook of the necklace had left on my skin. My face was speckled with red. It was a violent business. The priest shook my hand. Then he asked for a donation and a cup of tea.

A month before our wedding, I accompanied Dilip on the four-hour drive to Bombay airport to collect his mother. He hired a driver and a large air-conditioned Innova to accommodate all her luggage. By the time we arrived, she was standing outside with a porter, fanning herself with a brochure and shooing away taxi drivers. She wasn't a tall woman, but she took up space where she stood, bumping passers-by with her elbows and blocking the path with her wide stance. Her woven sunhat, sandals, trousers and T-shirt were all the same shade of pink. I thought I detected a scowl on her face until she laid eyes on her son. The sunhat drooped a little as she waved wildly in our direction.

'I haven't been back here in ten years!' she said in greeting. She was wide awake as we drove over the dramatic Western Ghats, pointing out every pile of garbage along the highway and shaking her head. I told her that the hills were beautiful in the monsoon, misty and wet from the rain, even though the summer sky now was an unimpressive bright sheet of white. Her incredulity skyrocketed at every toll booth, which, she noted, had been built without taking the average height of a vehicle or the length of a human arm into account, and two men were required as go-betweens to hand over money to the toll officer.

'This country,' she sighed. 'I suppose it's a way to give everyone a job. Hire three where only one is needed.'

When we reached Pune, the wide highway decorated with brightly coloured billboards gave way to narrow lanes with small businesses – motels, restaurants and bike shops dotted the road. As we waited at a traffic light, two young boys came out from a makeshift slum nearby. Both squatted, rubbing their eyes and yawning.

'Oh God,' Dilip's mother said, 'look at these guys. Can't they go behind their house? There is a toilet sign right there.'

I imagined the toilets were less than suitable but said nothing, hoping instead that the car in front of us would move. But it didn't, and the two boys were joined by a third friend who came closer to the kerb.

'This is crazy,' she cried.

'Leave them alone,' Dilip said, laughing.

'Shameless,' she said. Pulling her phone from her bag, she began recording them. I crossed my arms, hoping they wouldn't notice, but realized they had when all three stood up and faced our car at the same time.

Fortunately, the lights changed. Dilip's mother laughed as we drove away, and watched the video repeatedly for the rest of the drive. I tried to divert her attention – it was her first time in Pune – by pointing out the large green expanse of the army base, the deep shade that covered us as we passed beneath some ancient banyan trees. Pune was inland and the air was dry, cold in the winter and dusty in the summer, but never wet and putrid like what one experienced in Bombay. I suggested a list of places we could visit – the historical Shaniwar Wada fortress that had been the seat of the local Peshwa dynasty, a small but beautiful Shiva temple, and my favourite sweet shop on Main Street, in case she felt like indulging. We drove past the Pune Club, where our wedding and reception would be held, and I tried to impress upon her how special it was for me to get married there, that my grandparents had been members for over forty years, and even though my mother had never shown interest, Dilip and I would be given membership soon. It was also the first place where Dilip and I had discussed marriage, over a beer, after a late Sunday swim. I didn't mention some of the other memories I had of the place, of sitting like a beggar beyond those hallowed gates. Some things were better saved for after the wedding.

Dilip's mother peered in, nodding, and a thin smile appeared on her mouth. 'The British built some lovely buildings.'

*

The weeks before the wedding were the hottest of the summer. Only the brave ventured outside. Cows, dogs and humans dropped dead in the streets. Cockroaches came to pay their respects. It was a particularly hot day when my mother-in-law and Dilip came to our flat for lunch. I cursed Pune for making a bad impression. I felt responsible for everything abhorrent about it, things I hadn't noticed before. The heat was not just hot, it was unbearable. The air was not just thick, it was unbreathable. I believed I had become sensitized to the normal faults and dysfunction of our lives through Dilip's standards and preferences, but it was only with the arrival of his mother that I realized he had become immune to some discomfort over time. I was anxious about every flaw while being hyper-conscious that some flaws might add to the city's charm. How much did I want to misrepresent where I lived – and who I was – and could I even recognize what was a desirable cover-up and what was not?

Dilip and his mother drank coconut water and sour nimbu pani, unaware that I had spent the previous week arranging the wreckage of the home I shared with my mother, repainting the bubbling walls, taking down cracked mirrors and mending torn sofa covers.

My mother-in-law was fond of dressing in unusual colours and, we realized, of hats. Ma covered her smile when they walked in, and I, too, could not ignore the absurdity of the lady's attire. She was not, I knew, a woman of exceptional taste or perception, and yet her disapproval of Pune wounded me.

After lunch, we sat on our small terrace and discussed the wedding to-do list. It was the time of day when the neighbours crowded on to their balconies, which were designed to look like little boxes stacked on top of each other. They waved their arms to shoo away pigeons and crows, and fingered the laundry they'd hung to dry in the afternoon sun.

Perspiration appeared on our faces. Three storeys below, I could see the top of a head, a woman's head, with scanty hair at the crown and a thick salt-and-pepper braid that wrapped around itself. I could hear the sound of her broom, made of reeds and tied together, scraping the ground as the leaves and dirt rustled and fell, rustled and fell, into some version of their previous order. Smoke wafted in the air, carrying the smell of fuel and burning garbage, but we didn't move to go inside. The sounds within the compound were quiet in comparison to the low, billowing horn from the nearby railway tracks whenever a train passed.

I looked at the hazy sky and tried to feel content, content to know that even though I had spent so many years here, at last I would be leaving. I looked at Dilip. He was handsome and tall in a way that let everyone know he'd grown up abroad. Baseball caps, good manners and years of consuming American dairy. He was saving me, even though he didn't know it. His mouth spread open in a smile at something my mother said, and I could see all of his thirty-two teeth, disciplined from years of adolescent braces.

Later, over a bowl of sweet and milky rabri, my mother-in-law turned to Ma. 'Tara-ji,' she said, 'the pandit wanted to discuss the wedding ceremony. He asked if you have any relatives, maybe a couple, who can sit inside the mandap and give the bride away in your place.'

'I don't,' Ma said. 'Cousins, maybe. But I can do it well enough myself.'

Dilip's mother opened and closed her mouth, sucking in and expelling air several times, before she spoke again. This was a tic of hers, as though the words needed resuscitation before she could send them out. 'Usually when the mother is a widow, some other relatives perform that part of the ceremony.'

'But I'm not a widow,' Ma said.

Dilip's mother put down her spoon. Her mouth opened and closed again. Then she began blowing in and out loudly, as though something in front of her was on fire. We all looked at Dilip, who was helping himself to more dessert, leaving a trail of cream on the table.

'It was less controversial,' he said later, when we were alone.

'Indians in America are conservative sometimes. I didn't want to tell them your parents are divorced.'

From the balcony of Ma's flat, I used to watch the stray dogs when I came home from school. They were usually idle, with mangled paws and chewed ears, sprawled out with their packs, only moving to dodge cars and auto-rickshaws or to mount their mothers and sisters. I suppose that was the second time I saw sex, sitting in my navy-blue uniform, watching the scene below, but it was hard to differentiate between dogs fighting and fornicating. Sometimes there were battles when other pariah dogs entered their territory. A high-frequency snarl or a branch breaking underfoot would set them off and, late at night, when I was supposed to be asleep under my mosquito net, I would hear them and their war cries. I remember, one morning on the way to school I saw a puppy sitting near the gate, her stomach trembling with worms and fleas marching across the bridge of her nose. In place of her tail was a bloody hole.

After I married Dilip, I inherited his family, his furniture and a new set of stray animals. The dogs near his house are calmer, overfed and neutered by a group of Pune housewives. They sniff the air and their tongues hang over their canines. Occasionally, they nip at each other's genitals and mewl for food.

I moved into Dilip's apartment in June, during the wait for the monsoon. The rains were late. A bad sign. This would be a bad year. The papers reported that the farmers blamed the priests for not inspiring the gods, and the priests blamed the farmers for lacking in piety. In the city there was less of this sort of talk, more about climate change. The river that flows nearby rises and falls with some regularity, but the monsoon brings down a flood of roaring brown water.

When Dilip goes down on me, he sweeps his nose against my labia and inhales.

'It smells like nothing,' he says. He is proud of this quality, says it's unusual and might be one of the reasons he could imagine us being together. His life is filled with intense smells now, at the office and even taking a lift, and it's a relief to him that I'm odourless after a workout and in high-stress situations. He grew up in Milwaukee, where his ears knew only soft Q-tips and suburban stillness. Pune, he says, is really loud, really pungent, but his senses can manage the onslaught as long as our home brings him back to neutral. He tells everyone there were no jarring changes when I moved into his flat, that my life merged with his seamlessly.

Sensible of his fear of upheaval, I made changes cautiously, first removing any bed sheet or towel that could have been used by other women. Then books or items of clothing that they might have gifted him. The books usually took the form of lovelorn poetry and could be detected by a note written on the first page. I slowly purged any remnant of their existence: old photographs, letters, mugs, pens collected from hotel rooms, T-shirts with the names of cities they'd travelled to together, magnets in the shape of monuments, leaves preserved in paper, collections of pale shells in jars from beach holidays. These measures were extreme, but I wanted a home and marriage free of grey, fuzzy edges.

My mother sets an eggplant alight on the stove, and we watch the flames feed on its purple skin. The beige flesh inside is smoking. She separates the seeds and throws them in the bin. It's a marvel her fingers don't burn. On a white plastic board, she chops chillies and young green onions. The board is stained with turmeric, and there is still a little earth stuck in the rounds of onion stalk, but she tells me not to nitpick about small things. She fries cumin seeds in oil and pours them on top of the steaming eggplant, followed by torn leaves of coriander. Oil splatters on the side of the stove. I cough while mixing the contents of the bowl. My maid, Ila, straightens her sari and sighs. She begins the work of cleaning our mess while we bring out the dishes to where Dilip sits at the dining table.

Ma doesn't come to our house often. She says the main hall disturbs her, especially the mirrors that cover each wall, reflecting everything in multiple directions. For Dilip, the mirrors were a selling point when he was house hunting, a sign that he'd made it, and the culmination of every fantasy he had about mirrors and pornographic films. For my mother, the room is too alive, with each object and body replicated four times, with each replication repeated further in reflection. She sits down at the table and her feet jump nervously, climbing on one another like mice escaping the midday heat. For myself, I've got used to the mirrors, have even started relying on them when Dilip and I fight because seeing a reflection shout is similar to watching television.

'So, Mom,' Dilip says, 'how are you feeling?'

He calls my mother Mom like he calls his own. I struggled in the beginning, but it was easy for him, calling two women Mom and calling two places home.

My mother tries to speak in an American accent when Dilip is around. She thinks he won't understand her otherwise, and if he tries to speak in Hindi, she replies in English. Ma attempts his Midwestern vowels and confident pauses which assume the rest of the world will wait for him to finish a sentence.

'Honestly, beta, when the doctor gave me the news, I started to fear the worst. I even started making plans to take my own life – you can ask her, isn't it true? Sorry, I'm not trying to upset your meal, eat first, eat first, we will talk later. How is the aamti? Not too spicy, I hope? Yes, to answer your question, I was scared at first but now I don't think I'm really sick. I feel very fine.'

Dilip nods and looks into the mirror ahead of him. 'I'm so happy to hear that.'

'Ma, the doctor says you're forgetting.'

'My scans were normal.'

'Yes, scans can be normal even though –'

'Why are you going on insisting I'm ill?' She is holding a slice of raw onion in her hand. It drops back to her plate as she speaks.

'You're forgetting things. You're forgetting how to do things, basic things, like using your mobile phone and paying the electricity bill.'

'Oh, I never really knew how to pay the bill. These online things are too confusing.'

I put my hands down. She hadn't said this to the doctor.

'And what about calling Kali Mata? You asked me to dial the number of a person who's been dead for ten years.'

'Seven years,' Ma says, and turns to Dilip. 'See how she lies?'

Dilip looks between us. When he frowns, a scar from an old lacrosse injury glimmers on his temple.

'I'm not lying.'

'You are. That's what you do. You're a professional liar.'

We drop Ma home after dinner and Dilip hums to himself quietly. I can't make out the tune, so I interrupt him.

'Can you believe what she was saying?'

He pauses and then answers. 'Maybe she doesn't believe she's sick.'

'She has to believe it.'

'You aren't an authority.'

It stings that my lack is so visible. 'I didn't say I was an authority. The doctor said she's sick.'

'I thought the doctor said she has the brain of a young woman.'

'But she's forgetting things – important things.'

'Important to whom? She may want to forget – maybe she doesn't want to remember her friend is dead.'

'Either way, she's forgetting.' I hear my tone has turned shrill.

'Voluntarily forgetting is not the same as dementia, Antara.'

'That doesn't make any sense. Why would she want to forget me?'

Dilip takes a breath and shakes his head. 'You're the artist, be open to possibilities.'

'She called me a liar.'

'Well, isn't that what you make art about? About how people can't be trusted?'

His face has dropped. He looks disappointed. I try to match his look but don't feel it, so I bite the nail on my middle finger or, more accurately, the cuticle area. Dilip reaches out his hand and brings my arm down.

My art is not about lying. It's about collecting data, information, finding irregularities. My art is about looking at where patterns cease to exist.

Before I got married, my grandmother let me use a room in her house as a studio. It was cosy, dark and bright in good proportion, a place where my interest in collecting had begun as a child, among the objects left behind by the deceased inhabitants of the bungalow Nana and Nani lived in. Tungsten bulbs, batteries, cords, pens, stamps, coins. I began by looking up the dates and designs of these objects, losing myself in encyclopaedias of energy and patents in the library, always ending up far from the place where I began. To avoid these tangents, I started to draw the objects myself, mapping them out as I saw them, copying as closely as I could. My handwriting may be bad, too mechanical, lacking in flourish, but my hand is steady and precise. I started to collect dead insects, which are surprisingly difficult to find whole and uncorrupted. One of my prized possessions is a number of moths fossilized in wax that I keep in a glass jar.

Museums collect milestone objects – the first cellular phone, the first computer – presumably to display one day to the future (presuming that museums will have a place in the future). I grew up in a time of landlines and Swatch watches and have my own collections stored away: glass bottles that read Thums Up and Gold Spot for when these brands no longer exist, but also antique tongue-cleaners and pastel autograph books that I asked strangers on the street to sign when I was a child.

Dilip says if volcanoes all over the planet started erupting, covering the Earth's crust in miles of debris, and our flat was the only thing ever dug up in the future, archaeologists would wonder at the strange preoccupations of their ancestors. I tell him Americans invented hoarding and have made an art form of it.

Dilip once told me that, in America, no one uses tongue-cleaners because they use their toothbrushes to clean away the white scum. He says that I should try it, that it's easier to have one tool for your mouth rather than two. The idea doesn't sit well with me and I ask him about cross-contamination. He shrugs. The mouth is one hole, one room, one city. Something that's happening on one side is going to appear on the other. I tell him if that is the case, he won't mind my emptying the contents of my glass of water on his lap.

When I moved in, Dilip said I should use the guest room as a studio. He rarely had guests anyway. 'Besides, I like the idea of you being at home all day,' he said.

The room is spare, sunny, not what one would expect from a place where art is made. The cupboard has been transformed into my cabinet of curiosities, where my objects are stored and locked away, some in boxes, some in sterile plastic containers. Images fill binders, divided by subject, category and date of collection. The room itself contains a wooden desk and a chair that Dilip brought home from his office. On the wall is a calendar where I mark off the day's work once it has been completed.

I have been working on a project for the past three years, and I have no idea how long it will go on. It began by accident, after I drew the face of a man from a picture I found, but the next day, when I went to compare my work to the original, the picture was nowhere to be seen. I searched all day without any luck. By the evening, I had given up. I took another piece of paper – the only paper I work on, nothing fancy, made in China, but it holds graphite well – and drew the face from my own drawing, copying my own work as faithfully as I could, the careful shading, the exact thickness of line. This has become a daily practice. I take the drawing from the day before and copy it to the best of my ability, date it, return both to the drawer and cross a square off on the calendar. There are days it takes me an hour, and there are days it takes me several.

A year into the project, I was invited to show the works at a small gallery in Bombay. The curator, who is also a friend, compared the dynamics of time and duration in my work to On Kawara, and said that this was the diary of an artist, a phrase she used for the title. I thought the connection to On Kawara was erroneous. His work is mechanical, without any implication of the human hand. My work celebrates human fallibility. If On Kawara is about counting, I am about losing count. The curator didn't want to go into this – the essay for the catalogue had already been spellchecked, and she said complicating the issue wouldn't help me sell in this climate. A collector showed interest before the show opened – this sort of slowly built work was so important right now, he said.

The series didn't sell.

I blame the title. A diary. What does that even mean? A diary sounds so trifling, so ridiculously childlike. Who wants to spend money on a diary, really? I never even saw the work as a diary. I confess I was only thinking about how impossible it is for the human hand and eye to maintain any sort of objectivity. But isn't that how it always is? Intention and reception almost never find each other.

I dressed carefully for the opening, tried to look alluring without showing any skin, and felt completely unprepared while knowing this was the most important day of my adult life. I didn't tell anyone about the show, but Ma found out. She came to the opening, walked through every room and stood in front of all 365 faces. The first and the last picture met each other at the front of the gallery, hanging on either side of the entrance, creating a dialogue of difference. They could have been the images of two different men, two different faces, done by the hands of different artists. My project to copy perfectly had been a failure, and because it was – had to be – a failure, the local art scene deemed it a tremendous success. A few newspapers carried short reviews, calling my work exciting and compulsive, remarking that it was as disturbing as it was fascinating, wondering how long I could go on.

Ma called it my game of Chinese Whispers.

When I got back to Pune almost a week later, Ma cried and came at me with a rolling pin. Weeping, she said I was a traitor and a liar. She wanted to know why I would do a show like this.

Holding the rolling pin I had forcefully prised away from her, I perched myself at the edge of the dining table, trying to catch my breath. What was the problem, I asked her. Why couldn't I make the kind of art I wanted?

She told me to move out of her house that day, and did not see me again until I came one afternoon with Dilip by my side to tell her I was engaged.

I decide to see my father, to tell him about Ma's diagnosis. Trees and pesky chipmunks surround his bungalow in Aundh, on the other side of Pune, and the sound of air-force drills overhead rattle the windows. In the sitting room, a large grandfather clock spits out a bird and a German nursery rhyme on the hour.

My father's eyebrows are stitched in thick dark thread across his forehead. 'I called five or six times yesterday.'

I nod. It is the sort of reprimand I am accustomed to from him, and five or six is an approximation for any number. I don't listen carefully to the details of what he says. I am used to compartmentalizing him to these brief visits, and relegating his face to a corner of my psyche.

No question is explicitly asked. I answer the reproach in his voice: 'I was at the doctor's with Ma.'

The sofas in the hall are arranged like a railway waiting room, and we sit across from each other. He taps his hands together, waiting for me to say more, and I lean forward and hand him the doctor's report. He opens it slowly, taking an unnecessarily long time with the outer plastic file, carefully separating the glued sides of the envelope. When the envelope tears slightly, he gasps as though he's cut himself and examines the tear with some pain. Then he reads the pages inside, holding the paper away from himself and mouthing the words.

'Sad, very sad,' he says when he's finished. 'You must let me know what I can do, or if there are any calls I can make.'

He tosses the papers on to the table by his side and asks if I will have some more tea. I shake my head and break the caramel-coloured skin forming in my cup with a spoon.

'It's a shame,' he continues. 'I would like to be involved. But none of this was my idea.'

This is usual, and always accompanies a reproach from him – he divests himself of responsibility or choice in all past, current or future situations at the beginning of any conversation we might have. He means to head off any blame I might be ready with. He doesn't know I always empty my pockets of that stuff before I pass the threshold of his house, that even once I am inside, I know a different kind of door remains closed in front of me.

I wonder if he truly believes in his state of choicelessness, if there is a decision in his life for which he will accept accountability. The one-sided narrative has always been painful and interesting for me, the singularity of the voice that he speaks to me with. I wonder which voice speaks in his head.

My father's wife comes into the room at this moment, and he stops talking. She hugs me and pats my back. Their son also joins us, sitting down across from me.

The woman's arms hang by her sides like pins. The boy is no longer the baby I always think of him as, but a teenager of an age where it's difficult to be sure of how old he is. We don't resemble each other, except perhaps in our colouring. I've always thought my father and his new wife look alike, thin and woolly like finely woven sweaters. I smile at the three interchangeable faces.

I ask my brother about college, and as he answers I notice that he is sprouting hair on his chin. I rarely consider him, mostly focus on my father. And the wife. I can barely see her eyes through her thick bifocals.

As I leave, my father bemoans the sad problem of my mother one more time and tells me to see him more often. He says this every time we part, though inevitably six months pass before our next meeting.

On the way home, I stop at Boat Club Road. The doorbell sounds like birds chirping and I can hear old Chanda bai's Bata shoes squawking like rubber ducks as she comes to the door. She smiles with a trembling lower jaw and lays her hand against my cheek.

'You're looking very tired,' she says.

I go to the bathroom and wash my face in the sink. It's slanted, attached to an errant pipe – a small porcelain afterthought. The tap splatters on full and wets my feet. The backsplash of floral tile is now faded, scummy and damp. Grey water circles the drain.

Nani is seated cross-legged on a charpai, with three cordless phones in front of her. She sees me and raises her hand in greeting. We look alike, the three of us, my mother, my grandmother and me, besides the differences etched by time. Other variations are subtle: my grandmother has heavy ankles, and her hair is slicked down to her head, the parting glistening like an oily tributary. My mother has fair skin with ingrown hairs as black as mustard seeds populating the backs of her calves. I am the dark one, with curls that loosen only when they're wet.

When I sit down, Nani complains about the lane outside being dug up to introduce an electric line. She says it's a municipal corporation scam. When I ask her to explain what kind of corruption the local government is guilty of, she shakes her head and looks away.

'I grew up breathing Gandhian air,' she says. 'I cannot imagine the minds of goondas.' Her English is wobbly, the kind learned from television rather than books.

I follow her eyes out the window. The lane is full of tatty double-storey bungalows and flowering gulmohar trees. The sun shines in, like it does most days, drinking colour from the blue ceramic floor.

She and my grandfather purchased this house twenty years ago from an aged Parsi spinster with marshmallow arms. The spinster had not wanted to sell to Hindus, but there were no other offers. My grandparents arrived with their old furniture: my grandmother's chairs made from sheesham wood, and large Godrej cupboards as secure as tombs (she still hangs the keys from a rope at her waist).

Nana and Nani were eager to move; their old flat was still inhabited by apparitions of my grandfather's affairs and Nani's many stillborn children, and load-shedding was a daily occurrence. Ironically, they moved into a house that felt haunted by the last owner's dead ancestors – my mother said they were trading their bad memories for a stranger's.

On the day they took possession of the house, I watched as lace tablecloths were balled and packed by the movers – a group of some dozen men who came with a Tempo Traveller to transport the boxes. Open closets revealed the contents of many generations: old light bulbs no longer useable, unpolished silver ornaments, porcelain tea sets in their original boxes. Glass chandeliers were covered in a mist of cobwebs. The men lifted a chintz settee with sagging cushions that reminded me of the grey calico undershirt I wore beneath my school uniform. They left the smell of their bodies behind as they wrapped furniture in old blankets, and the forgotten Parsi owner sat in her wheelchair by the window, waiting for her nurse.

That was many years ago, but the house feels the same, with the stench of unfamiliar musk and a coating of dust.

'I need to talk to you about Ma,' I say.

'What about her?' Nani asks.

'We went to the doctor. She's forgetting things.'

'It's because she isn't married. Women forget things when they aren't married.' Then she adds, 'Anyway, forgetfulness runs in the family. Her father was forgetful.'

I shrug without agreeing, though I remember my grandfather would, on occasion, absent-mindedly offer Nani his newspaper, forgetting she could not read, and in response she, always imagining he was mocking her, would whack his hand away and stalk out of the room.

'This is different,' I say. 'The other day she forgot who I was.' She nods and I nod in return, and together we seem to imply that something has been understood, though I am not sure what. Miscommunications emerge from mislaid certainty. I consider whether I have told the whole truth or given something a meaning that never existed – whether I have, with a couple of words and the movement of my head, made my mother sicker than she truly is. Maybe that isn't a bad thing. Maybe we all need to be careful, alert.

I consider whether to share what happened at the doctor's office, whether to draw the picture of the cloud and the amyloid plaque.

Nani places her hand on her cheek. 'She's become so fat, your mother. Her knuckles are swollen to double what they were. How will we pry the jewellery off her hands when she dies?'

Morning is the time for deep breaths, and discovering ourselves anew in our bodies.

I read this in a magazine while Ma covers her greys at the parlour. I have started accompanying her everywhere I can. I double-check bills before she pays them and make sure she puts on her seatbelt. Sometimes, when others are within hearing distance, she shouts that I am torturing her, that she wants to be left alone.

For some couples, a sound sleep can erase discord from the night before, the magazine continues. Does it follow that marital bliss must evade insomniacs or those with irregular circadian patterns?

In the morning, I stretch and feel my arms and legs pulling in opposite directions, and my torso is the interstice between my heavy limbs. The hole in the middle of me is gnawing. I always wake up hungry and my mouth takes up my entire face, dry and warm, a dark, sandy pit. Dilip is beside me and the sheets below his body are damp and cool. He suffers from night sweats but never remembers the contents of his dreams.

I wash the sheets every day after he leaves for work and dry them in the outer corridor of the building where the midday sun shines in. The neighbours have told Ila they don't approve of seeing our bedding while they wait for the lift. The plaque outside their door, made of dark-blue-and-white painted tile, reads 'The Governors'. They're both retired, an ex-school teacher, an ex-navy man, and when she goes to visit her sister in Bombay, Dilip and I have seen Mr Governor sitting on their balcony, smoking cigarettes and crying.

'He must miss her,' Dilip says.

'Maybe she doesn't really visit her sister on these trips. Maybe he knows it.'

Dilip looks at me, surprised, as if he never would have thought of it, and then intently, as though it means something that I did. There was a time when this might have amused him.

'I don't think you're being generous or compassionate,' I say. The magazine at the parlour mentioned these traits as vital to any thriving relationship. He looks into the distance as I talk, mesmerized by whatever it is he sees, as though by looking away he can understand me more fully.

'I didn't say anything,' he replies.

In the evening, we go to the gym in the building. He wears a sleeveless shirt made of polyester that has to be washed twice after every workout. He lifts free weights a metre from the mirror and exhales swiftly with every count. I find his noisy breath embarrassing, like the passing of gas or the exposure of innards. I've never liked the idea of someone hearing me snore.

I use the stair-climber and tune my headphones into one of the music channels playing on the televisions overhead. Post-work is busy and I have to sometimes wait for a machine. I never worked out when I was younger, but since turning thirty, my body has started resembling an overripe pear.

Dilip says the workouts are making a difference, but I can't see it and tell him I don't like working out with him.

He doesn't understand why I am offended, why I feel insecure when he compliments me, and why I never believe him anyway. I wonder, sometimes, at the pathways in his mind, at the way his thoughts move, so disciplined and linear. His world is contained, finite. He understands what I say literally – a word has a meaning and a meaning has a word. But I imagine other possibilities and see the heaviness of speech. If I draw a line from point X to all its other connections, I find myself at the centre of something I cannot plot my way out of. There is so much to misinterpret.

Dilip believes a single thought mirrors an entire landscape of the mind. He says it must be tiring to be me.

'Your mother is upside-down up here,' Nani says, knocking on the side of her head. She sits cross-legged on her charpai as I look at old pictures. Occasionally, she checks for a dial tone on her cordless phones.

There are photographs of Ma as a young girl with long, difficult hair. She spent hours straightening it every week, lying across an ironing board with her hair between pages of newspaper. Rumours persist of what she was like at fourteen and fifteen, disappearing from school every afternoon to a roadside restaurant off the old Bombay–Pune highway. The dhaba bore a sign that read 'Punjabi Rasoi'. There, she would order a large beer and drink straight from the bottle. From her school bag, she would dig out a pack of Gold Flake cigarettes and smoke one after the other. Travellers would break at the restaurant, arriving in taxis and scooters, stopping to take a piss or have a meal – foreigners especially, carrying little luggage and almost no money, on their way to the ashram. Ma would introduce herself, get to know them, sometimes catch a ride back into town. Nani believes these unchaperoned days piqued my mother's interest in the ashram, but I wonder if her self-destructiveness was just another symptom of something there all along.

It was around then that my mother started wearing white. All white, all the time, like the followers of the ashram. Always cotton. Thin, almost transparent, though the texture of the fabric is hard to tell in these faded photos.

'Strange, she wanted to wear white when she never knew a single person who had died,' Nani says. 'Other girls wore miniskirts, bellbottoms. Not Tara. She looked like an old-fashioned aunty. Only, she never wore a dupatta.'

Among the pile are some pictures of Nani from her wedding day, where she looks wide-eyed and small, no more than fifteen years old. She is a red bride, or so I must assume from the black-and-white picture, and her sari has a single line of embroidery. So bare, it wouldn't even do for a wedding guest nowadays. Her nose ring glints for the camera. Behind her is her father, his stomach straining through his bush-shirt. Around her are other relatives, some semblance of people I know, her sisters and brothers, nieces and nephews.

'What does a dupatta matter anyway?' I say. Dupattas always seemed useless to me, an extra length of fabric, neither top nor bottom, serving no purpose except to re-cover what was already covered.

'A dupatta is your honour,' Nani says. She pulls the picture out of my hand, and I try to imagine the kind of honour that is so easily left at home.

There are other pictures that Nani doesn't keep with these, ones that have been hidden away, where Ma is about eighteen. Her hair is shorter, manageable, and she wears blue eyeshadow and pink lipstick. Her blouse is silk, printed with some hybrid tropical bird and tucked into high-waisted jeans. Shoulder pads come up to her earlobes. Her mouth is open, and I cannot tell if she is smiling or shouting.

I never knew her like this, but this is who she was when she fell in love with my father.

It was a golden age, a time when all the wrongs of the past were righted and the future was full of promise – that's how Nani describes the time when Ma met my father.

The match was arranged after my father and his mother were invited to Nani's for afternoon tea, and Ma walked in late, sweating, with brown nipples showing through her chemise.

He was thin, gangly, still learning the way around his new body. A dusting of dark powder seemed to coat his upper lip and his eyebrows scampered about before meeting in the middle. Even his joints inched towards each other as if by some magnetic attraction, elbow to elbow, knee to knee, his torso closing in on itself. His mother had to give him an occasional knock to straighten him up. He looked at the ground while Ma talked loudly, her weight on her feet as she spoke.

For a while it seemed that Ma had shifted in what she desired, that her teenage rebellion had been quelled and she would fall in line with what her parents called a good future.

She cut her hair, bought colourful clothes and started spending time at the Club. She professed a desire to study further, and even announced that she would take up hotel management or catering while my father finished his engineering degree.

A year after the wedding, I was born.

Five years after that, my father filed a petition for divorce. My mother was not present for this.

A little while later, he was on his way to America with a new wife.

'What are you going to do with all of these?' Nani asks as I stuff the photographs into an envelope.

'Show them to Ma,' I say. 'We have to make her remember.'

'Why don't we spend more time with him?' Dilip says.

He is talking about my father. I don't look up at him.

We are at the Club, waiting for our friends to join us. He is having a beer and I am drinking Old Monk with Diet Coke. We order dosas and chilli cheese toast.

Dilip never understood how important a Club membership was until he moved to India. Up until that point, he always came for short visits, stayed with friends and family and was escorted around in air-conditioned cars. But for many of us who grew up here, our lives have always revolved around the Club. Where else could you find such a sprawling green space in the centre of the city? The building is a landmark, something every taxi driver knows the way to. My grandfather always joked that he didn't consider the railways to be the only worthwhile thing the British left behind – it was the clubs, where we came to play sports after school, where our parents and grandparents would socialize, where we learned to swim. For many of us, it was where we had our first kisses behind the wild bougainvilleas that grow along the boundary walls, where we attended our first concerts, or New Year's parties.

I lost interest in the Club for many years, preferring to go to the new bars, cafés and restaurants that were sprouting up all over the city. It felt stodgy and old-fashioned. Something my grandparents did. But in the past few years, I've returned to it, finding comfort in greeting the same people year after year, in seeing the same broken steps, the same cracks in the walls that never quite get repaired. For me, it has been a constant when life was otherwise. Dilip has come to like it too.

He likes to joke that the Club membership was the dowry for marrying me.

On the tables are bells to ring for service. The alcohol is the cheapest in town. On Thursday nights, families gather on the lawn to play tambola, and there are eight tables in the card room just for rummy.

'We can even invite your dad here,' Dilip says. 'To meet at the Club. So everyone is comfortable.'

'I'm scared,' I simplify for my husband. Dilip can understand only some of the repercussions which keep falling, to this day, like a line of dominoes – like when his mother insisted we keep up the charade of my father being dead for our wedding because an explanation of the truth might be complicated. And then, of course, Dilip likes to fix things. He believes every problem has a solution. He will search, dig, scratch until he finds it.

'You don't have to be scared,' he says.

I realize he is trying to be kind to me, so I am kind back. I smile and nod at these words and Dilip smiles in return with the belief that he has done his work, but I am only trying to move on, change the subject, settle on some other pasture before our friends arrive, because for thirty-six years this peace of mind has eluded me, and a few caring gestures on this clement night can't ease a sickness that pre-dates us both and has no remedy.

1981

My father grew up as an army brat, moving schools every year, and had to resort to bribery to turn classmates into friends. The most common gift was imported liquor from his parents' stock. His father was a lieutenant general, and their homes changed with the seasons, but they were always filled with beautiful objects from foreign lands. Wooden shoes, knitted tapestries, and crystal so expensive his mother would oversee the washing of it herself. She didn't like to enter the kitchen, and once proudly told my nani that she had never cooked an entire meal with her own hands. She could trace her lineage to some royal Marwar blood, which she brought up often. She knew the right people, and married her two daughters into what she considered good families, but received a blow when her husband died without warning one afternoon while travelling on official business to Delhi.

In his wedding pictures, my father is a young groom mounted on a bedecked horse. A little boy sits in front of him, a nephew, looking terrified as the horse lurches forward with each blast from the horns. The boy and the groom are dressed alike, too, with matching safas wrapped around their heads and stiff collars edged in gold thread. The band that leads the procession wears red-and-green sherwanis and can pass off as wedding guests.

The men make a circle around the musicians, cheering and whistling with the beat of the dholak. Women dance a little behind, managing their saris and waving one arm in the air, watching the young men but not joining in their play. There is a picture of the party halting outside a gate, presumably a wedding hall, where my mother and her family wait to receive the wedding guests. Others from the street in regular clothes appear now and again. They have joined in the spectacle, creating enclosures of laughter and outstretched hands. A spotlight falls on the groom, a stark yellow beam held up by the photographer's assistant. The bright light floods the young man's eyes. He blinks away perspiration in every frame. When his eyes are open, his gaze is on the horse.

Photos, too, from inside the banquet hall. Barricaded in by furniture and distant relatives, the wedding party ready themselves for the real work, the export of dowry and daughter.

The women flank the bride, congregating in a fear only they can understand. The men dawdle with downturned mouths.

What did she look like in person, without lights blowing out the colour of her skin? How did she react to the unfamiliar faces of her new family? The groom, my father, looks bewildered, too young to comprehend the sanctioned kidnapping he must now commit.

By morning, the girl will be transformed. A new husband, a new life. And when she finds herself alone, perhaps she'll still cry, thinking of the past, mourning an end that did not culminate in death.

Nani says she always worried about how Ma would manage in her new surroundings. 'Your mother was a strange girl. No one knew what she wanted out of life. I guess nothing has changed. But your father's mother was also very strange. No good came of them living in the same house.'

My mother recounted the strangeness of her early married life to me on several occasions. Her mother-in-law ate pickled Kashmiri garlic every day since her husband's cardiac incident. The house had the particular smell of digested allium.

On the first day in her new home, her mother-in-law gave her a coarse bar of white soap and a hand towel to use for her baths. She also passed on a stack of old saris that had belonged to her mother-in-law. Ma was to wear them from then on. Ma smelled the fabric, inhaled the years of dust and mothballs. She shuddered.

On the second day, when she saw Ma moving around the house, my father's mother called her new daughter-in-law to the hall, where the radio was blaring, to ask her what she was doing. 'Nothing,' my mother answered. It was true. There was nothing to do.

'Sit with me, listen to some music.'

My mother sat on the sofa until she grew bored of the classical voices. She preferred The Doors, or Freddie Mercury. But when Ma tried to stand, her mother-in-law held her arm. 'Stay here. I like the company.'

Their time together on the sofa by the radio would last up to six hours. Meals and tea were brought by the servants. My father's mother kept a pair of tweezers in her hand. She would feel for the hard bristles on her chin and yank at them. She did this without the assistance of a mirror and, to Ma's horror, would often tear into her own skin. Her jawline was edged with a chain of scabs and bristles.

'You know what would be nice?' the older lady said. 'If you wait by the door when it's time for my son to come home. I used to do it for my husband when we were newly-weds.'

She pointed at a large photograph of a man hanging on the wall. His eyebrows formed a dark line across his forehead, and he looked off to the side with a scowl. The portrait was garlanded with dried flowers.

'Is that something you want to do?' her mother-in-law asked.

Ma stared at the thick gap at the bottom of the front door, where an unobstructed ray of light curved in. Watching, waiting for something to break the line in half. A pair of feet. The shadow of a body approaching.

She wished she'd said no and found a way to avoid this chore. They were backwards, the people in this new family. Ma had preferred sitting in the living room.

Why don't you try it? You might like it.

Like what, exactly? What was there to like about standing by the door like a dog?

At five minutes to six, she took her post by the door, swaying from side to side for up to thirty minutes, depending on traffic and how long it took her husband to come home.

The mother-in-law kept the door to the living room ajar so she could glance through and make sure Ma was at attention. Four days in, the older lady acknowledged that the act of standing for so long was tedious, and an elaborate plan was hatched for a servant to stand by the window in the kitchen and holler when he saw the young sahib approaching. At that moment, the mother-in-law would flutter her arms with excitement and motion for Ma to bound towards the door.

It came to pass that at five minutes to six, even though the arrival time was on average closer to six-thirty, the mother-in-law would turn off the music and shout for the servant to look out. Ma liked the silence, but was not allowed to put her head back or close her eyes without being tapped by her husband's mother.

'I don't want to do this any more,' Ma said one day.

The mother-in-law said nothing as Ma stood up and went to her room. The voice of Kishore Kumar seemed to forever hang in the air.

The room was a cage, but it was the only place Ma felt relief. Sometimes she would bang her body against the wall and scream silently to herself. Other times, she would lie on the bed, close her eyes and travel, knocking her arm against the pale, ginger-coloured side tables. The mattress was thinner than what she was used to. The bedcover was made of grey synthetic cloth, and she wondered how the servants managed to wash it. The floor was a burning red marble that in some lights looked like an endless abyss to fall into. On the dressing table was a cup that held her hairbrush and comb. She would tip it over and pick it up again, listening to the quiet crash. She would pull out all the hairs the brush had taken from her head and wrap the long strands between the comb's teeth. Sometimes she wrapped the dark wire around her fingers, watching it cut into her skin. When this bored her, she put her feet up against the headboard, watching her thin ankles, drifting in and out of daydreams about her husband, imagining what he would be doing at that particular hour, before her mind would wander to the bed she was on, and other men she knew or had experienced only in fleeting interactions but who had imprinted themselves on her with an intensity she continued to long for. My mother knew marriages were generally unhappy, but she was young and had not fully metabolized the idea that this would be her reality. She still believed she was special, exceptional and had thoughts that no one else did.

She watched the hands on the small Seiko alarm clock move, waiting for the day to end, listening for voices outside the door, for steps passing in the corridor.

In time, Ma worked up the courage to pull open my father's closet. There was so much there she had never seen him wear, items of clothing that probably no longer fitted him. She mentally marked what had to be given away without removing a single garment from its place. Ma touched the sleeves of each shirt. She inspected the way the soles of his shoes were worn, and the places in his undershirts that were thinning. There was something she loved about looking with leisure, something she didn't let herself do when the man himself was present. Sometimes she wasn't sure she knew what he looked like at all.

When he came home from his day of studies, my father greeted his mother before going to wash and read his books. After dinner, he often joined his mother in the living room and put his head in her lap. She would press her hands against his forehead, stroking the short baby hairs, willing them to grow in the opposite direction. From his mother's lap, my father would watch my mother. His mother watched them both. Over months, lines were drawn.

Days would pass when husband and wife said little to each other. Ma thought he was strange, moody and distant. His mother was determined that he should excel in his studies, and he was keen to make her happy. The prize for his efforts would be America, where he could earn a master's degree in the snow, eat burgers every day and buy acid-washed jeans. Ma learned to long for that dream too. For a while she wanted my father to be proud of her, to wear her on his arm at the Club, so she chopped her long hair off and dressed in floral silks when they went for lunch on Sundays. She planned and plotted, imagining a time when they would be in America, together and in love, and he would show his romantic side, the one that was not full of mathematics and mother.

Ma found out she was pregnant around the time she learned her mother-in-law planned to join them when they went abroad. 'I will have to come,' the older lady said, lifting her tweezers. 'You will never be able to look after the house alone.'

The depth of Ma's gloom and her alienation from her own family – Nani refused to hear any complaints – made her lonely, and desperate. Or perhaps it was me, the surge of prenatal hormones, and a fear of the new life that awaited her, but she began to turn back into her former self.

She let her hair grow, stopped wearing make-up and shoulder pads.

She disposed of all her mother-in-law's hand-me-down saris, and blamed an aged servant for stealing them.

She smoked in secret, though she knew it could be dangerous for her foetus.

Ma went back to her old cotton comforts, forgoing the bras she had enthusiastically purchased, and announced that she wanted to start attending a guru's satsang, to hear him speak.

It was an odd request from a girl who had never shown any interest in religion, and her mother-in-law tried to stop her, but Ma was determined. She was on her way to no longer caring what everyone thought. Even after I was born, she would disappear every day, dripping with milk, leaving me unfed.

'Take her with you,' my Dadi-ma said when I was old enough. The relationship between my grandmother and Ma had soured, and my father's mother had no great love for me, another girl, another nuisance.

And so I went with my mother, leaving in the morning and coming back late in the evening. She returned to the house every day smelling of sweat and joy – and one day they realized she had not come home at all.

The history of my mother's life is not to be found in old photo albums. It is kept in a dusty metal cupboard in her flat. She never locks the door – maybe because she doesn't value anything inside, or maybe because she hopes one day the contents will vanish. Still, the cupboard is hard to prise open. Pune isn't wet enough for rust, but the hinges are almost solid and brown, and a light fuzz of rot covers the inside of the door. A cupboard that looks as though it was rescued from the bottom of the sea.

Inside is a pile of saris, metres of fabric carefully folded with paper between the creases, the cloth of another time – Banarasis woven with shimmering thread. There is one that is particularly beautiful, particularly heavy – the one my mother wore for her wedding, where it was draped in crisp, well-defined pleats. The fabric is stiff, almost crunchy, and smells of mothballs and iodine, but the gold never darkens or dulls, a sign that it is real, precious, a small fortune spent by my grandparents on their only child. The red makes it richer, almost oppressive, a true bridal red. Below this, the rest of her bridal trousseau – carefully selected saris and fabrics in colourful silks and ornate brocades – clothes to carry her into her new life as a married woman, the most important role she will have, enough fabric to last her an entire year so that her husband would not feel the burden of his new wife, at least not immediately. There are tussar silks in jewel tones, an embroidered dupatta covered in French knots, pastel Kanjivarams, even a parrot-green Patola peeks through the piles of material.

And then, one shelf below, are the other clothes. These are more familiar to me. There are a few faded block-prints on worn cotton, but mostly everything is white. If I hold them to my face, I can still smell her body, as though she wore them just yesterday. I can smell the neglect, the damp, the misery that grows in the absence of sunlight. These cottons are coarse, the kind worn for work. The whites are still bright, some glaring and some almost blue, the white of widows, of mourners and renunciants, holy men and women, monks and nuns, the white of those who no longer belong in the world, who have already put one foot on another plane. The white of the guru and his followers. Maybe Ma saw this white cotton as the means to her truth, a blank slate where she could remake herself and find the path to freedom. For me it was something different, a shroud that covered us like the living dead, a white too stark to ever be acceptable in polite society. A white that marked us as outsiders. To my mother this was the colour of her community, but I knew better: the white clothes were the ones that separated us from our family, our friends and everyone else, that made my life in them a kind of prison.

I can walk from my flat to Ma's in about forty-five minutes if I take the shorter route and run across the main road while the light is still green. On the way, I pass three shopping malls that are situated in a triangle. One has a multiplex, and the circular road outside gets jammed on opening weekends of big films.

A two-lane bridge crosses the narrow river, which floods in the monsoon and dries up in the summer. Sometimes the smells from the stagnant puddles reach Ma's flat. Buildings are coming up on the banks, a combination of luxury condominiums and five-star hotels that boast water views on their websites. Giant hoardings for Hindi soap operas and fairness creams are dividers between the construction sites.

The morning traffic collects at every corner, and Pune feels like one long bottleneck. Each eruption of horns is a torrent of bullets, and before long I am riddled. It will be winter soon and the temperature drops suddenly. Human beings need to be eased in slowly. Sudden movements lead to schizophrenia and sore throats.

Turning into Ma's lane, I pass Hina, the fruit lady who once had a small cart but now owns a proper store. Dilip says she's a modern Indian success story and should be written about. I wave at her but she doesn't see me due to a detached retina that she refuses to get operated. Beside her is a salon called Munira's Hair Garden. Dilip once pointed out that the placement of their logo, a pair of scissors, makes the word 'Hair' look like 'Hairy'. And then there is a pharmacy that sells electrical products and, across the street, an electrical shop that illegally sells medicine.

At the gate, the doorman salutes me. I wait for the lift and say hello to Mrs Rao, who frowns at me while her Pomeranian defecates next to a flowerpot. The dirt lodged between the tiles at the entrance is a permanent fixture. Rot and years of disrepair have loosened the flooring. This building has been defeated, like so many others. I let myself into Ma's apartment with the key I have copied.

Seven sticks of incense burn by the door. I cough and my mother pops her head out of the kitchen. I can smell that she is frying peanuts with cumin seeds in oil. I slip my feet out of my sneakers, which have stretched at the mouth because they're never unlaced. The floor is cold and smells like lemongrass milk. Light pours in through the east-facing window in the kitchen, and Ma is a silhouette. She dumps a bowl of bloated tapioca balls into the pot and covers it to steam.

'Have you had breakfast?' she asks, and I say I haven't even though I have.

I set the table like we used to, with glasses for water and buttermilk, and no spoon for Ma because she likes to eat with her hands. She brings out chillies, red and powdered, green and chopped. The pot is placed directly on the table, and when she lifts the lid, the cloud that conceals the meal inside evaporates.

I help myself to a large spoonful. The tapioca balls bounce on my plate, leaving a glistening trail behind them.

My mouth fills with a first bite. 'Something is missing.'

'What?'

'Salt. Potato. Lemon.'

She takes a bite and sits back in her chair, chewing slowly. I wait for her anger, but she gets up and goes into the kitchen. I hear the suction of the refrigerator door separating and meeting, the clanging of utensils. She comes out with a small tray and places it on the table. There is lemon juice and a shaker of salt.

'What about the potato?'

'Sabudana khichdi doesn't have potato.'

'You always make it with potato.'

She pauses. 'No potato this time.'

I push the food on my plate around and look at her.

'Don't keep looking at me like that.'

'You're not taking this seriously.'

She throws her head back and laughs, and I can see creamy tapioca clinging to the dark fillings at the back of her mouth. 'Taking what seriously?'

'Why did you tell Dilip I'm a liar?'

'I never said that.'

It seems to me now that this forgetting is convenient, that she doesn't want to remember the things she has said and done. It feels unfair that she can put away the past from her mind while I'm brimming with it all the time. I fill papers, drawers, entire rooms with records, notes, thoughts, while she grows foggier with each passing day.

She takes another bite. 'They say when the memory starts to go, other faculties become more powerful.'

'What kind of faculties?'

'There are women who can see past lives, who can talk to angels. Some women become clairvoyant.'

'You're mad.' Reaching into my satchel, I pull out my sketchbook. I turn to the last page and add today's date to a list that contains some forty entries. Next to the date, I write the word 'potato'.

Ma squints at the book and shakes her head. 'How does your husband tolerate you?'

'You're not even married, how would you know?'

Her mouth is open as I speak, and for a moment I think she is mouthing my words as I say them. Have we said these exact sentences to each other before? I wait for a reply but the moments pulse by. My armpits are damp and I feel something inside of me rearing up.

She smiles. Her teeth look sharp in the sunlight, and I wonder if she enjoys these moments, has grown to expect them. My heart is beating faster and my breath is shallow. I welcome this too.

She taps my hand and points to the notebook. 'You should worry about your own madness instead of mine.'

I look down at the list, at the careful lines that form each column, before shutting the book soundlessly. On my plate, the tapioca begins to harden. The temperature between us cools. Within minutes, we forget that harsh words have been exchanged.

We mix a few drops of lemon juice in cups of hot water and go out on to the balcony. Ma has hung a dozen hand-washed bras along a clothing line. Some have been patched and mended.

'You need new ones.' I finger the murky lace of one battered specimen.

'Why? Who's looking at them?'

Below us, in the building grounds, a baby is crying in her ayah's arms. The woman rocks her maniacally while talking to the watchman. The cries are like that of an animal in pain. We sit silently, waiting for the baby to tire, for her vocal cords to give way, but the screams continue without intermission. The ayah keeps rocking, panting, in panic, perhaps hoping her employers in the building above don't hear.

'I don't understand why you won't buy new bras,' I say. I wasn't planning on returning to this, but somehow I have. The baby is still crying. I wonder what the child could possibly want, and why it seems like the only thing that matters.

'I have to be an example.'

'An example for what?'

'For you. You don't have to care what others say all the time. Not everything is a show for the world. Sometimes we do things just because we want to.'

If our conversations were itineraries, they would show us always returning to this vacant cul-de-sac, one we cannot escape from.

I start by taking the bait: 'What have I done that I don't want to do?'

She feigns benevolent dismissal: 'Anyway, let's not get into all of that.'

The refusal to let things go: 'Then why did you bring it up?'

More dismissal and rejection: 'Leave it, it doesn't matter.'

The outright anger: 'It matters to me.'

The rest unfolds predictably. She asks why I am always after her, behind her, chasing after her like a rabid dog with my fangs out. Don't I have anything better to do, she asks, than bully my own mother?

I do not hesitate for a moment when I tell her she only knows how to think about herself. Her expression moves towards injury but turns back, and she says, 'There's nothing wrong with thinking about oneself.'

I halt at the usual impasse. Where do we go from here?

I want to tell her all the things that are wrong with it, but can never find the words. I want to ask her what's so terrible about doing what other people want, with making another person happy. Ma always ran from anything that felt like oppression. Marriage, diets, medical diagnoses. And while she did that, she lost what she refers to as excess fat. She has no interest in being lean of body – but she doesn't need repressed know-nothings around her, she says. The feeling has become mutual. Certain contemporaries at the Club refuse to acknowledge Ma. The elder relatives, who might have had a soft spot for the child they remembered, are infirm or dead. Yes, Ma has people around her, people who love her, but to me they seem few. To me, we have always been alone.

There are repercussions for living the life she's chosen. I wonder if the loss is worth it, and if she believes it's worth it. I wonder what she feels after I leave to go back to Dilip and she looks around her house. Maybe this isn't her choice at all, but another path she has mapped over and over, one she cannot unlearn. I want to ask her if, in all the years she has run away, any part of her screams *come after me*? Does she want to be caught, brought back and convinced that she is important, that she is necessary?

But these questions dissolve when I see her leaning back in her chair, eyes closed, humming to the soundtrack of the crying baby and sipping her sour water.

Dilip wants to become a vegetarian because a lion killed a lioness in America yesterday.

The lions grew up in the same zoo, in captivity all their lives. They mated many times, produced cubs that were taken from them at a young age. One busy weekend afternoon, they were sitting in their cage as usual, and a bunch of children were running about, pointing at the animals, asking their parents if the lions were real, like the ones they had seen in the National Geographic programmes on television. The newspaper added that last bit, as though the lions had heard, turned to each other and said, *Those kids want to know if we're real. Should we show them how real we are?*

And then the male bit the female's head off.

Not exactly like that, but he swallowed her face and held her, incapacitated, while she suffocated inside his mouth, in front of all the screaming humans.

The article left the reader with a series of questions: Were the lions depressed? Is this part of a larger cover-up, like SeaWorld? Are they trying to hide a common occurrence by suggesting the incident is isolated? Can captivity ever be a normal thing – and should it be such a big part of our culture or something that we encourage as a childhood amusement? Doesn't the public have a right to know the truth?

Dilip says he hated going to the zoo, even as a child. There was nothing that could be worse than looking at a creature in a cage. He had the same feeling as when he studied colonial history and his text-book had a full-page picture of the Hottentot Venus, chained up at the neck and smoking. The entry described how, after her death, she was dissected and her organs put on display. He tells me that, when he was a teenager, he avoided going to Juhu beach on family trips to Bombay because a cousin told him the camels there were suffocating in the damp air, their giant lungs sodden like wet pillowcases.

Some things move my husband, but I can never predict what. He ate kale before it was fashionable and once tried to make his own soap. He leaves bowls of water out on the window ledge in case birds get thirsty on summer days. Racism, sexism and animal cruelty come from the same source, in his estimation, and he speaks about them interchangeably.

I tell his mother about the lions when she calls that evening – and she laughs at her son, says she doesn't know where these ideas have come from, except maybe that one summer he went to Surat to stay with her in-laws, because she knows they're a veggie-preaching lot. She wonders why she didn't hear about the lion incident in Milwaukee, and why the papers in India have nothing better to do than report on American zoos.

I tell him what his mother said, and he shrugs. 'Everyone's entitled to their own opinion.'

He smiles without showing his teeth, and I have a sudden desire to confess something. 'I loved killing slugs as a child.' I realize I am sweating, as though a poison has been released from within me. 'At the ashram.'

He looks at me, but his face is unreadable. 'Okay.'

'I poured salt on them, and they would shrivel and scream. Kali Mata taught me.'

He looks in the mirror as he answers. 'I don't think they scream.'

'They do. I remember there were screams.'

'It's not a big deal. You were just a kid.'

'Today I fought with Ma.'

'About what?'

'Our usual fight.'

'You know how to push each other's buttons.'

He eats dal and two vegetables that night at dinner and says he already feels better, lighter, after just three meals.

Two days later, over quinoa and spinach soup, he tells me that his mother was actually right, that something did happen when he went to Surat in Gujarat all those summers ago. He heard a story about his aunt, his father's aunt actually, named Kamala. She was born in 1923 and her father was the first man in the town of Bhavnagar to buy an automobile. He was also the first to educate his daughters as well as his sons. But when it was Kamala's turn to attend university, she begged her father to let her become a Jain nun, to live near the temples in the small city of Palitana, and climb the thousands of steps with the other pilgrims and devotees to the top of the Shatrunjaya hills every day. She told him of a recurring dream she'd been having, of the face of the Jain deity Adinath from a statue of him that sits in a temple in Palitana. But as she drew closer, the face would disappear into darkness.

I know enough about Jainism to know that Jains are some of the most extreme vegetarians around, forgoing not only meat and eggs but also plants that must be uprooted for consumption. Jain food was commonly made without onions and garlic. I run through all the recipes I will have to change if he decides to take this further. The nuns often tie white cloth over their mouths and sweep the ground before they take a step so that they neither inhale nor step on any living being, even by accident. However, the Jains I knew still wore leather and didn't seem to notice what industrial dairy farming meant for cows all over India.

I feel betrayed, as though some dark secret has been revealed. 'You never told me you were a Jain.'

'Only a quarter. On my dad's side.'

'How did Kamala know which temple it was?'

Dilip taps the table. 'I don't know. Maybe she had been there.'

I nod, and he continues, but I detect less enthusiasm than he started with.

Kamala's request was refused, and she was beaten and locked in her room. For seven days after that, her mother knocked at the door with a plate of food but not a single morsel was consumed. On the eighth day, Kamala's father opened the door and saw his child was already wearing the thin white cloth of the Jain nuns. In anger, he pulled at the white cotton covering her head. What he saw stopped his hand. Her hair was all but gone. Her scalp was red and inflamed.

When he asked her what she had done, she told him Paryushan, the Jain holy days of introspection and abstinence, had begun, and it was a time when Jain nuns plucked every hair from their heads as penance.

'How many hairs are on the average head?' I interrupt. He shrugs.

'How many thousands of steps is it to the top of Palitana?' I ask.

'I don't know exactly,' Dilip says. 'A lot.'

'Most of this story has been exaggerated.'

'We don't know that.'

'Yes, we do. In a generation, she'll have walked on water.'

'I'm just saying, the people in my family, they have the calling.'

'The calling for what?'

'For a life of radical non-violence.'

'But they also have a calling for the opposite,' I say. I bring up his mother's love for American holidays with big birds on the dinner table, and the fur she wears to shield herself from the Midwestern winters. I mention his uncle, the wife-beater.

I didn't understand what was non-violent about pulling hair out of your scalp, or running up and down thousands of steps every day. I want to ask if Jain monks are expected to violate their bodies in the same way, but Dilip's expression stops me.

'Something about this is making you uncomfortable,' he says. 'Don't worry, you don't have to stop eating meat if you don't think you can manage it.'

My earliest memory is of a giant in a pyramid. The giant sits at the centre of the pyramid, on an elevated platform. He mimics the structure he sits within, forming a large white pyramid composed of white clothes, grey hair and a thick beard. Around him are smaller pyramids, also white, and Ma is one of them – one among a sea of pyramids – and when I look up, the ceiling of the room meets in an apex high above my head, pointing upwards to the sky outside.

The smaller pyramids sit cross-legged. The aim of the congregation seems to be to copy the giant. I am the smallest in the room and I don't know how I would manage being any bigger. Some of the pyramids are terrifying if I get too close; they have hair and pimples, and large pores on their noses.

There is one other who is about my size. She waits in the corner, a dirty rag in her hand, watching us. From time to time she shuffles forward to refill water for those who ask. Before, when we entered the pyramid, I saw her crouched outside, collecting shit left by the ashram dogs.

The giant opens his eyes; his lower lids fall away from the upper. Hair grows all over his face, but somehow I can make out he is a man and not a beast, and Ma is not afraid so I try not to be. Three strings of beads hang around his neck – brown, pink and green – forming a tangle. I want to pull them off him and wear them myself because I have no necklace of my own, but I dare not go near him. His mouth opens and his tongue pushes out, and I can see darkness at the back of his throat, teeth covered in darkness, a never-ending recess.

I move close to Ma. She is looking at him, sweating with the rest of the room, but I can smell her particular smell, and I love her because she is known to me in some way I cannot explain.

She draws me to her and kisses me full on the mouth. Then she squeezes me into her side and tickles my neck. I am embarrassed, and wary of her affection because it's often followed by something unpleasant.

The giant draws his tongue back in and swallows, preparing before once more pushing it out. Saliva falls a metre in front of him, on to a medium-sized pyramid, a man with yellow hair, but the yellow-haired pyramid does not move – he is mesmerized and copies the giant, sticking his tongue out of his mouth, and a light spray of spit falls just beyond his shadow. I look around and my mother and all the other pyramids are following. The giant laughs or coughs, I am not sure which, and laughs and coughs more, in a continuous stream, and his belly, which sits a little in front of him, is shaking and his hair is bound into tentacles. The rest of the group follows, coughing, laughing. I even hear a belch. A woman beside me starts to cry, but when I look at her, no tears are falling down her face.

The room smells warmer, like my finger when I rub it in my navel.

The woman beside me screams between her cries, and some other pyramids scream in response. I look at Ma and her face is red from coughing. I hold her hand, but she pulls it away and begins to stand, and I see that the giant is also standing and all the pyramids are transforming themselves into white columns.

I stand and hold on to the edge of Ma's kurta, curling it in my hand, working my fingers against the fabric.

The giant has lifted his arms and is shaking them, and they wiggle and fly away from his body as though he is loosening, as though he is going to let his limbs go and give them to the sea of white, the way he gave his breath and his saliva.

The ground is moving because they are moving – all the pyramids, jumping, stomping, dancing, holding each other. Someone taps me on the forehead, and someone gathers me into her arms. I cry for Ma, but I cannot see her for a moment, until I find her behind me. Her breasts are bouncing below her white kurta, and the sea of people envelops her, fondles parts of her body and releases her once more.

The giant is croaking and his eyes bulge, and his face is like a frog's. He croaks again and again, and some follow him, adding to the croaking, but others heave their bodies around like different animals, neighing, bleating, bringing up sounds from inside themselves that are unfamiliar to me. They are all around me, closing in and receding, and I sit on the ground and they seem to forget I am there, but I can smell the skin of their feet as it rubs against the tiled floor.

Ma, I think to myself as I watch her. I want her to look at me, but she is elsewhere. I can see it in her face, a face she wears when she cannot see me. I don't know where I have seen this face before because I can't remember what came before it, but it is familiar and something I know to fear.

Ma has her arms in the air and is spinning around in circles. There are two men on either side of her and she disappears between them as they dance. She stops turning and teeters here and there, and one of the men holds her steady, laughing, but her hair is stuck to her head and her mouth falls to one side, still finding its balance. Others are shouting, retching, crying out at the top of their lungs, charging the air with nonsensical sounds.

'Ma,' I say.

Her mouth is regrouping, starting to point upwards at its ends, until she is smiling for someone. I follow her eyes and the giant is there.

The giant is returning Ma's smile, or perhaps she is returning his, but this I will never truly know because I did not witness whose mouth broke first. He is on his hands and knees, springing himself up. His long hair falls on to his face. Saliva bubbles on his lips, collecting between the strands of his beard.

I slap Ma's leg with my hand, and she looks down at me and pushes me away.

'Don't do that,' she says.

I feel my arms unravel at my sides. She pushes me again and I stagger backwards. Her breasts are moving in a way that makes her ugly.

'What's wrong with you?' she says. 'Dance! What's wrong with you?'

More bodies appear between Ma and me, other bodies in white that are travelling from the back of the room to the front, hoping to get closer to the giant. Their faces distend, their jaws pulse with blood. They're afraid to go too close.

I stand up again. 'Ma,' I say. She cannot hear me over the hoots and laughter and tears.

'Ma,' I shout, and I feel an urgency in my abdomen, something that I didn't feel a moment ago but is now ready to burst.

'Ma!' I am screaming, but the sound I make is lost.

'Ma! Ma! Ma!' I am flapping my wings, but she doesn't notice.

'What's the matter, pretty girl?' The voice is close to my ear, and I pull away when I see the face. A woman painted with chalk and dressed in black is crouching beside me. The only black in the sea of white. 'What's the matter?'

'Ma,' I say.

'Ma? What do you need to tell your ma?'

I point, but there are too many around her.

'Okay, okay, let me help you. Is there anything I can do?'

I point to my stomach and back to Ma. I feel bubbles in my throat, ones that have risen from my stomach, not the soft ones that form with soap but hard, plastic bubbles, lodged in place and growing. No sound comes out of my mouth.

The woman looks from my stomach to my face, and the dark kohl that circles her blue eyes stretches when she raises her glistening eye-brows. 'Tummy ache?' Her voice is strange, has a lilt I haven't heard before, as though she is singing a song.

'Susu,' I mumble.

'Okay. Well, lemme take you. I can show you where the potty is.'

She holds my hand and we snake through the white. Her skin is rough, and when I let my fingers wander in her grip I feel the edges of her talons. I turn back for a moment, but Ma has vanished in the white sea.

The toilet is quiet, and the lady in black holds me under my arms as I squat above the hole. We look at each other as we listen to my urine hit the bottom of the bowl, and I nod at her when it has stopped. She adjusts my pants and ties a bow with the string at my waist, and I see her nails are ridged and grey, and her hands are covered in brown spots.

'Pretty girl, will you wait outside for me?'

I nod, and stand outside the door, listening for sounds within. The lady in black lets out a steady stream, far louder and faster than mine. And I notice the bathroom door is one of many, that there is a vast corridor of doors and they are mostly shut. I jiggle the padlocks one by one. They feel heavy and metal and cold. Exposed bulbs buzz overhead, and I can hear a voice on a radio. At the end of the hall is a latticed railing that looks down to an open courtyard, and raindrops the size of fruit flies are misting the air.

I turn when I hear panting, and I see one of the doors is ajar, and through it come the sounds of animals and radios, and other things I cannot name. The padlock is hanging on its hinge like a severed limb. I push the door and it opens fully.

The other small one is there inside the room, without her rag, and she is flattened like a cross. While she lies on a table with her arms spread, a man in white holds her legs open. He is from the sea of white. He is the yellow-haired pyramid. His pants sag around his ankles and he grunts as he moves his body over hers. 'Pretty girl, pretty girl.'

I hear the lady in black call me. I turn away from the open door and run. She is standing outside the toilet. She shifts from side to side when she walks, and the long drapes of her clothes sweep dust across the floor.

'You want a little snack?' she asks. She produces a packet of glucose biscuits. I fill my mouth with them, the surface soaking up the saliva from my palate before they melt. I feel like throwing up but I cannot stop eating. The lady smells like fabric, and the fumes of many days are embedded in her clothes.

She asks me if I want to rest while I wait for my ma. 'Yes,' I answer.

We lie down together on a damp mattress in the courtyard. It is stained and faded, camouflaged against the brown tiles it sits on. The rain has stopped for now. I can hear shrieking coming from the pyramid, but it's faint and could be from the throat of any person, anywhere. I feel myself distancing from it, pulling away from the source, reassigning it to someone I don't know, someone wholly unconnected with who I am.

The space between the noise and me grows, I feel my ears hollowing out as the sound withdraws, and softness spreads to the rest of my face. The muscles around my eyes relax, and the atmosphere is whiter than before. I don't know where I learned to do this but I am good at it, and it's a trick I repeat often throughout the rest of my life.

The lady in black asks if I have ever seen stars. I tell her I have, and we look up at the cloudy sky. I want to say something more about the stars, but can't recall what they look like, how many there are in total, and if they cluster in some recognizable formation. Are they static or moving, do they flicker or glow like bulbs, and I begin to doubt whether I have seen stars at all – or if I know of their existence only indirectly, through my mother or my father, or someone else who had taken it upon themselves to teach me what I don't remember, because the only reality that remains from that time are feelings and ideas, and whether I authored them or they were placed within me is impossible to know.

'What's your name?' the lady in black asks.

'Antara,' I say.

'Hi, Antara. I'm Kali Mata.'

Before she became Kali Mata, her name was Eve and she lived on two acres in Lanesboro, Pennsylvania, with her husband, Andrew, their daughter, Milly, and Andrew's mother, June. I know them with their tongues sticking out, and in profile, from the pictures Kali Mata left behind. The family said grace at every meal while Grandma June was alive – Kali Mata said June was a stickler for that kind of thing, not because she necessarily believed, but because it was the right thing to teach the children. Eve didn't care much for Grandma June's advice, but even after the old bat bit the dust (just fifty-nine with all that praying) Eve decided to keep up the tradition. Grandma June had been the first body she'd seen devoid of life, one moment animated like a marionette strung up by the devil, and the next nothing more than a shadow on the floor, her limbs lying brokenly. Emergency services said something about a blood vessel exploding, but Eve just didn't believe that. Grandma June hadn't passed away with that kind of fireworks; it had been quiet, sudden, leaving the family disbelieving.

Eve never saw her own parents die, and even though she didn't like Grandma June's long lectures, the sight of death alarmed her. Andrew found himself explaining more about the phenomenon of death to Eve than to little Milly. Milly held her father's hand, said she understood, and told him that she hoped he would be okay. But Eve, a mother, well into her thirties, could only stare at the wall for weeks. 'They were really close,' people murmured at the wake. 'They were very close and she loved the old lady like her own mother.' Eve didn't correct people, didn't tell them about the occasions she whispered to herself that she hoped the old lady would drop dead, but she had to admit that death, when it stared her in the face, looked as final as it was.

Eve insisted on grace every night and Andrew was happy to oblige, but when everybody put their heads down and thanked the Lord for their daily bread, Eve began her own private negotiations with the Almighty: if God saw fit to take food from her table and the roof from her head, she would survive. But, if he was listening, and if all those Sundays spent in a dusty barn in Bible Study were penitence enough, she would ask for only one thing now, one thing that the Lord should grant her, because it was really nothing at all. She asked only that the Lord take her first, that he welcome her into his kingdom before anyone else who sat at the table in front of her. She wouldn't survive, she reasoned, if she had to bury one of those dear souls while she still walked the Earth. Those were wakes she did not plan on attending. And so, if there was any way this one small request could be arranged, she would be happy to keep insisting the family say grace at the table. In Eve's eyes, she kept up her end of the bargain, but the Lord didn't keep his, and when news of the car crash reached her Eve was inconsolable for the next five days. Then she packed a bag and left town. She'd meant what she'd said – no wakes, no identifying bodies. She would never see them as they looked in their final resting places. Eve lived in Philadelphia with her sister for a while, got a job as a sales girl in a bridal warehouse until she met a man who called himself Govinda. He was handsome, with light brown hair and glasses, possessed a melancholy she, too, felt, and made money selling marijuana. He took her to the Hare Krishna Mission, where they sang songs, and then to his apartment, where he said he was saving up to go to India to see the Brahma temple in Pushkar and escape the cycle of suffering. He asked her if she wanted to come.

In Pushkar, she started dressing herself in black embroidered fabric. It was weighty and forced her to move slowly. She had been a fair child, with orange freckles on her forearms, but that year they spent living in the desert darkened her complexion and puckered her skin. Her hair formed a short trail of dreadlocks behind her. Eyeshadow hung like turquoise dust on her clenched eyelids, settling into the grooves, creating patterns, and black kohl encircled the entirety of her eyes. Her lips were dark raisins. In her hair she kept an arrangement of ornaments collected along the way, feathers and trinkets hanging from threads.

They wandered the desert, living on the outskirts of villages, forgetting the lives they had before.

No one was sure where she came from. Some said she was ageless and had been meditating in the Thar desert for as long as anyone could remember. Villagers bowed to her, some even touched her feet, and the children called her oont bai, camel lady, because she could survive without water.

It was there that she met a giant dressed in white who asked her to join him on his journey. We never learned why she wore black, only that he had found her this way, and that she was quite perfect, quite complete the way she was. Perhaps she was still in a kind of mourning, and mourning for her would always be black. She had been at the ashram in Pune for more than a decade before a pale, bewildered pregnant woman stumbled into the meditation hall. Kali Mata was no longer the giant's consort but she thought of herself as the mother of his children, as the nurturer for his many followers.

She invited the new devotee to sit down, but Ma shook her head and her eyes darted around the room. She said she wasn't sure she wanted to stay. But when the giant entered, Ma rushed to the front and found a spot at his feet. She meditated there for more than four hours, still like furniture. When Ma opened her eyes, she looked up at her guru and said she would devote her life to him. Then she placed her head in his lap and wept.

I must have been no more than three years old when Kali Mata told me about America for the first time, and about the ashram where I found myself living. She told me we were still in Pune, but when I looked around I couldn't believe it. The ashram was nothing like the rest of Pune.

She taught me that the giant was called Baba, that he had other names, many others, but this was how we should refer to him. He would be a father to us, a leader, a god. But he was also a humble servant in many ways, because he had taken a human form once more to relieve us of our ignorance. His lineage of teachers and masters included several famous maharishis and acharyas, and even certain sages who appeared in ancient texts. These are outlined in his autobiography.

Baba travelled in a Mercedes Benz and collected VHS tapes of Brigitte Bardot films. He was more than eight feet tall, a height that doesn't seem as remarkable now. His voice was gentle and soft, even through the speakers he used while addressing crowds of thousands. And his teachings appealed to everyone, a carefully layered narrative that drew on the Buddha, Christ, Krishna and Zorba. Baba liked science and was interested in computers. He watched India play in Test matches and enjoyed Japanese food. There was something familiar for everyone to come home to.

As a teenager, Ma had admired the ashram from outside, the freedom that festooned its devotees, but she herself entered only years later, when she found her husband's house was full of loneliness and boredom. Ma was looking for a way out.

The ashram's marketing materials show the beginnings, when they lived in makeshift structures with tin roofs and little light. The ashram grew around a banyan tree which was twenty metres tall, sprawling, coiling, its branches growing up and down, staking claim to the earth. The sanyasis planted saplings of lemon and mango trees, which would one day bear fruit. Slowly, they got permits for piped water and electricity. They explored the possibility of a well. Septic tanks were required. Concrete was poured and foundations were laid. Then the frames went up and the trusses were set in place.

This picture fades into a new shot of the ashram today, a resort, a sanctuary. The master is dead but his vision lives on. All rooms are now fitted with flat-screen televisions, and they offer couples massages and Tarot readings. AIDS testing is mandatory for admittance.

Only some part of those four years of my life left an imprint. There was the ratty mosquito net that hung over my bed in the room I shared with Kali Mata. She let me use the colours in her make-up palette to paint my face. The kitchen was my favourite place in the ashram, where hundreds of steel plates and glasses shone as they hung to dry, and where Kali Mata taught me how to steady my hand and peel an apple with a knife. It was also where I saw Ma, where she would be cooking for Baba. And I remember running my fingers over carvings of birds and snakes while I knocked on the heavy wooden door that led to a room my mother shared with him.

And then there was the day when my grandfather came and told my mother he couldn't bear the thought of us staying there any more, among this gathering of foreigners and whores. He told her that she had shamed her family, that she should go back to her husband's house immediately. Ma ignored him and said this was her home now. She said that Baba would be my father and the sanyasis would be my family.

As for the girl with the rag, her name was Sita. She cleaned the meditation hall, watered plants, never speaking. After lunch, she used to rest on a patched-up straw mat, her eyes shining through the crevices of her elbows. I have asked about her in recent years, but no one can remember that she existed.

I've collected some images of Baba that I keep in an envelope. Baba loved pictures and always had photographers on hand. 'Pictures,' Baba said, 'do not record history. They decide history. If there are no pictures of you, you never existed.'

Ma poses next to him in a number of images. In one, she wears a sari. It was the first time since she had left her husband's house, and she wore it on the occasion of her symbolic marriage to Baba.

The cotton looks coarse and bright white, two sheets cut and sewn together. There is no petticoat, and a brown ribbon is tied around her waist. The rope has a plastic tassel on one end, much like a shoelace. The pleats are tucked in place. Only three, and narrow, half the width of what is normal, but that was all the fabric she had. She must have taken small steps that day. She is sitting on a jute mat, beside Baba but a little behind. They arranged her hair over her bare shoulder.

The short pallu is left to rest on her head. Ma clutches at the loose end. The sun must have been bright because she is fighting a squint.

I have pictures of Baba in the form of postcards and keychains that I got from the ashram bookstore, and also a copy of his obituary that I converted from microfiche.

The obituary states that the possible cause of death was a drug overdose, though a group of his followers insist he was poisoned by local authorities. He was fifty-seven years old and may have had a condition called gigantism that explained his notable height. He left behind no widow or known children.

When the moon was full, my mother would burn sandalwood incense throughout her flat with the windows closed. Kali Mata had told her to do this to vanquish evil spirits and mosquitoes. We stopped the practice for a year when the doctor said it was giving me asthma. Ma believes that was the year everything went wrong.

Today, the smoke is heavy as Kashta performs this little ritual, and I watch the baroque plumes for shapes and faces. Nani sits surrounded by haze in an upright chair while I cough. I cannot tell if she has fallen asleep. Ma is next to her, looking dazed. She hasn't been very alert today.

I stand by the window. The moon is white in the sky and I imagine the tides rising into tall peaks and crashing on moonlit shores. The newspaper, folded on the coffee table alongside stacks of magazines and unopened mail, calls it a supermoon. I look at its surface through the window again, glowing but battered, as though it has been struck too many times. I pull the page with the article from the newspaper, and over it I sketch the skin of the moon with a pencil, mapping these brutalities.

The article says the moon will look larger than normal, that this is the closest it has been to the Earth since 1948.

'Nani,' I say, and she looks at me, blinking. 'The last time the moon was this close to the Earth was in 1948.'

Nani smiles and scratches her nose. 'The year you were born,' I add.

'Yes,' she says, 'I remember that year.'

There are no birth records of when my grandmother was born because most children in the refugee camps died before their mundans, when babies have their heads ritually shaved. Her husband invented the date of birth for her passport. But when Nani tells the story of her life, she starts at the very beginning: the midwives are screaming in Multani and they use a dirty cloth to wipe the fluid from her body. She's hungry and crying, searching frantically for her mother's breast, so anaemic that they name her Gauri, the fair one.

I ask her how she can be sure she remembers when the rest of us can barely piece together our childhoods.

Nani scoffs. She says I couldn't understand unless I had been there. Partition was a different time. Things happened then that never happened again.

Her eyes quiver and move to the wall behind my head. I turn away and reach for my laptop, open up several pages detailing the structure of amyloid plaque: a side of Velcro that misses its coordinating opposite. More diagrams showing brain tissue submerged in plaque, a mess of tatters, trapped in a grid where they don't belong.

This is what Alois Alzheimer found when he dissected his patient Augusta's brain after her death in 1906. Poor Augusta couldn't keep anything straight.

Scientists don't know where the plaques come from, or why the protein divides incorrectly. It reminds me a good deal of what I've read about cancer, but I don't say this to anyone for fear of sounding careless with words.

Amyloid plaque may only be a symptom. What's the cause? The length of telomeres, which sit at the end of chromosomes like the handles at the end of a skipping rope, could be one. They shorten over time, a sign of biological ageing.

Is this a cause or another symptom?

Ageing, it seems, is not everyone's destiny. Neither is cognitive decline.

I wonder if there are examples of agelessness. I wonder if there are immortals.

Nani seems in good health, sharper than she was when her husband was alive. But ageless? No. She seems old. There is stiffness in her joints and her mind.

I draw X and Y axes, marking them as age and decline. I plot my mother and Nani on the graph. Between them is a little family of krill.

I always imagined Kali Mata defying the limits of this graph, an asymptote to the infinite, until she dropped dead one morning in her home.

How many krill will die on this mission to make Ma remember? In the top corner of the page, I begin a flat depiction of the moon.

'You have your period.'

I look up from my drawings. I have transformed the moon into a peppered omelette. My mother turns off the bathroom light and sits down on the sofa. The smoke is settling. Nani's head droops on to her shoulder.

'Yes,' I say. 'How do you know?'

'You leave a smell behind. Pineapple.'

I've never had a smell before, not one so specifically categorized. Dilip has never mentioned it. I wonder if he knows what pineapple smells like. He once had an allergic reaction to a kiwi and his lips broke into ulcers.

I stare at the moon a moment longer. When Dilip is home, I will ask him to look at the moon with me.

My mother yawns. 'Did it start today?'

I need to think for a moment. 'Yes. This morning.'

Ma nods. She leans back against the cushion. 'With the moon, as always. Kali Mata, you always smell like pineapple.'

The moon has migrated across the sky, now hidden behind some buildings in the distance. I begin another drawing of its surface, this time from memory.

'What is this?'

I look up. Nani is holding a crumpled piece of paper in her claw.

'I was leaving notes for Ma around the house. So she can find them and read them. Maybe it will help her memory.'

Nani smiles. 'You're a good girl. Read it to me.'

I hesitate and press the scrap against my palm. In a few weeks, it has begun to look like ancient parchment.

'The time you added chilli to Antara's khichdi,' I read.

Nani laughs, and coughs when I finish reading. 'When was that?'

'She wanted me to learn to eat spicy food, I guess. She wouldn't stop, even though I developed a bad case of the hiccups.'

Nani shakes her head. 'Your mother didn't add the chilli to your khichdi. I added ginger to it because you had a very bad cold.'

'That's not true,' I say.

I was sure I remembered it, the taste of pain in my mouth.

'I'm telling you,' she said. 'Have you asked her? She will tell you.'

I had read that one to Ma and she had looked at me vacantly before I stuffed it into the sofa for her to find again.

'Even if I ask her,' I say to Nani, 'she doesn't remember.'

'Maybe she doesn't remember because it never happened.'

I feel the backs of my legs stiffen. Has she been speaking to Dilip? Has Ma convinced her that I'm lying?

The paper is carried out of my hand, but when I look around, all the windows I see are closed. Above my head, the fan moves with a soft swoosh as it completes its rotation, returning to the part of its hidden mechanism that sends it forth again. I bend to retrieve the paper but it floats away from me like a flattened ghost. Nani begins laughing and her voice is raspy, as though the mirth and the cough have become one and there is no boundary between her amusement and discomfort. We watch the paper vanish under the sofa.

From my pocket, I produce a key and hand it to my grandmother.

'What is this?'

'To open Ma's bank locker.'

Nani puts on her reading glasses and examines the keychain. It is a faded and muddy orange Garfield the cat. She looks up at me and arches an eyebrow.

'Just in case,' I say. 'We have to be prepared.'

A new doctor smiles when we enter the examination room. The one from last time is on holiday.

Ma shifts in her gown. She tells the doctor it smells distinctly of another woman's sweat. On the doctor's desk are his instruments, standing in a steel cup. A slick tongue-depressor, a curved pair of pincers. I don't have words for the others. In his hands, they look sharp, unkind. The room feels unclean. My eyes move from Ma to the ceiling, the white light, the air conditioner.

'Have there been any other episodes?' he asks.

'Yes,' I say. 'She's been having nightmares. The maid says when she enters the house in the morning, she finds Ma sitting in a corner, frightened.'

The doctor's expression does not change. He makes a series of notes on a page in Ma's file. His handwriting is typically illegible. 'I feel,' I begin, 'that everything is moving very quickly. Her symptoms are worsening.'

'Everything seems to be as good as can be expected,' he says. The hair on his face grows in patches of black and white. His two front teeth taper up, and he whistles when he speaks.

'She's been taking the medicine,' I say.

'I've seen cases, especially when it is early onset, where the degeneration occurs at a faster rate.'

'Is that what's happening here?'

'We can't be certain.'

'Then what are you saying?'

'Actually, the studies on this are rather inconclusive.'

I open a notebook and begin to read off a list. 'I have been showing her pictures, old videos. We've been watching her favourite films. I have been taking her for walks and drives in places where she used to spend time. We've been cooking, especially from recipes she hasn't made in a while.'

I lay a folder on his table, and begin to remove printed sheets of paper where I have highlighted sections in combinations of yellow, green and orange. The effect is citrus and difficult to look at for too long. He clears his throat and pushes his glasses back. 'I have a suspicion that my mother is leaking,' I say, pointing to a passage that lays out this thesis.

'Leaking,' he repeats.

'Yes, all over and from everywhere.'

Moving aside an article from a science journal I had annotated, I open a pamphlet I have made by hand and reveal my magnum opus. A flow chart of my mother's bodily functions, and a history of her life, starting from birth, where I note that my grandmother did not have a C-section and, therefore, properly inoculated Ma with microbes in the vaginal canal. From there, the events of my mother's childhood spool downwards: lists of possible vaccinations and penicillin use.

The next page focuses on the damage done to her mitochondria, the ageless centres of her cells, which were inherited from her mother and continue to live in me. The word 'mitochondria' labels the centre of a giant spider, whose legs tangle and cascade into a web of faltering Krebs cycles. The web is shortened telomeres down-regulating the production of enzymes, the turnover rate of mitochondria declining. Along its edge hang little cages overflowing with reactive oxygen species, their production increasing exponentially, perilously, as the lipid bilayer, the membrane which holds the whole architecture in place, begins to crack and collapse.

On the other side of the paper, my mother's intestine is a curving corridor, porous and full of holes, compromised from years of senseless eating and medication. Dead soldiers are piled up, their pyres already waiting.

'What is all this?' the doctor asks.

I look down at the sheet. 'I have been researching. This is what I've found so far.'

'Are you being serious?' he says.

Suddenly I cannot look at him. I feel like crumpling it all up.

'Please take this away,' he says. 'There are some new experimental treatments we can look at.' He lists some of the side effects. Stroke. Heart attack. Depression.

I say we will think about it, and wish the floor would open up and swallow me.

'Do that. And also, I recommend you find someone to help you with all of this.'

I wait for him to continue. He regards me with a tilted head. 'There are therapists you can talk to,' he says. 'About how to handle the position you find yourself in now. Caregivers in this role can suffer as much as the patients. It can be very stressful.'

We go home from the doctor's office, and pass the hordes going to Mass at the small church sandwiched between the local dairy and the German bakery. Ma and I don't speak to each other but stare out the window. The church hangs decorations on Christmas Eve, which twinkle like stars from a nursery rhyme. The queues to light a candle at midnight cause a back-up, cutting off the flow of traffic, and horns and angry shouts drown out the hymns.

A short walk across the busy street, over a broken footpath, is the neighbouring mosque, where the call to prayer is observed five times a day. Christmas is no exception. The popularity of Christmas in Pune has never been limited to the Christians in town, especially because of the general belief that the statue of the Virgin erected near the entrance of the church bestows good luck on her worshippers. Diminutive and dressed in pink gauze, she is the object of an informal pilgrimage. As we pass by, I say an involuntary prayer for everything and nothing in particular.

The keepers of the mosque know many Muslims are waiting to receive benediction from Mother Mary and her son, and the evening azan bellows through the loudspeakers with particular force after dark on the twenty-fifth, a reminder that the duty of believers isn't eclipsed by bright lights and a sparkling pine tree in the tropics.

I look at Ma. Her eyes close as the car brakes. I wish we weren't such failures.

'Why don't you stay with us for a night or two, Ma?' I whisper, partly hoping she doesn't hear me. 'Maybe next week? After New Year's?'

She opens her eyes and looks past me on to the crowded street. 'Maybe,' she says. 'Maybe one or two nights only.'

The date changes after midnight, and the commotion from church, mosque and bullock cart continues to swell. Voices are dissonant. Screams are indistinguishable from prayers. The streets heave with disorder. The uproar continues to escalate, but no one seems aware that the holy day has passed and the time has come to purge after the glut, to reflect on the excesses of the past day.

I have trouble sleeping that night. The wires by my bedside table disappear into a mess on the other side of the wall. Above my head, the ceiling light is an eye that watches me.

The next morning, relative calm returns to the town, and the church promptly turns off the festive lights to save on electricity. The traffic – machine, human and animal – resumes its normal flow.

On Boxing Day, Dilip has a conference call and I go out by myself. The black top of the rickshaw flaps over the sides like an awning, and the rubber conceals my face, keeps it hidden from the sun, the eyes of leering men and other disasters waiting to happen. But the men's eyes reach the parts the light reaches, and even when I don't see them looking at me, through the cotton-ball clouds I can feel the warmth of the sun on my skin. Those are the parts they can see, my feet in my chappals, my ankles, the full length of my body, my bare arms. It's easier for them to look at this headless girl riding around in a vehicle without doors.

Sometimes, their faces appear below the hood, ducking to catch who's inside, but we are moving too fast for me to tell them apart and they all belong to the same body and road.

We pass the commotion of MG Road, the booksellers, the jewellery shops, the women and men calling out to one another over the hullabaloo. Things have changed around here, I'm sure of that, but the city clips by too quickly to know how. Through the dry, salty membrane in my nostrils I can smell Kayani Bakery. The rickshaw stutters and halts, the engine smoking at a traffic light. Two men lean against the dilapidated gate of the old telephone exchange. They share a bidi and, above their heads, shards of glass line the top of the boundary wall, glinting in the sun. I sneeze and the driver glances back at me. Orange saliva gathers at the side of his lips. He spits on the ground and empties his nostrils one by one.

At the bus stop, men catch hold of the back of the bus, pressing themselves against the red metal shell. A legless boy sells day-old newspapers at the corner, and a flea-ridden dog rolls on its back.

College students on scooters sit three to a seat, howling back to their friends left behind in the dust. The girls are smiling and their earlobes are full of holes. They are girls like Ma used to be, girls of single colour, head to toe, girls with hair that hangs back like creatures flying behind them. I watch the eyes on them, on their clothes, their limbs, their open mouths. The day feels warm and bright.

I meet my friend Purvi for lunch at the Club. The afternoon is for eavesdropping. We circle the walking track, and Purvi describes the nightclub she went to the night before. I listen to some of the account but also to two men discussing the benefits of forced sterilization programmes, and to the lyrics of a song some teenage girls are singing as they stroll the Club grounds.

The path loops around, and at one point it is only separated from a crowded intersection by a line of shrubs and an iron fence. I hear the screech of traffic piling up, drivers on either side refusing to give way, jerking their vehicles forward into small gaps. Drivers alight and gather to give advice over the endless toots of horns. Heads shake and curses are thrown about, first insults about someone's mother, followed by a passing remark about a sister and a female cousin too.

The cacophony ignites with fumes of petrol. We stop and watch from behind a low wall of plants. I can smell burning rubber. The noise fights for space, bursting into an indecipherable clatter. An arm reaches out, and then several more. Throats are caught, shoulders pushed, and dust rises with the scuffle. Among the bodies, I see one fall, trapped under the weight of insults and rage. The heat beats down on their heads. A man looks up at us. His face is narrowed with a scowl. The shade sways as the trees above the path drift from side to side. I glance down at my hands, laced around the wire fence. I stretch them and let go but, in the distance, the fight continues. The man is lost in the fray.

Purvi is still talking. She is animated, sculpting the air with her hands, or rubbing one against the other, as if to erase some unwanted words. She says that rubbing palms or the soles of feet together is a yogic technique that integrates the left side of the brain and the right. When she was younger, she was a boyish girl who hated her hair and hid her hips. Now her nails are painted and filed into points. She's one of my friends who married young and for the right reasons. She and her husband go on cruises, rent holiday homes and learn to ski. They buy and sell horses, rarely repeat clothes, and never turn off the air conditioning in their apartment. Sometimes, when we are alone like this, Purvi interlaces her fingers through mine and swings our arms, like a little boy trying out his bat. She touches me as we walk, brushing elbows and the vulnerable parts of our wrists, stepping into my path. A year ago, at the Club, she fingered me in a bathroom stall while our husbands ordered drinks at the bar. We've never spoken of it.

'It's my father, with his family,' I tell Purvi once we are seated at a table.

They are enjoying Boxing Day. The new wife leans back in a white cane chair and he sits upright on the arm. They don't touch, but look at each other often. She nods at whatever he says. Then she smiles in a way I haven't seen before. Her shoulders shake, laughter breaks through. The sound washes over my body. Purvi glances at them before turning back to the menu, but I keep watching. The table they have chosen is bathed in sun. There are only a few metres between us but the light turns their world into a foreign one. When I lean back in my wicker chair, I could be looking at a painting, framed by the white pillars of the building, something almost Victorian. There is a past and a present, and a gap which cannot be closed. Can they see me? They must be able to see me. I am right here. They often look in my direction, but perhaps the sun blinds them. I am invisible.

Waiters pass back and forth. I blink and look away.

My father liked my mother a long time ago. He liked the way she looked, at least. Maybe he agrees to see me sometimes for the same reason, because I look like a girl he once liked – because I sit in his living room, imploring, confused, with the look of a girl who once hurt his pride.

I wonder what the upstairs of their house looks like now, since the new wife has been there for decades. If I asked to see it, would they show me which room belongs to whom, show me the changes they have made to the bedrooms since I was there as a child, the upgrades, a new sink, additional cupboards, retiled floors? Maybe I will suggest that, next time I endure the humiliation of a visit to their house. Of course his wife will offer to show me how they live. Or maybe the boy would want to show me around, since, technically, I am his older sister. Maybe through my humiliations, my father can witness the humiliation of my mother, feel avenged for the way he was made a fool of so many years ago. Or maybe he sees himself in my face, the way he sees himself in his wife. Maybe my father will show me the rooms he has designated for his child, and then the bedroom he shares with the woman he married, the one he inherited from his parents, a bed his son must have jumped on when he was young, where he fucks his new wife now but maybe still imagines my mother. Maybe I can fuck him – this man who likes to look at himself – on the same bed, quietly, careful not to disturb the others, while his wife makes tea a floor below.

My stomach squeals loudly. 'Are you hungry?' Purvi asks.

I shake my head. My stomach isn't growling, just speaking out of turn. It's always done this during quiet exams, dinners, the suspenseful pauses in films – it always says the things I haven't been able to, when maybe I am hungry but the hunger is of another kind.

I look towards the entrance, which is still decorated from the Club's anniversary. The balloons once floated in the air, and now they hang lifelessly from the nooses of metallic streamers.

We watch television in bed after dinner, and Dilip does not lower the volume when I mention children. His eyes are on a news anchor who is talking over his guests. They discuss whether non-Indian brands have the right to appropriate Gandhi's image for commercial purposes.

I am not sure if he has heard me. I wish we had more art on the walls. What's the point of always looking at blank white? Dilip says it helps him clear his head.

'I'm sick of India,' he says.

I look at the television and tell him to change the channel. 'No, I mean I'm sick of everything here.' He looks at me and back at the screen. 'Except you.'

'What's the issue?'

'This life. This job. This town.' One of his legs slides off the bed, and he is between sitting and lying down.

I nod, but he doesn't see me, so I put my hand on his. On the television, the advertisement plays at a louder volume than the scheduled programming. A couple is sharing a melting bar of chocolate, licking each other's fingers. It is meant to be romantic, but I think it is disgusting and have to look away to keep from throwing up. I hate this apartment. I want to live in a spread from a magazine where every surface has the right amount of beautiful junk. Where I can stand in the centre of the room, unmoving, like a statue, and dust would never collect on me or my clutter.

'I can't imagine where else we would go,' I say. He looks at me, waiting, and I realize he has an answer in his mind that he wants me to come to.

'I have a family too,' he says when my time is up.

I look at my feet, at the chipped nail polish on my big toe. The top of my foot has a few fine hairs. I have forgotten to pluck them for several months. He doesn't notice them. Or maybe he does but they don't bother him. Or maybe they do but he is too kind to say anything.

'Do you want children?' I repeat. As I ask him, I realize I don't want children that sound like him, as though their tongues move too freely in their mouths.

I had asked him this question three months into dating, over a bottle of wine, when we were contemplating the misery of our parents.

'I think I do. Don't you?' he says. It is exactly the same answer he gave me before. He is the same man. He has not changed. Tomorrow, the moon in the sky will begin to move into shadow.

'Why?'

'Why, what?'

'Why do you want children?'

He shrugs. 'So we can be like everybody else.'

I cannot remember what I said the last time or if this is something I want, too, but it feels familiar, feels like something I would say. Isn't conformity something I have always craved?

I look at Dilip and he is smiling.

'You haven't left the flat today, have you?'

1986

The floor of the ashram is white and cold against my cheek, and there are cracked heels all around. Everyone is dehydrated but perspiring. Arms belonging to bodies in white reach down to lift me. They hold my limbs, the hands closing around my legs, ankles, wrists, forearms, and I float a few centimetres above the ground before meeting it again. They are whispering, discussing what to do with me.

Kali Mata runs her hand against my cheek. 'Darling, stand up. Please stand up.' I close my eyes at the cool skin of her palms, at the smell of green onions and ghee in her nails. I love her. I want to do it for her. But I can't. I want water. I feel water coming out of my mouth. Saliva. The fan is turning above our heads. A lizard scurries across the wall, vanishing behind the white legs of the sanyasis. I try to curl myself up into a ball but the hole in my stomach screams when I move my legs. I look up at all their faces.

I know the others, but only Kali Mata is truly mine. Her blue eyes are like marbles. I can see myself in her eyes, lying there, a dried splatter of white paint. They have gathered to peel me off.

The floor reverberates – I can hear it, my ears are so close to the ground, so sharp – and I can hear her voice. Ma appears among their faces and they make way for her. I tense at the sight of her – I haven't seen her in weeks, I thought she had forgotten about me, I wondered if she was dead. No one will talk about her in front of me, no one will let me see her. Why do they want to keep us separate? Why does only Baba get to have her?

She picks me up off the floor, carries me to another room, pushes a glass against my lips. It hits my teeth with a clink. I take a sip of the water and sigh. My body is parched from within. I look around and see the room is my room, a room that I inhabit without her, and I cry, throwing my arms around her as my stomach protests.

'She hasn't eaten a thing in days. She just asks for you and points to her throat, says something's stuck.' I don't know who is speaking, but I feel the arms I am in stiffen. Ma is angry. I can already smell it.

She throws me down on the bed, and my head feels the hard wood beneath the thin mattress. I cry out, but Ma has climbed on top of me, is holding me, my arms and legs incapacitated, and the flailing I feel, the panic, stops short and rolls back inside, turning over on itself. Her hand hits the side of my face, and like lightning, I see the streak before I hear the sound. She wraps her arms around me and I feel my lungs shrinking as they lose air. I shout but my voice is muffled.

The light begins to darken at its edges, moving in slowly towards the centre. Is it a beating if there isn't a bruise? I cannot recall the nature of the pain.

'You better eat when you're told,' Ma says. 'You better be a good girl.'

There was a time when I knew the ashram well, when its particular topography made sense to me. I learned to walk barefoot, to feel gratification in the pressure of pebbles. Kali Mata cleaned my cuts and scrapes, carving out the inner flesh from an aloe vera leaf and rubbing it on my skin. We spent time in a little orchard she tended, populated mainly with burdened papaya trees. She listed the many health benefits of the papaya when she cut open a fallen specimen with a blunt pocketknife and handed me a sliver. These lessons continued even when I was older. When I was sixteen, she taught me to dry papaya seeds and boil them in tea as a form of birth control.

Kali Mata and I went for walks together in the ashram and I learned the shape of the land, where the ground curved like a cradle and the roots of trees rippled above the soil, unfettered. I knew the crevices that could hide my body, among the snakes and the tall ferns, below the notice of the world.

In the ashram, when the sky blackened there was no light except the faint glow of torches which disappeared in the grove. I walked with my hands in front of me, feeling for obstacles in my path. Baba liked to tell the story of how he had sat in silence for one hundred days, alone in a solitary cave near Gaumukh, the mouth of the river Ganga. Not speaking heightened his other senses, gave him supernatural abilities. He knew the feeling of levitating from those days, and from observing the life cycles of cells on his skin. Kali Mata said I shouldn't take him literally, but I did. I do. When I walked in the dark, I felt every spider's web, every rock underfoot, and whispers in the trees, the fragrance of jasmine blooming in the distance. My sandals marked each step. The leather soles slapped against the bottoms of my feet. That was the quality of the quiet there.

In the early days, I thought I would never be happy in that strange place. I stayed up all night, huddling in a corner by myself. I could cry without sleep, water or food. The sanyasis tried to coax me, hug me, even scold me from time to time. Kali Mata pinched me and told me not to be ungrateful. I had to eat, drink, sleep, they all said, I had to look after myself, give in to my state of nature. They said I should do it for Baba. They said I should do it for Ma.

They didn't know that when I did close my eyes I couldn't place who I was, and that staying awake was the only way I knew the ends of my own body. They gave me a kurta that belonged to Ma, white and worn, frayed at the edges. It smelled like her and I held it through the night. When I lay in bed, I could hear the sounds of the crickets and bats. Their voices echoed as though they were in the room with me. The springs of the mattress hummed under me. The building creaked, and even the ground felt loose, fragile. One wrong step and I would be swallowed up.

The days were easier and, as I got older, I did chores like everyone else, I helped in the kitchen. Kali Mata said we had to give back as much as we took, but I never knew how to measure those things. I ate tomatoes like they were apples. Certain stones uncovered colonies of worms, and I spent hours watching them burrow, sometimes giving in to the desire to smash them between rocks and bury their carcasses. I bathed myself, even during the monsoon, when the drain regurgitated cockroaches. I learned to wash my own underwear and hang it to dry. Kali Mata taught me how to hold a pencil, and control my hyperextended thumb, how to still my hand.

After four months of living there, I found ways to go to sleep by myself, to listen to the sounds of Kali Mata's breathing across the room, to find a pocket of warmth in the centre of the bed and fill it with any heat I could muster, until I could spread my limbs out without dread of the cold.

But I never managed to control what happened at night. When I woke up in the morning with blood on my pillow and scratches on my face, they told me that I suffered from bad dreams and cut my nails close to the skin. When that didn't work, they put mittens on my hands. Sometimes, I would wake up in the morning with a sheet tightly wrapped around my body, straitjacketing my arms and legs in place. I would scream until Kali Mata heard me and came to let me loose. She said they did it to stop me from thrashing my limbs about.

When I arrived at the ashram I didn't wear a diaper, but within a month they put me in one. It was too much to wash my sheets every day. I wore one on and off until we left the place four years later.

Sometimes Kali Mata would hug me, holding me so close that I could smell under her arms. 'I dreamt about you, you know,' she said. 'I dreamt that there would be a child to need me.'

There were days when I wouldn't see Ma at all, and I was not allowed to see her, or even know where she was, and I learned not to ask questions if I didn't want the answers. When she did appear, she was an apparition, and we sat together, both in white, me once again an extension of her body. She held me and kissed me, and fed me with her hands, softened rice with buttermilk, like she did when I didn't have teeth. Sometimes at night, she would come when she thought I was sleeping. I would lie still and heavy, let her find a way to fit our bodies together. Her face and kurta were often wet, and she would breathe raggedly into my hairline. And other times, her voice would rise, piercing through the air, and her hand or foot would find a way to come down on me. There were pinches, slaps, kicks, beatings, though now I cannot remember what they were in retaliation for. For me they were accompanied by surprise, fear, and a feeling that lasted beyond the pain of the impact, cauterizing me from the inside out. I understood that sometimes Ma was there and sometimes she wasn't, but this was neither bad nor good, and this is how our lives would be. Being together or apart was independent from wanting and happiness.

There were times when I hid. Sometimes for days together. I could be invisible, soundless, odourless. When they found me in the end, it was only because I wanted to be found.

In time, the bottoms of my feet hardened. I don't remember exactly what they were like before, but I remember they were different.

In the ashram, some people wept like overwrought children when they saw Baba, while others sobbed silently. There was a lady whose skin looked like milk curdling in tea, and she fell to her knees, shaking, as he passed by. Then she touched Ma's feet too.

But most people at the ashram were dabblers. That's what Kali Mata liked to say. She turned her nose up at that type, the ones who sampled everything on the market. They were promiscuous in their beliefs, like fickle lovers. They discussed their ambivalence openly, in front of Baba, wore blue jeans under their kurtas and cut off their sleeves to sun their dark shoulders. Vegetable sellers set up stalls and pawnshops proliferated just beyond the ashram gate for these occasional visitors. They sold white chemises and pants ready-made, in different sizes and styles.

And then there were those who pulled their clothes off in the meditation hall and, bare-breasted, lay on the ground, arms and legs spread, eyes rolling back, cackling.

Those are the ones I will never forget. And Baba, laughing, clapping his hands.

In the ashram, Baba's voice was soft yet thundering, and I always looked away when I heard it. He spoke about desire and joy – he said he would teach us how to know both together. I never understood how to achieve this, but as I sat watching the meditations every day, which always began in silence and ended in frenzy, I found there was a life in being a spectator instead of a participant. Each evening, as the followers broke out into cacophony and flailing, releasing whatever animals had been captive within, letting them escape into the vortex of the pyramid, I collected my various feelings, about Ma, the ashram, the moments that made up my day. I placed them in a dish during dinnertime and observed them. They lay there, limp. Unwilling to fight. They would not win, they did not want to try. I looked around and heard the many voices, and saw the many bodies that seemed to make one giant form, a giant larger than Baba, but a mirror of what he was, a collection of so many desires. I knew these desires were there, that they were powerful enough to control weather patterns and bring floods every year, but I could not fathom how they passed, how they were handed around and pocketed in front of me. Adult desire was something I did not yet understand. There was no place for me around it and nowhere for me to go. So I left the dish next to me, occasionally observing its contents, watching them grow. One day, I mixed them into my food and swallowed them whole.

By the time we left the ashram, it was 1989. I was seven years old.

Sometimes I can feel that girl crowning at the back of my throat, trying to come out through any orifice she can. But I swallow her until the next time she wants to be born again.

Every six months, I wash the curtains in all the rooms of the house and we hang sheets on the rods at night to keep the light out. Ma and I used to wash our curtains at home, but now we have to send them to a special cleaner because Dilip has blackout drapes that are too thick and heavy to fit in our washing machine. Had I ever slept in a truly dark room before I met Dilip? He says in the US it's different, different in a way I won't know until I visit. I've grown up in a place that's always at war with itself, accustomed to its own inner turmoil. The walls are permeable to sounds and smells, even light seems to seep through. I ask him what is so bad about that. Nothing, he says, except that isn't how it's supposed to be.

I tell him he is too concerned with everything being sterile. He looks around the house, at the careful order I have imposed, and laughs.

I shake my head. 'No, it's different. I know what I have is an illness, but in America you think it's a privilege.'

He crosses his arms and says I have no idea how different this life is from the one he grew up with. I look around at our television and bed and curtains, at our shopping malls and diners, and I can't see how.

'Imitations,' he says.

I spend the majority of the afternoon in the studio. My graphite pencils have serial numbers and a logo branded into the sides. I hear Dilip walking around the house, not by his footsteps but by the faint static sound his body makes as it moves through air. The first time he saw my work, Dilip asked me how I decide what kind of art to make, or what to work on. I answered that I don't. In fact, I have never been particularly thoughtful that way. The work appears as though by chance, and then it selects me.

The maid knocks on the door, asking me what she should cook for the evening, but I ignore her. Dilip and I fought once because he heard me tell her off. He said this is something that will always separate us — Americans don't behave in certain ways. I asked him not to idealize the polite veneer of his childhood because everyone knows what Americans are really capable of.

I begin my day of work by sketching from memory, something loose and formless, a fleeting impression, to warm my hand. I usually choose something I have had contact with — a toothbrush, my car keys, a part of Dilip's body. Sometimes I embellish, try to complete the object, give it context — the toothbrush in an open mouth, the car keys in a hand, an additional part of Dilip's body. Then I add the detail, even if the overall form is just a faint outline. I add texture with short, sharp strokes — shadow, crosshatch, or spirals of black hair.

I know I'm finished when I have gone too far, when the picture has moved away from its original subject, altered to the point of being almost grotesque. Animal into man, man into object. I do this as preparation for the real work, to get the gibberish out of my system. It's a kind of catharsis, if catharsis really works. I know it feels good to cry sometimes, but Dilip says that football players in America who tackle each other all day are more likely to beat their wives, so maybe only love begets love.

From the drawer in my desk, I take out my drawing from the day before. The face always looks the same to me, though every day adds another subtle difference, moving one step further from the original. Sometimes I am tempted to look back to the beginning, the first image. But this temptation is part of the process. I don't look back until the drawing for the day is done.

I wonder if one day I will tip over, making that small mistake which will turn him from a man to an ape, that slip in proportion that indicates an entirely new species. Or maybe I will do too little, flatten him out with my lazy hand and turn him into a mannequin. But these fears are not constant; over time, I have seen them inflate and pop.

There are days when the dread of making an error causes my hand to shake, and there are days when errors seem like a small affair in light of so many years of work. And there are days when I want to stop, when I never want to see this face again.

I put the drawing in the drawer when it is finished and let it shut with a solemn bang.

In the evening, Dilip and I are invited to a party, and we do lines because everyone else is doing them. I stand on the balcony without a shawl and feel the hair on my arms poke through the pores. When I look down from the ninth floor, I want everyone on the road to be as small as ants, but we aren't high enough for that and I feel thwarted and a little angry. We all chat for a while and I get tired of everyone quickly, but my heart will not stop pounding, and I'm nostalgic for the days when parties felt innocent with Ecstasy and dancing.

Everyone is curious about how Dilip is managing as a vegetarian. They ask one question at a time and wait for him to contemplate his answer. The hostess makes sure to pass him the dishes that are free of animal flesh. He says he feels better, cleaner than he has in a long time.

A female friend of ours says he looks younger than before. He smiles at her and they begin discussing vitamin B deficiencies in the Indian population.

The lanterns hanging along the terrace twinkle and swing in the wind. The discussion moves from the relative benefits of vegetarianism to how hard it is to be paleo and alkaline with an Indian diet, and who has switched entirely from white rice to brown.

'Have you noticed,' I say when we are on the way home, 'when men change their diets everyone is so respectful, but when women do it everyone tries to convince them to cheat?'

'But being vegetarian isn't just a diet. It's not about vanity.'

I put my head back against the seat of the car and look out of the window. 'I told my mother to come and stay with us.'

Dilip is about to nod, but he pauses. 'Stay with us? Or live with us?'

I look at him and my mouth opens. 'Stay with us. For a few nights. A week at the most.'

Dilip sits against the seat and looks in front. 'Sure.'

We go over a few speed bumps that are close together before I say, 'I think, eventually, Ma has to live with us.'

Dilip leans forward and makes the music louder so our driver can't hear. 'When?'

'I don't know. I can't tell you an exact date. Soon.'

I slide out of my shoes as we enter our apartment, and I can smell the cheap leather. I wipe my feet against the legs of my trousers.

My husband lies on the sofa with his shoes still on. We're looking at each other in spite of all the mirrors. Around us are eight sofas, sixteen lights, four dining tables and thirty-two chairs. I see finger-prints on the glass that I didn't notice in the afternoon. There are countless other objects in the room that do not make it into reflections; they are cut off, halved and quartered, by other objects. The room in square metres cannot accommodate this profusion, these partial, smudged realities. Our flat feels too full and I have the urge to throw something away.

'Do you think she should live with us? You can't stand each other for more than a minute.'

My jaw grows rigid and I can barely open my mouth. I have an answer but I am not satisfied with it. He knows too much about my mother and he can use it against me. Sometimes I wish I hadn't con-fided in him. I wish he were a stranger.

'She needs me.'

He nods and shrugs. Does that mean he agrees but doesn't know how to respond? Or he hears me, hears the words, but doesn't think I mean what I'm saying? To be indecipherable in this moment seems unkind, unlike him, but perhaps what he has to say would be worse.

I want an answer about what he means, but I see that he wants an answer too, an answer to a question I have already forgotten. We wait in silence for one of us to go first, for the confusion to be broken. The alcohol, the comedown, makes us irritable and too lazy to be considerate.

'It's hard,' he says, 'for me to understand your relationship with her sometimes. Being around her is very stressful for you. And the other way round. To be honest, I wonder if you'll make her worse or better.'

I nod. He's right. But I want to cry for being stupid, for giving him the tools to make this incision.

I tape white index cards with names and emergency numbers written in block letters on the wall above Ma's telephone. The paint is peeling and some of the cards float to the floor. I persist. Ma is sitting on the sofa, watching me. She puts her hand on my bottom and moves it around in a rough, circular motion.

'You're having a baby.'

I look at her. 'No, I'm not.'

'Soon, very soon.'

'I don't think so. We aren't ready.'

'I know it. I've seen it in a dream.'

She's been talking about her dreams a lot recently. To me, to the neighbours, to people in the street. Apparently, she advised the watchman to get his affairs in order. He took it as a threat and now refuses to open the gate for my car when I visit her.

'You have so much here already,' she says, her hand still on my bottom. It feels like she is trying to wipe it away. 'And you haven't even had children yet.'

I don't answer.

She continues. 'And you're always on a diet.'

'Everyone is always on a diet.'

She shakes her head. 'I'm never on a diet. And at your age? At your age, I ate Parle-G biscuits coated in white butter.'

I shudder. I have done that, slathered biscuits with butter, eaten them by the plateful, delirious and hurried, afraid of getting caught in the act by the nuns at boarding school after we had raided their pantry in the middle of the night. The taste remains illicit for me, something swallowed too quickly, something in danger of coming back up, something that immediately went to my brain, which was always foggy, deprived of fat, forcing me to drift off into space.

Ma doesn't know. I never told her that for a portion of my child-hood I was always hungry and have been searching for some fullness ever since. Talking has never been easy. Neither has listening. There was a breakdown somewhere about what we were to one another, as though one of us were not holding up her part of the bargain, her side of the bridge. Maybe the problem is that we are standing on the same side, looking out into the emptiness. Maybe we were hungry for the same things, the sum of us only doubled that feeling. And maybe this is it, the hole in the heart of it, a deformity from which we can never recover.

In the kitchen, I can smell something sour, something fermenting. Inside an open cooker by the sink is a mountain of yellow split mung beans, soaking in water. The beans are melting, dissolving, white and bubbling. I ask my mother how long she has been soaking the dal. She walks slowly into the kitchen and peers into the pot. Her head is still, but her thoughts run through the past few days in circles, the loop continuing to be unrecognizable with each pass.

I push the cooker into the sink and turn the tap to full. The water on the metal sounds like crashing waves.

My mother tilts her head and looks me over, as if I've returned after many years away. 'You look different,' she says.

Cracks originating in another apartment climb up the wall, sprouting into full bloom in the corner of my studio. There are days when neighbours are a comfort and there are days when the closeness feels like danger. If cracks travel, I wonder what else makes it past the walls. Moisture, voices. Sometimes, while we shout at each other,

I imagine the neighbours on the other side pressing their ears up to the plaster. Or maybe they sit on their sofa side by side and watch the sounds invade their rooms, sounds that nearly take shape, shifting weight.

It is a struggle to remain present wherever I am, because my mind travels in time and space, not just to past and future but also to the homes that surround us in this compound, to the bodies that inhabit this city. When I see population graphs, the country seems like a heaving mess, numbers skewed to the young and the hungry, and I imagine them all just outside, climbing over one another until they find their way through an open window, a hatch or even a crack, and they are all in here with me, or nearby, advancing, sweating, crying out, bleating, neighing, sometimes a sea of white, sometimes of colour, and I feel the menace at the back of my neck even as Dilip and I continue our quarrel about what kind of furniture will fit in the studio.

At the department store, we look at a single bed with a red Sale tag blown up and draped across the frame like a sheet. The bed will do for my mother and won't take up much space in the room, but Dilip wonders if we will regret not buying a bigger bed in the future. 'Why would we regret it?' I ask, though I can already think of several reasons, and we decide on taking the small bed for now, postponing remorse for the future instead of managing it in the moment because, after all, who knows how long we will live in this apartment. Dilip adds to this: Who knows how long we will need a space to make art, or how long we will live in India, or how long we will live at all? And while he sees these questions as heartening and comical, they fill me with irritation. We stand in a queue to pay for our new bed, and I imagine myself living far away from the only home I have known, dying in a foreign land, until the salesman who rings up our purchase asks if the bed is for our child.

'No,' I say. 'It's for my mother.'

*

'I won't be able to sleep in this cupboard,' my mother says, looking around at the books and drawers and the boxes in the corner stacked one on top of the other. I wrap the pale, thin curtains around themselves in a knot and they swing gently. The window of my studio overlooks a swimming pool that no one in the building seems to use. Feathers and decomposing leaves merge into a landmass on the surface of the water, and everything looks more unwashed than usual.

'I can move everything out of the room,' I say, still looking outside.

'No, no. No need.'

She doesn't say more, but I sense she is thinking, *I won't be here for long*. We haven't discussed whether this is a trial run for an impending event or an adult slumber party, and I think it might be better that both of us continue with our separate illusions. But when the small canvas bag she has brought with her gapes open and we discover that she has forgotten her toothbrush, medicine, underwear and nightgown, I realize that one of us at least must be clear-headed and perhaps the time for my illusions is past.

I am alone in the car on the way back to Ma's flat to pick up her things, and I am caught like a ribbon in a cassette, stuck on how to prepare her to say goodbye and the best way to do it. Because we have to comprehend the finality of this end as much as she does, even though it might be difficult to register since she will still be there when we return the next day, not looking or acting different from the day before. This is a long and drawn-out loss, where a little bit goes missing at a time. Perhaps, then, there is no other way besides waiting, waiting until she is no longer there inside her shell, and the mourning can happen afterwards, a mourning filled with regret because we never truly had closure.

The inside of her apartment verges on disaster, kept at bay by the half-hearted attempts Kashta makes at cleaning, but she, too, knows that her employer is unwell, and takes liberties when she can. I wonder how I will love Ma when she is at the end. How will I be able to look after her when the woman I know as my mother is no longer residing in her body? When she no longer has a complete consciousness of who she is and who I am, will it be possible for me to care for her the way I do now, or will I be negligent, the way we are with children who are not our own, or voiceless animals, or the mute, blind and deaf, believing we will get away with it, because decency is something we enact in public, with someone to witness and rate our actions, and if there is no fear of blame, what would the point of it be?

The tattered and mended bras are in a drawer with her underwear. I scoop them all out.

'What are you doing?'

I turn. Kashta is standing in the doorway, scratching her scalp with her middle finger.

'These are torn. I want to throw them away.'

Kashta shifts weight. 'I can take them.'

I had planned on throwing away the lot of them, along with a pile of magazines I feel certain Ma won't remember. But Kashta watches me and the exposed underwire in my hands. I give the bras over and the secret is safe. I expect this exchange will go unnoticed, unless Ma begins to suspect Kashta is stealing from her. Maybe she will be relieved that those wretched things she couldn't get rid of are finally gone.

'Don't keep them in the house,' I tell Kashta as I leave.

By the time I get home, the mood has shifted with the help of dusk and whisky. Ma takes healthy sips from a cold glass. Rings of condensation are on every surface. Dilip looks up when I come in.

'Will you have anything?' he asks, holding up his own glass so the ice cubes bang against each other.

I shake my head.

Ma has changed into a dress that I realize is mine. The cotton block-print fabric strains against her heavy torso, turning her breasts into a single unit. The sleeves cut into her underarms. She is beginning to sweat. The buttons at the back of the dress barely cling to their holes, and when I sit next to her on the sofa I can see creamy patches of flesh that have never seen the sun.

'Ma, why are you wearing my dress?'

She looks at me and then at Dilip. He blinks and my mother begins laughing, still looking at him. 'It's my dress,' she says.

'No. It's not. It doesn't fit you.'

She shrugs as best she can in the confines of my clothes. 'I have the same one.'

Dilip is peering into his glass, avoiding eye contact with us, even though we both seem to be watching him, perhaps hoping he will play referee. He must be wondering if this is how we will be before long, if this is how every evening will pass. What can he be looking for in his glass? Maybe a way out.

I reach into the bag I came in with and pull out a housecoat. Ma ignores it when I hold it out to her and picks up a magazine from the coffee table with her free hand. She flips a few pages without looking at me, then scoffs.

'Look at this,' she says. Her voice is withering. Dilip leans forward.

'Little marks, here and everywhere. What is this, a leg?'

She has found a small passage in the text that I have marked up, a doodle that is somehow so offensive she cannot let it pass. 'Does it even look like a leg?' she asks Dilip. 'This is her habit from childhood, you know. She draws on everything. She can't leave anything as it is. This was one of the biggest complaints about her when she went to boarding school. I think it is really the reason they threw her out. What did that nun say? Your daughter defaces everything she gets her hands on. Can you believe it? They threw her out of school for this.'

Dilip's gaze finds me and travels down to the small scar on my hand. He clears his throat. 'She has a talent for it,' he says, continuing to speak as though I am not there. 'It was her calling, think of it that way.'

Ma throws herself forward and laughs, and her forehead almost touches the glass. Hair falls in front of her eyes as she turns to look at me. 'Her calling is being strange. She did odd things as a child and now as a woman also. What kind of strange art do you make? The same face, day in and day out. What kind of a person does such a stupid thing?'

'Mom,' Dilip begins, 'I think we should –'

'I have to explain when people ask me, and I don't know what to say. I feel ashamed.'

'That is what you feel ashamed of?' I cry. My mouth trembles. This person, who never did a worthwhile deed in her life, thinks I am an embarrassment?

'Why don't you just tell me who it is? Who is the person in the picture?' Her face shrinks and her eyes are troubled.

'I've told you a million times,' I say through gritted teeth. 'The person is whoever you see – and everyone sees someone different. The original picture doesn't matter any more. It was a picture of a stranger and now I've lost it.'

Ma holds the side of her face. Her hand migrates to her forehead and her eyes close.

Dilip clears his throat and finishes what's left in his glass. 'Mom, are you ready for dinner?' he asks.

She opens her eyes and looks at him, her mouth set into a hard line, and then she rises to her feet, slowly, drifting, so that for a moment we are unsure if she is standing or falling. With composure, she shakes her head. 'I want to lie down for some time.'

I watch her leave the room, glass in hand, and I feel I cannot breathe. Every part of me wants to do physical harm to her, to tear my clothes off her back and humiliate her. I bury my face in my hands, and when I finally feel I can bear the light I turn to Dilip. He is watching me, leaning forward with his elbows resting on his knees. I know what he is going to say. How can she live with us? How can we let this hideous creature poison our home?

'Those drawings really bother her,' he says.

I feel my eyebrows draw down. I swallow and attempt a shrug.

'You still want to continue it,' he says, 'when it bothers her so much?'

I hear my pulse in my ears. Folding my hands, I look at my lap. 'Haven't I spent enough time making decisions based on her?'

I move quietly around the bedroom, even though I feel wild inside, a mad rollicking horse, as the evening opens up before me like I'm living it again, first her words, her crazed laughter, her disgusting body oozing from my clothes. And then Dilip's input, which might be worse because it came from behind me like a treacherous knife. Wasn't he the one who didn't want her to live with us? Didn't he say I was too close, that I needed some distance from her madness? And now he thinks I should stop my work because it distresses her? Why, why should everything be about her all the time? I feel his body adjust itself on the bed and listen for the rhythm of his breath as I imagine turning around and fastening my hands on his throat while he sleeps.

I sit up when a sharp sound cuts through the room. It is coming from the studio.

I open the door and see the glittering shards of a glass of water I had left for my mother catching light on the floor, while she sits like a witch, mesmerized by a small fire in the wastepaper bin. Where did she get a lighter or matches? I feel Dilip appear next to me, and together we watch her throwing balled paper into the flame, waiting for each one to be consumed before she adds another. She is methodical and doesn't seem to see us, and I barely notice the pile of my notebooks that she has disembowelled, the fragments of images that lie on the floor. I sit paralysed, in awe of the light in the dark room, this whole scene which must be a dream.

In the flame, I begin to see a body, the beginning of some dancing deity, and a primordial terror rises in me. Ma laughs and pours the contents of a glass in the basket, and the fire erupts, rushing out, rising like a lit column to the ceiling. I turn my face as the warmth hits me like an open hand. Paper, flaming and disintegrating, jumps out of the basket in particles of white and ash before falling like embers to the floor. Ma hovers close, and the edge of her dress is alight but she doesn't notice, and we both start when the lights go on and a bucket of water comes down over her and the flame.

My mother blinks, burnt and wet. The cotton turns sheer with water, and I see the angry blisters on her hands. She shivers and wraps her arms around herself.

How long have I been here? The acrylic flooring that looked like wood has melted down into a fuming plastic puddle. I cough and Dilip throws open the window. I look up at him from my place on the floor. From here, his shoulders look heroic.

I dress her in dry clothes, ignoring the pustules on her fingers. We put her to bed in the living room. The leather couch is too slippery to accommodate sheets, but we do the best we can. Dilip and I do not speak as we watch her curl into herself. We lie awake, watching shapes flash across the ceiling like fevered clouds.

The next day, I take Ma home wordlessly, without listening to Dilip's request to call a doctor. I am unaffected by the idea that she might do harm to herself. Whatever she wants to do, let her do it in her own home. She wanted to destroy my drawings, and she did – years of life studies, preparatory sketches, some more than ten years old, have vanished overnight. All the images that were a record of moments in my life, memories, but also my becoming, the making of me that is separate from her. Maybe there was something more she was after – maybe she wanted this home to disappear, my marital home, the one that keeps me away, the only place where I am safe. Maybe she hoped to incinerate my marriage. Maybe my life.

The remnants of that disaster take longer to manage. A painter overcharges me to cover the grey spot on the ceiling, and the flooring has been discontinued and requires a full redo. For two weeks, the studio is taped off, covered in dust, a danger zone of chemicals and confusion. All of my belongings are removed, stacked in a corner of the living room. It doesn't escape us that none of this would have happened if I had cleared the room out in the first place.

I wake up to dim, pale light and all the boxes open. My drawings are scattered, with the butter paper unfolded. Some in piles, others separate. That face unprotected, vulnerable to the elements – that same face with little differences, repeating itself like an endless stammer around Dilip.

'You said there was no picture,' he says.

My eyes are still on the drawings. I haven't seen them all opened like this in a while. I barely register what he says.

'You said there was no picture,' he says again. 'You said that you had lost it.'

I take a step towards him. In his hand is a photograph with a creased corner. It hovers lightly on the skin of his open palm. I step back again.

'Why did you lie?'

My mouth is dry from the night.

'What was the need to lie? Who is he?'

I try to swallow.

'I'm not going to ask you again. Who is he?'

'I found the picture,' I hear myself say. 'In her things.'

'You found it? Or you took it?'

'I found it.'

'Antara, who is he?'

'No one. No one to me anyway. He's a man my mother knew.' My shoulders fall. 'They used to be lovers.'

1989

I knew that night was different when Ma came into the room I shared with Kali Mata. She had the beginnings of bruises on her face. She didn't close the door gently.

'Wake up,' she said.

She put a bottle of water and a hundred rupees tied with a rubber band into a cloth bag. She spoke to Kali Mata in a low voice.

I knew they were talking about her, the golden one, the new favourite who would be taking Ma's place, who would now live on the other side of the carved door with Baba. It had been decided. Kali Mata sighed and shook her head. 'This is no reason to leave. Did I leave? Did any of the others leave? We all love you. You're one of us. There will always be a place here for you.'

Ma laughed and cried at the same time. She wiped her dripping nose with the sleeve of her kurta. Her eyes were wide, her mouth taut.

'The truth is, I hate it here,' Ma said. 'I always have.'

I'd never seen her like this before. I began to shake. Kali Mata held me in her arms and told me she loved me.

We left without a word to anyone else. No one came to watch us go. We walked for some time. The night was filled with the tang of diesel fuel and the sounds of trucks. Ma's mouth moved as she talked herself out of turning around. She covered her lips with her hand to stop the words.

A decrepit vehicle halted in front of us. It was a Tempo Traveller and the driver's face was obscured. A jagged parcel lay in the back, held down with old rope.

'What's that in the back?' Ma asked. He looked at her but didn't answer. 'Furniture?'

'Maybe,' he said. 'Which way?'

He wore a woollen cap and a frayed muffler in the heat. Grey hair sprouted on his face, a thicket from his ears. Behind his spectacles, his eyes were magnified to twice their size. Blue flowers bloomed in his pupils.

'Poona Club,' she said.

He nodded. 'Pune Club.'

I sat in her lap on the passenger seat. She wrapped her arms tightly around my waist. My bladder was full but I didn't mention this. A small metal Lakshmi hung from the askew rear-view mirror. The goddess sat on a lotus. She had four arms. Or six. She jerked with the sputters of the vehicle. Ma sighed and let her shoulders rest against the vinyl seat. I could smell the driver's last meal and a whiff of sulphur when he leaned over to adjust her door. His arm lingered, pressing against me, against Ma's arms around me, for a moment. 'You won't remember this hardship one day,' she whispered in my ear. 'When you're older, all these moments will cease to exist.'

The sun was beginning to come up when we reached the Club, and the guard recognized Ma in her dishevelled state and let us in. Ma had asked to be dropped at the Club because it was the only location, besides the train station, that the driver was sure to know. Also, it was the only place where we would be able to use the phone. I didn't realize it at the time, but Ma had not made any plans before leaving the ashram. She had no idea where we would go, who would agree to take us in, and under what conditions. She hadn't spoken to her husband in years, and she had told her parents she didn't want to have anything to do with them if they were going to insist she give her marriage a second chance.

Ma told me to wait in the playground by the entrance while she went to make a call. I sat at the bottom of the metal slide and lay back, looking at the sky. I watched birds landing on the electrical wires criss-crossing the trees, swinging back and forth like small children. The playground was empty and there was no one else around. I knew children liked to play in them, but I never had, and I wasn't sure what I should do there. I decided that I hated playgrounds, strange metal landscapes with no purpose. Hating the playground felt good, gave a direction to my feeling of unease, grounded it in an object that I could see. This contempt still draws up the moment I feel uncomfortable. I disown so I can never be disowned.

When Ma returned, I had mud on my knees and dirt under my fingernails. Or did I have this from before? The day was brighter. Ma didn't seem to notice. I could feel her heart beating in her hand when she grabbed my arm.

'They won't help us.'

'Who?' I asked.

'Your disgusting father. Or your Nana–Nani.'

They wouldn't help us? That didn't sound like them, from what little I knew – the woman who held me to her creased skin and the man who stuck out his top dentures like a cashier's tray because it made me laugh. And my father. My father, surely, would help me.

Father. Father. Father. I couldn't remember anything about my father. I was a baby when I left his house. And, as far as I knew, he had never come for me.

I would dream of him sometimes, when I was in the ashram. Sometimes I would picture a man whose face I couldn't recall taking me away from my mother. (Did I picture that, or did Ma plant it there when she told me I always wanted to leave her, that I always wanted to hurt her?)

My father was unknown, and sometimes I could be persuaded into imagining that was better.

'They're trying to rule over us like tyrants, but I won't let them,' Ma said. Her eyes were wide and red in the corners, and her breath smelled of day-old banana. 'I will look after us. You trust me, don't you?'

I wanted to nod or say something in return, but I didn't. Or maybe I couldn't. I wonder now if I even understood the question at that time. Trust her with what? What choice did I have, and what else did I know?

We lived at the Club. Sometimes within the walls and sometimes right outside. I met a stray dog whom I called Candle because the tip of his tail looked like a burnt wick. I kept him with us to keep away the bandicoot rats I saw burrowing in and out of the flower beds in the darkest part of the night.

Ma took to begging. I wasn't young enough to evoke sympathy so she made me stay near the gate. On the first day, we learned there were rules for begging, that certain streets belonged to certain women and children, and that encroaching on their space was an act of war. They had missing teeth, dust embedded in their hair and spoke a kind of Marathi I had never heard before. They were quick with their hands and on their feet, the kind of beggars who could persist, the ones Ma had told me never to make eye contact with. They looked different from us, smelled different. But as the days passed, the differences began to recede.

The Club members who knew us, and knew my grandparents, looked at us with confusion, unsure of how to react to our pleas. Some shielded the eyes of their children and walked on. Others laughed and patted me on the head, as though it were a kind of joke. They all passed us with a little hatred because of what they knew of Ma and because we were proof of how easy it was to fall. One night, she held her hands up in front of her face and made a little box. She peered inside.

'Look in here.'

I looked, but there was only the street in front of us. Candle was lying on his back. A lady in a magenta sari walked by.

'The world exists only as far as you can see,' Ma said. 'What's above, what's below, that's no concern of ours. What they've told us before, none of that matters.'

I looked straight ahead, at what was in my eyeline. Bottoms, hands. A couple sitting on a bench, waiting. Some scrap metal on the side of the road. A girl sitting in a car with her cheek pressed against the window. I looked back at Ma, and she was crying.

I remember sleeping sitting up against the gate, lolling over, waking up with my head in Ma's lap. But I don't remember being hungry. The security guard brought plates of food and water at regular intervals. I later found out that my father had been calling the Club manager to instruct him to feed me. I'm not sure how long we lived like this. I was with Ma and she was with me, and there were no rules or chores or time-tables to observe. I had not bathed, and fur grew along my gum line. I slept with Candle, napping on his mangy coat, watching creatures mow little lines in his hair, resting my hand on the pustules that my mother called scabies. Soon, I itched like him, looked like him, was converted by his presence, and I knew I had met a member of my family.

One morning, when it was still early enough that the Club security guard could openly sleep in his chair, my father came to collect us in his off-white Contessa.

He looked the way he does now, a full-grown man whose beard begins to show itself a few hours after shaving, but thinner, with a sharper nose. He looked nothing like Baba or any of the men I had seen in the ashram. His ears were clean and there were no hairs coming out of his nostrils.

He held the door open. Ma stood up slowly and tugged my arm. We climbed into the back seat and shut the door.

My father did not turn to look at me, and I admired the back of his head. He did not speak a word to Ma. He put the radio on. As we drove away, I called out for Candle, who rose from where he was lazing and jumped forward, the muscles in his hind legs pressing against the damaged fur. The dog chased us for a moment, but then stopped to scratch.

*

No one made any mention of us looking like beggars. There were no questions about the ashram. In my grandparents' house, I soon learned, Baba's name was forbidden. Nani was waiting for us with hot breakfast on the table and a kettle of steaming tea. The milk had malai on top and everything was cooked in ghee.

My father, having dropped us here, now stood back, hovering in the doorway, a driver, a baggage handler, ready to make a hasty departure when this job was done.

Nani's arms were crossed in front of her, her bangles catching on her fleshy forearms, her bottom spreading on the red semicircular sofa.

'I hope your tantrum is over,' Nani said. Her voice echoed in the flat. I didn't know whom she was speaking to until I saw Ma's sullen face.

'Antara,' she said. 'Do you remember your Nani Ma? Come here.'

I walked across the speckled tiles towards her but stopped when she put her face in her hands. She started to heave and her shoulders shook. I turned around to my father and Ma, who stood in the shadow. Ma waved her hand, motioning for me to go forward. When I turned, I noticed the colour of my feet, covered in dust, in stains, and the footprints I had left behind me. One of my toenails was black, and the nail bed bloody.

I was taken for a bath, scrubbed clean by a servant I hadn't seen before. Her hair was in a knot on the top of her head, and her cotton sari sat high on her waist so her ankles and calves were exposed. I smelled her hands as she washed my face and neck. Garlic, chillies and soapsuds. Not so different from Kali Mata. Afterwards, I sat limply between her legs as she used her fingers to plough rows through my hair, checking for foreign creatures.

Nani looked in on us. 'Bai,' she said to the maid, 'yeh amchi beti hai.'

'Kasa hai,' the woman said to me.

'Baby, this is Vandana,' Nani said.

Vandana began looking after me because Ma spent most of the day sleeping or locked in a room with Nana and Nani. I could hear them shouting at each other through the door, but that stopped when they came out for lunch or dinner. Ma looked down into her plate, mixing her food, pretending that none of us existed.

My father often stopped by in the evenings before returning to his house and his mother. He and Ma sat together for a while, sometimes without speaking to each other. On other occasions they would whisper, sometimes even shout. I hid under the dining table, even though I was too old for that sort of thing. I tried to read my father's lips, but a table leg blocked him from my vision.

He never asked us to come back with him. Sometimes I thought he looked at me with the same eyes he had for her. One day, he came with another man and a briefcase full of documents. Ma glanced them over and signed her name.

I had questions that I never asked: Why were we at Nana and Nani's house? Would we ever go back and live with my father again? It seemed to me that parents and children all lived together, that husband and wife should be inseparable, even in their mutual dislike of one another.

Vandana took me to the Club in the afternoons to play. She packed a tiffin and carried it in one hand while she held me with the other. In the auto-rickshaw, she taught me to speak a bit in Marathi. She was from a village that we only called gaon. She laughed at my pronunciation, which made me redden and not want to try again, but it didn't occur to me to tease her when she said she couldn't read or write. I suppose that was because I couldn't do either myself. I made a pact with her that she would teach me more Marathi and I could teach her the English alphabet. I never really enjoyed the playground, but when she got on the swings and started pumping her legs back and forth, flying higher into the air, I wanted to join her.

Sometimes Vandana pulled her sari up behind her and brought it through the middle of her legs. She squatted down so far on her haunches when she swept the floor that I was sure her bottom would touch the ground. It never did. She could stay in that position for what seemed like for ever, and once I tried to time her, but she went so long that I forgot I was watching the clock and never made an accurate reading. The teeth at the front of her mouth were missing, and I saw the pink gaps of her gums when she smiled. She brought fresh green chillies with her every day and cooked me poha for breakfast.

One evening, I watched Vandana tie her keys to a string at her waist and put on her chappals outside the door.

'Bye-bye,' she said, showing me her toothless gums. I could hear Ma in her bedroom, humming. I waited for Vandana to close the door before I went out behind her, slipping down the stairs, confident she wouldn't see me, and defensive when she turned and said, 'Eh, what are you doing?'

'I'm coming with you,' I said.

'Coming with me where?'

'To your house. To meet your husband.'

She cocked her head and looked at me. 'You can't come with me. Go back upstairs. Your mama will be looking for you.'

Murli, the liftman, watched our tussle and laughed.

'Take her to her house,' Vandana told him in Marathi.

'No,' I said. I felt something scraping up the sides of my stomach and I pushed down on it. 'I want to go with you. You have to listen to me, you're a bai. I'm the boss of you.'

Four lines appeared on Vandana's forehead and her eyes became black slits. 'You're nobody. Your own mother barely looks at you.' She took me by the back of the neck and pushed me into the lift. I reached up and slapped her, and she slapped me back.

Upstairs, Nani opened the door to find me crying and Vandana scowling, with patches of sweat appearing on her lilac blouse.

'What happened?' Nani said.

'She tried to follow me home.' Vandana dropped my hand and nudged me forward. Ma appeared behind Nani at the door.

'Follow you home?' Ma looked at me. Her face turned the colour of a burn. I flinched, expecting to be slapped again, but instead I heard Ma shout at Vandana. 'You should be more careful.'

Ma pulled me into the house, but they continued shouting at each other, both becoming less and less intelligible. Vandana slapped her forehead and pointed at Ma. She didn't come to work again, and Ma told Nani to keep a manservant from then on.

Ma and I shared a bed after that, and she would invite me out on to the terrace with her to watch while she smoked in the dark. It was then that I first realized how beautiful my mother was. When she finished, she gave me the butt and taught me how to flick it far, into the traffic near the station.

Sometimes we took her cigarette downstairs. We walked past the dilapidated hotel, the one Nana owned and ran, with its art deco facade and peeling paint job. Families sat on straw mats on the ground. Once, we saw a drunk man stretched out in his sleep, muttering to himself, and we lingered nearby, trying to make out what he said. The chai-wallahs carried their wares away or dozed against steel posts, waiting for the crowds to arrive. Damp faces, clenched jaws and bloodshot eyes, they all looked past us, and we were dulled by the warm night. A steady flow of bloated rats hurried along the tracks, sniffing what had been left behind after the long day. Smoke and the smell of hashish wafted up to our noses, courtesy of a barefoot junkie who groped his testicles as he looked at my mother. A solitary hijra wandering through the train station tapped her shoulder and held out an ornamented hand. Ma gnawed on her dry lips. She wasn't usually superstitious, but the hijras were said to have inexplicable powers. Money could be traded for protection, but we had none. Ma fished out a red lipstick that happened to be in her kurta and handed it over. The hijra took the tube, said a word of blessing and moved on. The large board where the daily schedule of trains clattered across, a flurry of changing symbols, was illegible to me.

I cannot remember what I felt for Ma during that time because the feeling lacked a familiar name. At the ashram, I had lived without her and longed for her at the same time, but now that we were together I would turn corners towards dread, to feeling I had been mistaken, that maybe I did not want her or need her, only to return to the notion I had lived with all my life, that being without her was hell, misery. And even now, when I am without her, when I want to be without her, when I know her presence is the source of my unhappiness – that learned longing still rises, that craving for soft, white cotton that has frayed at the edge.

Ma wasn't well after the ashram. No one could deny it, but no one could tell me what this meant. Her eyes remained on the ceiling, in conversation with it, when she was awake, but most of the day, she slept. She slept as though she hadn't slept in years.

We later found out that this was because Ma was staying awake to contact my father late at night. He was going to be remarried, she had heard, and Ma would call his residence to abuse him. On the occasions that someone else picked up, Ma disconnected the line and called back. Sometimes I sat on her lap as she did this, and eventually she let me dial the number while she held the receiver to her ear. I still remember that number by heart, though I have rarely called him myself. When Nani found out, she pulled me away and told me to come to her room when my mother was behaving strangely. I asked my grandmother what constituted strange.

Nani sighed. 'I don't know what she is hoping to achieve.'

She received her answer two days later, when my father came to the flat and gave my mother a thick envelope of money. Whether he had done this out of a sense of responsibility or whether she had found a way to extort him, I will never know, but it was the first time I wanted to go with my father and leave Ma behind. I watched him, a tall, lanky figure with fuzzy hair, who made brief eye contact with me from the shadow of the doorway. He didn't smile, and his eyes looked troubled when they beheld me.

I asked Nani if Ma and I would be going to the house that belonged to my father.

'Your mother was gone from that house for a long time,' she said. 'Things change as time passes. A new woman is coming into that house now.'

Though the proceedings made little sense to me at the time, I could discern two facts: my parents were no longer married, and my father had found a new wife. Just like Baba had. I remembered how Kali Mata had told Ma to stay, had explained to her that she was a part of the family. I understood that Ma could remain and be like Kali Mata, discarded and respected. I wondered if that option was there for her now, with my father, but as I recalled her face on the day we left the ashram, the sadness and disgust, I knew Ma did not like new wives coming in.

I began to recognize the chaos inside my mother, to see how unlike her I was. Yes, I dripped on occasion, too, but I was always able to seal myself up again.

I asked Nani what divorce was. She was inarticulate when it came to such matters, but tried to explain.

'When a husband and wife are not husband and wife any more,' I said, 'does that mean that a father is no longer a father?'

Nani held my gaze for a long time before allowing her lips to curve into a smile. 'No,' she said. 'No, it does not.'

I waited below my grandparents' flat with a blue suitcase. My hair was braided in a neat plait that pulled at the skin beneath my sideburns. Nani had flattened my delinquent eyebrows with petroleum jelly. As she stood beside me downstairs, Nani told me to be a good girl.

'Make him love you,' she said. Her words seemed like a warning that I only had a single chance.

Ma had barely said goodbye.

My father arrived in his usual Contessa. He was a clean man, and prudent with money. His car, though old, was spotless and well maintained. 'I hope you packed enough for a week,' he said.

I had packed a little extra, the things that I didn't want to leave behind.

I don't remember how many steps we took to the house, but I dragged the blue suitcase up behind my father. The door was black and the handle was a gold bar carved like a column in a temple where the relief had been rubbed away by hands over many years. The doorbell was so faint I was tempted to press it again after my father, but I stood back and waited, surprised when the door flew open. She was waiting there, wearing the bangles from her recent wedding on both wrists. They were too large for her and must have belonged to my grandmother. The glass in her frames was bisected and smudged with fingerprints. My father did not seem to notice. He stepped into the house to greet her while I watched them from the outside. I touched the wall of the house, shuffling my foot until they both looked at me. A manservant came and prised the suitcase from my clenched hand.

The new wife bent down and embraced me, pulling my face into her hair. I smiled in the fog of frizz. It was woolly and smelled of coconut oil. In the antechamber behind her, I could see the maids peeking in on our moment.

They showed me to a room that was usually occupied by my grandmother. I would stay there because she was in Delhi, visiting one of her daughters. The room was damp and smelled of sweat and skin, but they didn't seem to notice. My suitcase was already there, open, and the manservant was separating my underwear into piles and placing them inside the dark cupboard. I leaned against the foot of the bed and looked into the face of the fan that stood in front of me like an open mouth.

In the morning, my father left for work after eating a banana in two mouthfuls and drinking a tall glass of milk. I set an alarm like Nani showed me so I could wake up when he did. I ate like him and tried to say something, but had to lie down with a stomach ache as soon as he left. I stayed at home for the rest of the day, with the servants and the guard dog, who rushed to the gate, barking, any time a car or cyclist passed.

I had carried only my best clothes to their house, finished all the food the cook served me and didn't ask for sweet shakkar-roti at the end of the meal. After my bath, I tried to comb my hair myself, plait it, even though I couldn't see the back, and I didn't ask for help when I could not find the switch for the geyser. There was no soap in the bathroom and the toothpaste burned my tongue, but I didn't say a word about it. I was resourceful after the ashram; I knew how to do things that no one else did.

I sat at the top of the stairs looking down for most of the week. The staircase curved around twice and reminded me of a snake that had been captured in the ashram. The smell of garlic always wafted up from the kitchen downstairs. The floor was a dark, cold marble, and when my bottom began to numb I walked up and down the corridor until I felt it thaw. I had forgotten to bring house slippers with me and kept my socks on all day to warm my feet, but the floor was as slippery as it was cold, and I took little steps until I found there was more pleasure in sliding back and forth. I imagined skating on ice was something like this. Once skating grew tiresome, I returned to the step, where my frame of vision consisted only of the landing, where I saw the occasional tops of heads rushing by – maids, the manservant, and sometimes the new wife, who moved around quickly, often disappearing for most of the day.

I wanted to please her. I made my bed and killed the cockroaches in the medicine cabinet for her.

My fifth day in the house, I saw the top of the new wife's head, her thin arms straining as she dragged three large suitcases across the corridor. Breathless, she called up to the servants, only to observe me in her line of sight. Her eyes widened, as though she had forgotten I was in the house.

'Your papa and I are going to America,' she said. 'For at least three years. He wanted me to tell you.'

My father's crystal decanter, full of amber-coloured Scotch, sat on a small trolley bar against the wall behind her. Light passed through it and adorned her like a crown.

In the evening, my father's friend came home to meet the new wife and the daughter. His name was Kaushal Uncle, and he looked between us, the two females in the room, unsure of whom to greet first. He settled on the wife, bringing his hands together and telling her how happy he was to meet her. He hugged me next, pinching my cheek and the point of my chin.

We sat in the hall, and my father brought out the Scotch and glasses. The table was covered in silver bowls and objects that glittered like jewellery. The men toasted each other while the new wife and I drank tutti-frutti punch. The glass looked odd in my father's hand. His wrists were limp, thin, and seemed strained by the weight of the beverage.

Fried pakoras and samosas and koftas came out of the kitchen. The servant held out a tray to Kaushal Uncle, but my father motioned to me. 'Offer the food to everyone,' he said.

The tray was heavier than the servant made it look, and my hands shook a little. I held it towards Kaushal Uncle. He laughed and nodded at me. Taking the tray, he placed it on the table near his drink and enveloped me in another hug. His shoulder smelled of perspiration and phenyl. He tapped the back of my head and said, 'What a lovely child you have!'

He turned me around and sat me on his lap. His arm slid around my waist. I stayed there for the rest of the evening, while my father spoke about his plans for America, the flat they were planning to rent, jokes about adjusting to the intemperate weather.

I wonder now why my father didn't tell me they were leaving, why he had his wife do it. Did Nani and Ma know he was going? In my notebook, I have grouped it with not knowing the details of my parents' divorce, and never discussing their marriage. It must have stemmed from the same impulse. Perhaps, married to an American,

I have forgotten that certain subjects are not discussed. But at the time, I didn't wonder about any of these things. I was sad, but it seemed proper that my father would not tell me. It seemed acceptable that he was leaving.

Exactly a week after I arrived my nana came to pick me up. That was the day I shut all thoughts of my father into a peripheral space, one that takes little room, one that needs no attention.

'Do you really put your bra on like that?'

Purvi watches me dress. She arrived before I was ready and let herself into my bedroom.

It's early in the evening and the sky is a faint purple. I turn away from her. I am tired and the muscles in my face can't conceal my thoughts.

When I'm dressed, we join our husbands in the living room.

Her husband is polite when he meets me, and we side-hug as he pats me on the back. He likes whisky with his cricket, which he has turned on, and he carries the scent of hand sanitizer with him when he walks into the house.

We move to the dinner table. I've made sure there are many things to eat – Purvi's husband likes choices at dinnertime. Papdi, kantola, drumsticks, cabbage. In the centre of the table are plump legs of chicken, charred and steaming, that have been marinated in coriander, garlic and chilli. Beside Dilip is a mountain of dahi aloo. He turns away from the dish and from me.

Purvi's husband grew up in Pune, went to college in Bombay and returned to join his father's business. Their company designed the first mall in the city, a bright red building – their signature colour. Now they have malls all over India, all part of the same brand, housing some of the best retail outlets in the country. This is the way he introduces himself, with a story of his background, his family and their estimable wealth. He sets the scene for how he wants to be judged and remembered, clinking a large cube of ice in his glass at the end of every sentence.

He asks Dilip if we have ever noticed the locking mechanism in his car. When Dilip says he hasn't, Purvi's husband insists we look after dinner.

'They had diamonds in them,' he says. 'They were real, you know. But that turned out to be a little unsafe. We have so many drivers.'

Purvi breaks her chapati into small pieces and scatters them around her plate.

Purvi's husband suggests that one night next week we all go to a new five-star hotel for dinner. 'The food there is excellent,' he says.

'We have been there together before,' I remind him.

He raises his glass to me and compliments the chicken. I tell him I didn't cook it.

Then he tells me about his father's latest property purchase. It's on a road not too far from my grandparents' house. His father bought a plot in a lovely little society and started building his dream home. But the society complained about the height and size of the structure, saying that it blocked the light for the other homes. His father had to halt construction.

'My father,' he says, 'was heartbroken.' He lets his head hang. Purvi coughs.

I say I hope he will eventually build something else he loves.

Purvi's husband laughs and hands his glass to Dilip, signalling a refill. 'You shouldn't worry about my father,' he says.

I want to explain that I was just being polite, that my concern for his father is a learned social nicety, a smile on the mouth that doesn't reach the eyes. But I sense he doesn't care much about these details, that he is using me to move along with this story.

He says his father is close to local politicians and permission boards. The clerks call him sir. The police chief is a regular at their home for dinner. The building society that dared to stop him has already been made to pay. He doesn't divulge the punishment but smiles at his father's ingenuity, musing that it is something he hopes to learn.

I don't say anything more but see that I was right, that my input was just a bump in the narrative.

I have a striking sensation that life is short, that I can feel the minutes ticking by, that I don't have much time left. I am tired of them, of Purvi and her husband. Not tired exactly, but something else, something nervous and frantic. I want them gone, want their stench out of my house, want their multiplied bodies to disappear from my mirrors. A year ago, we argued after drinking too much gin and the evening ended with Purvi's husband threatening to put a cigar out on my face. The next day we pretended it didn't happen.

I wonder what would happen if I asked them to leave, what new plot line would emerge from that? How would they reply? Would they look to Dilip to intercede on their behalf? What conversations would ensue on the car ride home? And how would the story be repeated at other dinner parties?

A hysterical laugh bubbles in me, but I swallow it and sputter. They look at me with wide, worried eyes, nervous that I may throw up, afraid that they will see the food we are eating chewed up and partially digested.

After dinner, the men turn the cricket on again. Purvi lingers in front of the television and cheers when an Indian batsman makes a century. She pumps her fist and turns, her eyes on her husband, and I see the deep thing they share, the skeleton underneath.

Purvi's husband pours himself another whisky and pats Dilip on the arm. 'There's a new business I want to get into.'

He leans close to my husband and speaks in a low voice. He says he believes that pharmaceutical companies are on the way out. New studies are showing that everything can be cured with turmeric or, otherwise, cannabis. He travelled recently to China and visited labs where they produce medicinal mushrooms. 'I think it's going to be a big business.'

He leans over and asks me if I have ever been to Bhutan. I say I haven't.

He says I must go, that there are mysterious things that happen there, miracles that take place in the mountains, above the treeline, where oxygen is rarefied and the plants are the heartiest on Earth.

He says he will take us, that he has been invited by a tribe of nomads that live there. Men, smaller than midgets, who herd yaks. If we are lucky, they will take us through the mountains in search of a fungus, a wily creature that latches on to caterpillars. The caterpillars, once infected, eat insatiably, feeding on everything in their path, feeding the fungus, building and disappearing into cocoons. But the fungus eventually wins, taking over the body of its prey. What is left is the most elusive mushroom of all, the cordyceps.

He smiles at Purvi and looks back to Dilip.

The Chinese have figured out a way of making them in labs, creating the effects of altitude in tanks, making super cordyceps, the likes of which you could find only on Mount Kailash, nay, the moon. He says we can make a lot of money together.

Purvi claps her hands. 'What do you think, Dilip?'

Dilip nods and shakes his head at once. 'I'm not sure. It doesn't sound vegetarian to me.'

Purvi's husband stumbles as he crosses the room. He leans towards me. I turn my face away from the onslaught of his breath. 'There is a species of trout,' he begins, 'found in America, with a red belly, that swims in deep waters. When that fish becomes a host for a certain parasite, it leaves its dark home and comes to the surface. There, it bobs around in the sun, and the light catches its red scales, attracting birds. The fish becomes the bird's lunch, and the clever parasite is excreted in bird droppings on land, where it can reproduce and begin its cycle once again. Parasites could be the greatest weapon on Earth. Genetically modify them and they could turn their hosts into zombies.'

*

That night in bed, I am quiescent. Still as a rock. Dilip takes a long shower and walks around the room with wet feet. The windows are closed to keep away the mosquitoes that will awaken at dawn. He lies down next to me. We haven't spoken in some days.

Tonight, the silence feels alive. I am not sure if I started it, but it seems like something I would do. Doubts tumble in quickly to bury me; maybe he and I, we were never quite what I thought. I believe that if we don't resume our conversation, if we never refer to it again, it will go away.

If we never speak about Ma, she will cease to exist.

The same might be true for the little picture he found, and the lie that accompanied it.

I am hopeful, if afraid.

But there is something else growing in the room, in the bed. A feeling I can't put my finger on. I try to imagine what he is thinking, what he wants to say.

The next day, Dilip's mother calls. I almost don't answer.

'I'm worried about the two of you,' she says. 'And now you want your mother to live with you? Do you think that's wise? Shouldn't she stay in her own home, maybe with a live-in nurse? You do your work from home, won't having her around the house make that difficult?'

A few days later, when we are on speaking terms and the past seems bite-sized and manageable, I wonder aloud about what this upheaval has been for Dilip, and what it has been for me, and in the future, how we will exact our revenge and make the other repent.

He is silent.

I say that these things are not always conscious, that sometimes the way we act is determined by equations we fall into over and over again. However simple the problem, and however clean the solution, there is always a remainder, a fraction of something said and misconstrued.

He rubs his eyes and says he would never hold on to that sort of enmity.

1989

Nani told me my mother pierced her own nose using a blunt pin, and flunked seventh standard not once but twice. The only positive memory my grandmother had of her own child was from the war in 1971, when her daughter, still young and docile, helped her tape brown paper to the windows of every room to prevent glass from shattering over them as they slept.

I remember sitting between Nani's legs as she poured oil on my head. It trickled down the side of my cheek and found its way to my neck. She folded it into my hair, holding me tightly with her knees. Oil reached her churidar and dripped on to the floor. 'Your mother, she never let me do this. She wouldn't sit still, she said she hated the smell. Imagine. I told her, keep it for one night and wash it out. She never listened. That's why her hair has become what it is. But you know your mother. Difficult.'

I knew my silence would be heard as an affirmation, but this was a time of uncertain alliances between all of us.

Nani may have been the architect of my short banishment to boarding school, but nothing can be proven. In later years, the adults took to pointing fingers at one another. My grandfather most vocally said he was against the idea from the start, though I remember he was the one who presented me with the small blue suitcase again, one morning in July 1989.

We piled into his red Maruti 800, all four of us, and began the drive to Panchgani. The car hugged the curving mountainside, and it rained most of the way, obscuring the view from the window. In the seat between me and Nani was a Thermos and a steel box of sandwiches. The narrow hairpin turns continued, and I began to feel sick. Outside, I caught a glimpse of a woman standing knee-deep in mud. The earth in Panchgani was full of water and sap.

We were already in the car when they explained where I was going. Panic expanded in me. I spread my body across the seat. I didn't know if I could stay away from home for so long. I hadn't packed for the journey. The bubbles returned to the back of my throat, the ones from the ashram, choking me, bouncing with the car. With the next bump, I threw up on myself.

My grandfather opened the windows and started humming the tune to *Amar Akbar Anthony*. Nani used napkins to clean my clothes. 'Do you know how to cover books with paper?' she asked.

We stopped the car and I felt the mountain breeze on me. My skin prickled under my clothes. The smelly wet patch felt wetter. I got out of the car and the mud found its way into my shoes. Ma glanced at me through the front-seat window and turned away. Nani patted my back, asked me if there was any more inside. I said yes, that the bubbles were still with me, crowding the back of my mouth. I felt them scratch my tonsils. I moved my tongue down my gullet, but the bubbles did not shift. I put my finger down and felt my tonsils. Then I gagged once more.

I opened my eyes to the sight of a brick building and a sloping roof partly covered by trees. The patterns of the Portuguese tiles. I traced the green diamonds with my fingers. Nana stood with a bent woman dressed in white.

'Sister Maria Theresa,' the nun said. She sniffled and leaned peril-ously to the right when she walked, and looked like she was hiding another head under her habit.

Inside the walls, the school was different than it seemed from the front. Red brick gave way to a sooty courtyard. Small monkeys were hanging from trees in the distance. The land beyond the back gate twisted into a ravine. Along the walkway, earthen pots were filled with dried shrubs. The champa trees had no flowers. Girls in navy-blue skirts and blouses filed past. Their shoes were polished and their shiny braids hung straight as they walked.

'There was a fire in the dormitories last year,' the nun explained. 'The girls are living in the gymnasium until it is rebuilt.'

Past the brown double-doors of the gymnasium, four rows of beds and cupboards extended from one side of the hall to the other. At night, the beds would be filled with girls in their dark uniforms and tightly wound hair.

'This looks nice,' Nani said. She touched the plaid bed sheets. Ma plunked down on a bed. She hadn't said a word for most of the day, and kept her eyes on her feet. Her mouth was still and straight.

The dining room was a large windowless cavern under the main building. I retched at the pungent smell.

'Not used to fish, I see,' the nun said.

Hours later, the red car picked up dust as it started down the road, away from me. I imagined Ma turning back, motioning for me to run after them. When I rubbed my eyes and looked for her, she was already gone.

My year in boarding school would be the last time we'd be apart until I was much older and left of my own accord, against her will and without consent – but we did not know that at the time, having only known the past, when my will and consent were the ones in jeopardy. When I returned to Pune, I entered my mother's new home like a stranger.

In boarding school, I resolved to keep my possessions light and limited, whittled down to what was most important in the event that I may need to leave. Objects had to be considered, prioritized, and life lacked the heft required for grounding, leaving me nauseated with the changes in pressure.

*

A thin girl with bifocals sat on my bed as I unpacked in the dormitory. My body was filled with a trembling I couldn't quell. The girl, by contrast, was easy and comfortable. She wore her socks above her knees and had a small scar above her mouth.

'I'm Mini Mehra. My bed is next to yours.'

Mini explained that life at Saint Agatha Convent was alphabetized in all things. Lamba and Mehra would be next to each other as long as they both attended the school, unless some other Ls or Ms came between them. She was from Mahabaleshwar and lived in a semi-detached house with her brothers and parents. During dinner, she showed me how to cover the fish in yellow dal to disguise the taste. She explained that the oblong balls were boiled eggs, which could be peeled and were the tastiest things on the plate. After lunch, I emptied the contents of my stomach into a flowerpot.

In time, I learned some things on my own. We were allowed to bathe twice a week in lukewarm water, no matter the season, but we could wash our hair only once. Every six months, spoonfuls of castor oil were administered to combat constipation, which afflicted students and teachers alike. I taught myself to clean my shoes, tie my laces, braid my hair and make my bed.

Headmistress Maria Theresa had another name given to her by the students – she was known as the Terror, and on my second day at Saint Agatha I learned why. While the other students were studying history, science, English and maths, I was to be locked in a small office with her. Behind her dark wooden desk, below a large, austere crucifix, was a picture of a young woman whose body had been stuffed into a stocking of a dress. The woman stood at an angle, dark-skinned. Her red lips were smiling, and the sun coming in from the window obscured the left side of her face. They looked alike, yet not alike enough to be related. I looked at the picture on my first day in that room and wanted to ask the nun who the girl was, but decided to wait for a while, until some time passed, until we built a friendly rapport. Later, I would wish that I had taken the opportunity at the start.

'I'm not sure how a girl can become a big, hulking thing of your size and not know how to read,' she said.

I waited, wondering if I should answer.

'Your forms list your mother's name and your father's name, but you have your mother's name. Why is that?'

I opened my mouth but my tongue was like felt.

'Never mind. I can guess what the answer is. Open your book of letters and stories.'

I fumbled through the small pile and found the book. Before I could fully open it, she slammed her hand on top of mine.

'What is this?'

The book had been covered in paper. The job was shoddy. Mini had tried to show me the fastest way. On the first page of the textbook were letters, scribbled in pencil, forming what must have been a sentence.

'Did you write this?'

'No.'

'Do you know how to write? Are you a liar?'

'No.'

She reached out and pinched my cheek, twisting the skin between her fingers. I felt her nail pierce through.

'Go through each page and erase every mark. These books were pristine when they were given to you. You will keep them that way.'

I began turning the pages, quickly but gently, so she would know I respected the book and its binding. She left the office, letting the door crash behind her. She was wrong, the books were not pristine. Some of the edges were turned, curled in. There were scribbles in corners. I wondered how many girls had read this very book, had sat in this office, before me. Rubbing my burning cheek, I realized these must have been the doodles of four-year-olds. By my age, they were all reading books, memorizing tables. I opened to a page of swathes of green and blue, sky and grass. Reading the picture was easy. I moved my finger over the black letters that ran along the bottom. They could have said anything. In the centre of the picture was a tree with a thick, broad trunk; smooth, unlike anything I had seen in Pune. Below the tree was a girl holding an orange ball in her hand. In the corner of the picture was a dark mark. I ran the eraser over it and it began to fade, taking some of the sky away with it. I didn't understand that mark. It seemed senseless. It didn't say anything or mean anything. It only cleaved the bright blue in half. The ball in the girl's hand was lined. Adding an extra line to it would go unnoticed. I pushed my pencil into the centre of the ball and carried it to the edge. And now there was a line. A line just like the errant one in the corner, but this new one had found a home in the picture and could reside there without causing trouble. Another line could be made on the girl's yellow dress, around the collar which curved in an S-shaped frill. I added a layer of frill.

A yank on my braid sent my head back. I looked at the ceiling. I looked at Sister Maria Theresa's face. Saliva collected at the side of her mouth.

'I tell you to erase the markings and what do you do?' She lumbered around and peered at the page. 'Only your first day and already a vandal?' She grabbed the pencil from my hand and pointed at the book.

I began rubbing, but the line would not disappear. Unlike the blue, the yellow turned muddy, almost green. The girl's dress faded at the neck. I stopped rubbing and laid my hand down on the table. Sweat had collected all over me. Sister Maria Theresa bent her head to look at the picture and, without warning, stabbed the pencil into the back of my palm.

We both looked at my hand, at the pencil erected in it, like the tree in the grass of the picture. Like the flag at the entrance, where Ma had left me. I screamed, first at the sight of it, but didn't feel a thing until a pain unlike anything I could remember went snarling up my arm.

Sister Maria Mathilda, who administered medicine, used two balls of cotton to check for particles left inside my hand. She was gentle, but didn't touch me any more than she had to. I was dismissed after my hand had been bandaged in gauze.

'What happened to you?' Mini asked.

'The Terror,' I said, trying not to cry.

Mini opened her mouth into a perfect O when I told her about the hole in my hand. 'She's not allowed to do that.'

I opened and closed my hand. I hadn't learned to be outraged yet.

The next morning, Sister Maria Theresa began my lessons. Neither of us made any reference to the day before. On days that I was slow, unable to keep up with her pace, she dug her nails into my skin, each time some newly discovered patch. If I or my work was slovenly, a ruler was applied to my knuckles or the backs of my calves. I learned words like 'sin'. I learned that cleanliness had little to do with bathing.

The bathroom we girls shared had a muffled light, even when the sky outside was sunny. The tiles under my feet were wet, and I could smell the lye and soap and a dampness that had entered the wooden doors of the shower stalls. The halo around the drain was dark, embedded with years of dirt that had circled and disappeared down the hole. I stood naked in the stall. Mini was dressed, but neither of us commented on this. The right side of her spectacles dipped down and rested on her cheek, and I looked at her face a little longer to see if it was crooked.

I didn't know why she had followed me in. She flipped over the upside-down pail and turned on the tap. Water hit the steel with a violence. I watched it rise and reached out to turn it off as it met the halfway mark. That is all we were allowed, I knew. Half a bucket, lukewarm. But Mini touched my wrist and pulled a long stocking from the pocket of her uniform. I stared at her and blinked, wondering what other miracles she had in there. She fitted the elastic waist of the stocking around the nozzle and placed the nylon foot in the pail. Looking at my face, she turned the hot water tap on full. Water soundlessly continued to flow into the pail.

'Lamba, are you in there?'

My eyes widened and my stomach dropped. 'Yes.' My voice was a squeak.

I heard the Terror's steps closing in on the stall. Mini put her finger to her lips and stepped soundlessly inside the steel pail. Water dislocated. The tap continued to flow.

I heard the Terror's breath catch as she bent down. She looked through the small gap below the stall, seeing my feet and the bottom of the pail. Her knees cracked as she straightened.

'Don't take your own sweet time,' she said.

I listened as her steps disappeared in the corridor.

Mini and I stood a little longer, I still naked, she in uniform, submerged to her knees in my bathwater.

One night, I lay in my bed, staring at the dark ceiling. Beyond that room was the foaming sky.

'Mini,' I said. 'I have to go number one.'

'So go, na,' she muttered.

It was a long walk down the unlit path, past the sound of the haunted trees, the wailing animals, the cold.

'Mini, come with me.'

Mini turned her head away, mumbling.

I lay back down. My fingers and toes were freezing, but a sweat had broken out on my body. I pushed my legs together and felt the pressure across my abdomen. If I clenched my eyes shut, I could almost see the sky lighting up as the night grew dark, streaming like milk. The stars twinkled. I felt my face soften, my mouth fall open and sigh.

I woke up the next morning to a sharp jab in my side. The morning light, unfiltered, warmed my face. I opened my eyes to see a strong chin and heavy jaw looming over me.

'Filthy little Hindu. Look at the mess you've made.' I was lying at the centre of my sopping bed.

That morning, I stood at the door of the gymnasium, holding the soiled sheets above my head. My knuckles burned and I longed to lick them. The blood had drained out of my arms. My body quaked. My classmates walked past, rushing to their first lessons, giggling under their breath. They did not know me yet, these girls. Though I had lived among them for months, I spent my days separately. They knew I was different, slow.

The beatings were not all bad. Sometimes they were the way we made friends. We would compare the red welts on our fingers and wrists. Those were our rings and bangles. The backs of the hands and calves tended to bruise darker. That was our mehndi. The girl with the darkest mehndi each week was the bride. We celebrated her and said she would be a favourite of her mother-in-law. The girl with most rings and bangles was our queen. We curtsied or kissed her hand when we passed her and did her bidding as was required.

Sundays were spent in Mass. I moved my mouth along with the words of the hymns, but in my mind I repeated other prayers. Jesus, pale in plaster, looked down at me from the altar. I spoke to other gods, the ones Nani had shown me at home, but in Hindi so they might understand.

I learned to draw so well, so finely, that the Terror could no longer see my mark. I learned to read, to write, to name the planets and multiply fractions.

Some nights, I squatted down in a corner of the gymnasium and went directly on the floor. Piss splattered against my bare feet, but I trained myself not to think of it. The nuns soon noticed the puddles and started monitoring the gymnasium in the middle of the night, drifting in and out like ghosts in their white nightgowns. For those occasions, I taught myself to bring my heel up between my legs and push it deep into my pelvis.

I learned how to regulate my body. How often I could bathe would determine how much I could sweat. How often I could urinate determined how much water I could drink. Part of me was sealed off. Little went in and little came out.

'What's wrong with you?' Mini asked.

I shook my head, but a sinking feeling pulled me down. The dining hall began to lose focus. The backs of my legs slid and scraped against the chair. The room turned black.

I woke to find my nose pressed to the ground. There were dozens of shiny black shoes as far as I could see. Murmurs and laughter. A cold hand came down on my forehead. I followed it up the veiny wrist and looked into the face of the nun above me.

'Call the nurse.'

The nurse began the protocol of checking my temperature, but at the sight of my fiery red urine she shouted for the headmistress.

'Infection,' she said.

I was admitted to the local hospital, where the country doctor administered strong antibiotics. For three days, I stayed in the blue hospital room. My nose burned from the smell of bleach and the naphthalene balls that sat over the drains.

Ma and Nana were called. They arrived and brought the smells of Pune with them. Nana shook his head when he saw me. Ma cried.

'We are taking her home,' she said.

When I was released from the hospital I returned to the school only to collect my belongings. A small blue suitcase. Some drawings I had made. I hung them in a room in Nana and Nani's flat, one that I would share with my mother.

No one ever asked me about what had happened, why I had lost so much weight and some of my hair, or why I had a round scar on both sides of my left hand. Life went on as though nothing had changed. Perhaps, in a sense, that was true. We all went on living in separate realities.

Nani spent a good deal of time trying to convince me to eat. When I told her I wasn't hungry, she said she would call someone to take me away. A doctor, a policeman, a boogeyman. Some man. Always a man.

The moment was awkward – I felt too old for it, old enough to know there was something artificial in the construction of her warning. More than anything, I was curious about the details of the punishment I should expect, the specifics of the pain or humiliation. Take me away and do what, I wanted to ask. For my part, I could see over the horizon of her threats, down to the other side – I had visited there, this place she only alluded to, but I sensed that the truth of this would terrify her. So I ate my food, and let her believe I was afraid.

There are incidents with Ma almost daily now.

She doesn't know who soaked the mung. Still, every morning, it's there. Why is it there? Sometimes she remembers soaking it but doesn't remember what it was for. Chila? Dal?

The same happens with the clothes in the laundry basket. She wonders if someone is living in her house, using her things. Who is this other woman? Is it one or several? She pays the maid her salary twice on the first of the month. The maid is uncharacteristically cheerful until I correct the mistake.

I don't mention this to Dilip. The less I mention her, the better. As it is, Ma's illness looms over us at night. Things are not quite the same at home. He locks the door when he's in the bathroom, comes to bed when he is certain I'm asleep, and I shiver if I think too long on the fragility of what we have.

I go to see Ma's doctor. He has cut his hair and isn't wearing his wedding ring today.

I ask him if he had a pleasant Diwali. He says it was pleasant.

I tell him about the mung.

He tells me he will look at my mother's dosage.

I tell him my mother is living alone again. 'There was an incident.'

'What kind of incident?'

'She lit a fire using our things, doused it in alcohol. The whole room was ruined. She burned her hand. It was scary. She seemed as though she was possessed.'

He nods. 'That sounds scary, but with the proper precautions I'm sure it can be avoided in the future.'

I shift back and forth. 'At the moment, she can't live with me.'

The doctor says that is unfortunate for my mother, but might be the best for me in the long run.

'For me?'

He says my mother and I have always shared some version of our objective reality. Without me, her ties to that may have loosened, sad, but true – yet on the other hand, as a caregiver, the distance might be good for me. It is difficult when everything starts to vanish.

He says memory is a work in progress. It's always being reconstructed.

'Maybe she will remember things from the past,' I say. 'Things we have all forgotten.'

'You'll never know if the memory is real or imagined. Your mother is no longer reliable.'

We run through the later stages of this together, he an expert of medicine and me an expert at searching for theories.

Hallucinations, inhabiting the past, an archaic sense of self, a deep feeling of isolation. The present is seen for what it is, a fleck always slipping through the sieve.

He nods at me and says I am well versed. I thank him but I feel flimsy inside.

He tells me to keep talking to her, to help her turn things over in her mind. Writing may help too. It activates different centres in the brain. Feelings may remain, but eventually those will fade. I will lose her in increments. At the end, she will be a house I've moved out of, containing nothing that is familiar.

'I have read,' I begin, 'that this disease is caused by insulin resistance in the brain. Like another kind of diabetes.'

'There isn't enough evidence to support that.'

'I've also seen some studies that link cognitive health with problems in the intestines.'

He leans away from me, as though he can smell something awry. Perhaps it is my mention of the bowels holding the answer to our question, a desecration of the dogma he holds dear. French intellectuals sniffed when Bataille suggested enlightenment could be found in shit, or God in a prostitute, and it is likely that now neurologists prefer to retain the screen that separates their domain from the rest of the body, the sanctity of the blood—brain barrier, because a turd can have no relation to the mysteries they seek.

At home, I turn the lights on and a fly whips past my face. It roams the parameters of its cage, bumping into mirrors and pressing against windows, tasting surfaces with its feet. I watch it fly in circles and wonder how many hours it has been in here. By now it has mapped this place, created coordinates in its mind. It knows the furthest distance it can travel, the sofa, the bookshelf, the door handle. I slide open the balcony door and stand aside. I wait for the fly to leave, to catch a scent from outside, a familiar breeze. But it doesn't. It continues crossing from one side of the room to another.

I return to the sofa, put my feet up on the armrest. Maybe it likes it here, a new home. It buzzes around my head, frustrated. Trapped.

Once more, the fly passes by the door, gaping as it is. I watch it and wonder if it can see the door at all, or if the map it has made of this era in its little life is so persistent that the outside world ceases to exist. It is blind to the way out. All it knows, as it hits its body against the mirror, against its own reflection, is that something is missing, something is amiss.

Ma leaves the house in the middle of night. She wakes up, uses the loo and heads out in her nightgown. The watchman finds her trying to hail a rickshaw. When he brings her back to her apartment, the door is wide open.

He calls me right away. Dilip and I arrive within thirty minutes.

The sky is beginning to brighten. The watchman tells me that she had left the tap running in the bathroom. I thank him and give him the smallest note I have for his trouble.

'Is she unwell?' he asks me just before leaving.

'No,' I say. 'She's fine. Just bad dreams.'

After he is gone, I turn to Dilip. 'Now he knows.'

Dilip blinks. My arms are trembling.

'He knows that she's not well,' I say. 'The whole building will know, all the servants, that a single woman living alone is unwell, maybe mad. She isn't safe any more.'

I tell Dilip I am staying with Ma until we find a solution. He doesn't ask me how long I expect to be gone. I try not to think about it, ignore the tightness in my face and the sense that everything is falling apart.

Ma and I share a bed, something we haven't done since before I went to boarding school.

The maid sweeps the house twice a day, bending low and inching along. She rubs her eyes with her free hand. Dust and hair form a pile near the sofa. The bristles of the broom graze my feet.

A lizard has found its way inside, either through the door that is always ajar, or through the open window in the kitchen. It creeps upside down across the ceiling, getting lost in the brown stains. I watch it edge forward like it's walking on ice. A scab of plaster hangs like a sheet, swaying with the rotating fan.

The maid finishes sweeping and moves away. Her pile stays on the floor like a nest of black wire.

I see new spots on the ceiling. They seem to darken. 'The upstairs neighbour's pipe broke,' the maid says.

I lean my head back, mapping the bubbling paint. Pune is hazy, but the universe within these walls gapes grandly. They mimic each other, the lizard and the maid, lingering around me. My head throbs. Ma has been waking up every night with bad dreams.

At twilight, we listen to the cars and trucks, all honking, fighting across the main road beyond the compound gate. Men holler at each other, their voices distant but familiar.

I pour Dettol on the shower floor and leave it overnight. In the morning, I pick up my loofah. It smells like ethyl alcohol. I use it around my knees, scouring the dead skin. The hot water hits my back. I keep rubbing. Soon, I glow red. I imagine that if I go long enough, hard enough, I will be a diaphanous cloud. I can forget that there is something underneath.

The ceiling trembles like it's alive.

Sometimes I think maybe it's this flat. It's easy to go mad here.

Other days it's unmistakeable: Ma has lost it.

She tells Nani she hears Baba's voice. He doesn't say anything out of the ordinary – comments on the weather, calls out her name. Sometimes it's no more than a grunt or a cough, or his laughter drifting up from the car park below.

She looks around at first, sure he's there, coming in through the window or the door – he misses her and knows where she lives. He sounds so close he must be here. It gnaws at her until she gives in, until she stops what she is doing and walks around the house, checking behind furniture and jabbing at curtains. I watch as she does this, but look away when she turns back with nothing.

Nani's mouth crinkles but she remains silent. I go into the bathroom and cry.

'I think she hallucinates about what hurt her most,' I tell Nani. 'She expected something different when she left the ashram. She expected he would come after her, demand she return and take up her place beside him. But that never happened.'

'That was so long ago,' Nani says. 'People don't hold on to things like that.'

I walk Nani down to her car. The gate has been left open. The watchman is sharing a bidi and chai with his friend down the road. Mrs Rao is nowhere in sight, but her Pomeranian barks down from the balcony, pushing his head through the metal bars. We kiss each other. I wave as she drives away. We have settled into a pattern of avoidance. My grandmother has never seemed more like a stranger.

In the evening, Ma falls asleep in bed with her slippers still on. I dial Dilip. He is eating dinner by himself, in front of the television. His voice crackles, as if he is far away.

Dilip says his friends in Dubai just moved into a nice place that has a garden and a garage for two cars. Five minutes away on foot from them there is a public beach. Would I want to move to Dubai someday? he asks. I listen to his bare descriptions, trying to imagine this other city, wondering how the beach becomes the desert, how the air turns from wet to dry.

Ma cries out in her sleep. 'What was that?' Dilip asks.

'Nothing,' I say.

My mother comes out of the bedroom. Her hair is pressed to the side of her face. She slithers into the armchair across from me.

'You have to stop,' she whispers. Her eyes are wet.

I sigh and rest the phone against my neck. 'Ma, it's not real. Should I put you back to sleep?'

'I know it's real. You have to stop making those drawings.'

The television is on. A female news anchor of open ethnicity is reporting on a suspected terrorist attack. I reach for the remote.

'Did you hear me?' she says. 'Stop making those disgusting draw-ings. They are an insult to me. They are an insult to your husband. You insult us every day that you do them. You insult us every time you hang them in some fancy gallery show.'

I place the phone on the sofa and push myself up. My heart pounds and my knees crack as I straighten. I put my hands on her shoulders, one at a time.

'Okay,' I say. 'Whatever you want. But I want you to lie down for a little while.'

She seems to calm down and allows me to help her from the chair. Her hands are cold as I tuck her under her covers.

Dilip is quiet on the line.

'So,' I say. 'What else?'

'Why did she mention me? Why are the drawings an insult to your husband?'

I rub my eye. White from the corner sticks like glue on my fingers. 'I don't know. I don't know what to make of it.'

1993

My mother and Nani could not abide the sight of each other any more and Ma decided to rent a small apartment not far from the ashram.

At the time, I was not sure how she paid for the place, but later my grandmother told me that Nana gave her the money to restore some peace in his life. Kali Mata, too, would come from time to time with envelopes of what she referred to as goodwill from the ashram.

I started attending a local English-medium school, ill prepared to keep up with the other students. The principal suggested daily tuition for several hours, but Ma only smiled in response. There wasn't enough money for that sort of thing.

The subject I dreaded most of all was Hindi. How could a language I heard and spoke all the time be so utterly foreign? Otherwise, my reading and writing skills were passable, and the teachers praised my mechanical handwriting. Submission was apparent in every line I wrote.

'Convent school,' my mother said. The principal seemed to understand.

Now that I had numbers, and letters, too, the whole world opened up for me. Kali Mata smiled. 'Reading changes everything.' But it wasn't language that held appeal, only the symbols that made it up, abstract and random, characters I infused with alternate meanings.

I began to keep a diary, but not the kind the other girls at school kept — no entries about romance and boys and dreams and wishes. Mine was a collection of moments from the past, the ones I could remember anyway, primarily a list of grudges. I coded this list carefully, contrived an order, one that could be read chronologically but also by the severity of the transgression. Entire tables were dedicated to Sister Maria Theresa, and several to my mother, too. Others were given their own form of data entry, coded by colour or numerically.

My father did not receive this treatment. In my journal, he did not exist.

I made few friends at school and even fewer in the building. My alienation intensified when I woke up one morning to find my left eyebrow missing. The hairs were scattered on my pillow like scraps of thread, so insufficient I couldn't believe they had once formed a neat row on my brow. I looked in the mirror and ran my finger over my face. My left eye seemed defeated, incomplete.

'What have you done?' Ma said when she saw me.

Kali Mata put down her tea. Her eyeshadow cracked like the top of a brûlée. 'What bad luck you have,' she said.

I begged my mother to let me miss school, but she wouldn't hear of it.

'It isn't so noticeable,' Kali Mata said. 'Well, it is, but only because you still have the other one.'

I kept my head down, brushed my hair over one side of my face. I leaned my head in my hand and favoured certain angles. That afternoon, I came home exhausted.

'It's nothing pretty,' Ma said. 'But why should you hide your face? Young girls are supposed to be brave.'

She was talking about herself, her own self-image. A rebel, a contrarian. But I was nothing like her. I didn't feel brave.

My anxiety produced a fever and I stayed home for a couple of days, reading Enid Blyton books and checking the mirror every hour. I searched for a glimmer of black somewhere, but my brow was a blank.

When the light moved on my face I saw two different people. The girl I had been and the creature I was now, something inhuman.

I swept my mother's razor along the other eyebrow.

In less than a second, it vanished. Black slivers speckled the wet drain.

The hair looked thicker on the bathroom floor, wetter, blacker than what had been on the pillow.

Nani cried when she saw me.

'I knew this would happen, it's some disease she picked up in the convent,' she said.

When I said I had shaved it off myself, my mother leaned forward at the dining table. Her arms were as white as raw chicken thighs.

'Well,' she said, 'you could scare the devil, but I'm glad you did the right thing.'

Leaving the house became daunting. Eyes followed me wherever I went. I spent time indoors. Only Kali Mata would visit me regularly. She brought books, old packs of cards, games that she had never heard of or seen. Then she brought other strange objects: oriental tea sets, old keys and some photographs of me as a child at the ashram. We laid out the faded pictures on the dining table. Kali Mata had gained weight and she leaned over heavily, her breasts resting on the table, separating like dough.

I knew Kali Mata was different from me because of the colour of her eyes, not the difference in our skin. Her eyes were a speckled shade of blue, and her pupils formed prominent black dots in the middle. I was sure the world would look different through those eyes, and I didn't think she could have dark, ordinary days.

'The world outside is moving on without you,' she said.

I considered this, but wondered if I had ever belonged there, with everyone else.

Once, I snuck out to buy a single cigarette from a shop down the road. The shopkeeper pitied me for my eyebrows and gave me an extra one for free.

I stood on the balcony before the building was awake. The awnings were inhabited by pigeons, carpeted in their fuzzy excrement. Hiding in a corner, I lit my cigarette.

Two storeys down, across the way, through an open window I saw an old man undressing in his bathroom. He let his clothes fall to the floor in a pile. He was thin, just skin and bone, and his penis was shrivelled to the size of a nub. I extended my arm and approximated his member across the distance. Barely as big as my nail. He turned on the shower and water spilled out as though from a hose. His buttocks sagged like empty sacks.

That night, I drew him as I remembered him, still under the water, his arms hanging by his sides.

The time of day Baba died escapes me. So does the season, but those details have been carefully documented by his followers.

The entrance of the flat was dark as always, as though we wanted people who came to the door to imagine that unhappy hermits lived within. I don't remember what the note on the table said, but my mother's scrawl looked anxious and unconsidered. Something seemed to be crawling down my back, and I shuddered. Was this the first time I was alone in the house? I walked by the mottled mirror that hung beside the front door, never looking directly at my reflection but aware that the mirror was seeing me, doubling me, even when I had my back to it. The porous tiles of the kitchen floor looked murky, as though it hadn't been mopped that day, but when I stepped in, I felt that it was still damp, maybe even a little viscous from the insect repellent that Kashta mixed with the soap.

I found two boondi laddoos in the fridge and fitted them neatly in my mouth. After that, I paced up and down the small living room, stopping only to eat all the cheese with the red cow on the label, and the curd balls that came wrapped in wax, until my stomach bubbled with trapped gas.

A red rocking chair sat beside the quiet telephone. We called the chair red, but it was really maroon, and it didn't rock but slid back and forth. The woven cane that constituted the seat was worn and tatty, and it was my favourite piece of furniture in the house, though I never sat on it any more because of a dim memory of having caught my finger in its mechanism when I was little. The mirror was still behind me, taking the back of my body in, and I didn't dare turn around.

Ma walked in wearing crumpled white. She was mussed, almost chalky in some way. I backed away from her at the sight of her face, and my spine pressed against the dining table.

The hard wooden edge lodged in my back. I felt it was separated from my bones by only a bit of stretched-thin skin. There was no pain, just a meek sensation, buffered by the padding that covered me. Sometimes my blood flowed loud enough to awaken my whole body, but at other times I felt I was wearing a suit I could unzip and step out of to reveal my real arms and face, the skin I was hiding underneath. I had gained thirteen kilos since turning eleven. Kali Mata thought it was hormones.

Ma opened a high cabinet where she kept some alcohol and, standing on her toes, took out a bottle of Teacher's whisky which had been kept only for male guests. Opening the bottle, she smelled the contents and closed it again. I could tell by now that she had been crying. Not recently, but maybe that morning. Her nose was greasy with a collection of blackheads.

'Baba died today,' she said.

Technically, it was at some point the day before, but they waited to do the cremation in the morning. There were disagreements among his followers. Some had wanted to have an autopsy done to determine the cause of death, while others had deemed it unthinkable to cut open a deceased deity. If he had wanted to be cut open, he would have left instructions, they argued. Some had thought a Hindu priest should be consulted, but Baba hated priests and that idea was dismissed. Others had wanted to embalm the body, at least for the time being, so his many devotees could travel to see him one last time.

'Embalming is only for communists,' Ma had said. The majority agreed that it would be irregular, not in the tradition of his forebears, and that he should be cremated as soon as possible. The last group won out, and a pyre was built for Baba in the ashram. The gates were thrown open for one day and many entered without knowing the reason why. Ma was present for the washing of the body and the changing of clothes. She said they split his skull from the back so his head would not explode in the fire.

Afterwards, they stood in a line, Baba's paramours, and offered consolation and blessings to the crowd. One man started shouting that they should all throw themselves on to the pyre. He was subsequently removed.

Standing next to Kali Mata, Ma had felt a sense of pride.

'I realized that it's no small thing,' she said. 'To be the lover of a great man.'

I told her that to me it looked small, cheap even, and was definitely nothing to brag about.

She grabbed me by the arms and shook me before slapping my face.

'You're a fat little bitch. Have some sympathy! I became a widow today!'

The word 'whore' came out of my mouth but it was mingled with a scream as I rushed into her body, knocking her over on to the floor. I sat on her chest and wrapped my hands around her throat, squeezing until the veins appeared under her eyes.

When I let go, she coughed and gasped for air. I looked down at her face.

'Fat little bitch,' she repeated.

When I wasn't eating, I had an urge to put other things in my mouth. My fingers, my hair, the plastic buttons on my school uniform. Forty-five minutes after eating, I was hungry again, though my stomach was not limber enough and food would ferment inside me. I spent sleepless nights with gas trapped in my rib cage, days of diarrhoea and constipation. Sometimes blood appeared in my stool. Sometimes the acid from my stomach appeared in my mouth.

At times, Ma was desolate at the sight of me, but otherwise she insisted a child should eat whenever she was hungry.

On days when the latter was true, she would take me for ice cream if I begged long enough. After school, I sat at the counter and slurped a vanilla milkshake at Uncle Sam, a fifties-style American diner hidden at the back of a five-star hotel. The vegetarian menu had fried potato cubes and pizza speckled with jeera. Families lined up for the pale, eggless ice cream that had mostly melted by the time it reached the tables. The white leather seat covers had turned a shade of distressed grey, but the walls, with vibrant flags and strange memorabilia, looked as though they had been put up yesterday. The jukebox didn't take money and played only Bryan Adams songs, and a miniature model of a classic Cadillac turned on a revolving platform near the cash register. Uncle Sam looked down on everyone from a picture at the front of the room.

'If this was a church, Mr Parekh, that's where the altar would be,' a waiter said to the ursine manager. Ma and I glanced up at Uncle Sam.

The manager shook his head. 'This is no church, Reza, and that lady wants two choco-sundaes.'

Our choco-sundaes were brought over without a tray. The waiter put an extra bowl of gleaming canned cherries next to me. I looked up at him. His palms were darker than the rest of him. His hair was overgrown and flopped over his pockmarked cheeks.

I tried to make the ice cream melt so I could eat it quickly, helping it along with the back of my spoon, pressing down on the little creamy mountains. The waiter leaned against the wall while I worked on the sundae. He looked between Ma and me, smiling occasionally.

'It must taste good,' he said, watching me take my first gulp.

I nodded and took another mouthful. Saliva burst in my mouth. The cold liquid warmed to the temperature of my body.

'What does it taste like?'

My mouth was full and I couldn't answer. I swallowed, but the sweet, milky liquid coated my throat and I coughed.

Ma laughed. 'I'm sure you've tasted it before.'

He shook his head and rubbed the front of his uniform with his blackened hand. No visible trace was left where he touched himself. I watched, mesmerized by the strange pigmentation.

'Food doesn't taste like that for me. Look at her face. It's something different for her.'

I looked up at him and saw he was looking at Ma, and it occurred to me that they'd had an unspoken exchange while I had been eating.

'My name is Reza Pine.'

We introduced ourselves, but the manager called out to him through the room of voices, the sounds of adults and children. He refilled the bowl of cherries before he went away.

1995

I already knew that sex smelled like fish and ice cream, but the first time I had sex was for a packet of imported Big Red gum. The boy in question would chew a piece and blow cinnamon breath on my face. He was sixteen, lived in the building and had pimples on his forehead. He'd watch me as I played badminton with his younger sister. We did it close to his flat, on the landing between floors. After the first time, it felt easy.

Thirteen years old. I was wearing women's sizes, and my feet fitted into Kali Mata's sandals. The liftman pressed himself against the wall of the lift when I entered. I shouted whenever my mother spoke to me. We were rarely in the same room any more. Something about me was expanding, taking up too much space, sucking the air out of closed areas. No one wanted to be around me for too long, but I didn't mind and hated them all in return anyway.

My father and his wife had returned from the US.

Three years had turned into six. They called to tell me that she was pregnant. I refused to take their calls and Ma had to give me the news.

I had started to suspect that someone else was living in my body, taking up temporary residence and making herself at home. She was opening me up from the inside, causing the appearance of stretch marks and discoloured skin. Hair had appeared in greater quantities where I didn't want it, and I couldn't keep up with the demands of depilation. And I was eating for a multitude, it seemed, satisfying a bottomless hole of hunger.

No one told me this was the age for these feelings, and even if they had I would not have believed them. No one told me that it would take years to accept my body at all, to feel that I knew where it began and ended. At that moment, the scale of existence was unfathomable. I could remember a time when I slipped through narrow cracks, when I could sit on my grandmother's knee without producing a groan.

And the confusion I felt within myself was nothing compared to the changes I witnessed from the outside world. Men looked at me in a way I hadn't noticed before. Had I been oblivious all this time? Or did they see this other woman living in my body too?

Women also were different, or perhaps I could read some shift in their eyes. The swelling of fat above my waistband elicited a reaction. Was it disgust? I knew there was anger. In fact, anger was the one discernible thing we all shared, and the one thing I could name. The world seemed forcefully, endlessly angry with me. Men for the desire I produced. Women for my inability to contain this new body.

Humans grow up flagrantly, messily, and no one was afforded the choice of looking away. Sequestering me for those in-between years might have helped – going into a cottony cocoon and emerging a completed woman.

I descended further into gloom when Reza told me that my skin might never clear up. He walked in just as Ma was taking a sterilized needle to a whitehead on my chin and said that his skin had erupted when he was about sixteen and now, some fifteen years later, had still left its mark. He pulled off his faded T-shirt to illustrate. His body was taut, slim, but covering the planes of pale skin were colonies of keloid, scars that had never gone away. 'I hope that doesn't happen to you,' Reza said. I looked once more at his spotted abdomen. 'You're a girl,' he said. 'It's worse for girls. Guys with bad skin can still get laid.'

My teeth clenched at this double damnation. I felt the other girl inside me rising.

He spoke again, as though he had read my mind. 'It isn't fair, of course, that this should be the case. But it's true, regardless.'

Our friendship with Reza developed slowly, over the course of afternoons after school. He did odd jobs, mainly things with his hands. The pay at Uncle Sam was not very much, but Reza brought us home the cakes and confections that didn't sell. During work hours, he was supposed to wear gloves to hide his hands. He often disobeyed.

Reza detested the job, but at the end of the month he got a thin envelope from the bank with unblemished notes. They reminded him of his mother, how she took pride in making sure the currency in her wallet was flat and fresh, how she tried to use up the faded bills as quickly as she could. She believed that crisp notes were the currency of the rich, like choice cuts of meat, tender greens or sweet mangoes. But by the time money reached his mother, it had passed through many hands.

Ma brought Kali Mata and me to the restaurant one afternoon. We sat at a table and kept drinking water because Kali Mata didn't eat anything with artificial colouring.

'We should order something,' Ma said.

The manager stared at us as we pretended to read the laminated menu cards.

Reza took a sip from his flask. 'No, don't worry. I'll bring some cake over tonight if you want.'

Reza Pine is difficult to sketch because he always spoke in terms of fluid reality. The truth was subjective, something he had little interest in, and experience continually altered itself as memory. He had picked up some of these ideas from his encounters with Baba and they had shaped him when he was still a young man. It was the reason he never found a place in the world of photojournalism and had to use his skills as a photographer elsewhere. Ma had never met Reza in the ashram, but people had mentioned his name.

'I feel like I know you,' she said. She touched his leg as she spoke.

'Then you do,' he replied.

I rested my cheek on Kali Mata's black-clad shoulder.

When Reza described himself as an artist, my first instinct was to mistrust him. What did it mean, to be an artist? He was the first I had ever met.

He said property developers in Pune were like war profiteers, exploiting the territorial instincts of men. He drew them in charcoal, gnarled figures walking around with urine dripping from their shrunken penises, marking off sections of the city with their stench. He drew anywhere, on paper or walls. It made no difference. But his hands, always black, were familiar to me.

'It's dirty work,' he said.

He was born to a poet who kept a shop to support his family. His father was his hero, a genius of Urdu verse, a man Reza could not remember but always memorialized.

Reza acknowledged he himself was something of an outcast with the press and the artist community in Bombay. It had to do with an incident that occurred during the 1993 riots in Bombay.

I said I had never heard a name like Pine. Not with a name like Reza, anyway.

He smiled at me and I looked away.

Reza had almost become an NRI. When he was very young, his family moved to Canada. When they arrived, there was ice on the ground.

His father thought a name like Shaikh would never do. He went outside of their one-bedroom apartment in the Portuguese ghetto of Montreal and read the sign. Pine Street, it said. From then on they would be known as the Pines.

'What happened?'

'They deported us,' said Reza. 'They thought my father was a communist.'

'Was he?'

'Yes, of course.'

*

In 1992, Reza Pine, a young photojournalist, travelled to Ayodhya in northern India to witness the demolition of the mosque and the rallies to celebrate Rama's birthplace. In Bombay, violence erupted in the streets of his city, and all was alight with flames. Bottles thrown into windows, shopkeepers terrorized, women beaten, raped, and children forced to watch.

Hindus killing Muslims, Muslims killing Hindus, unleashing a savagery that was dormant the day before, awoken with inflammatory words.

Communal violence was easy to dig up. The foundations had been laid by history. Reza saw how easy it was to kindle the kernels of fear, how the fear could be patted down but would eventually find another food source.

He met the men, the individuals who made up the mob. They wore their colours with pride and, standing side by side, admired the artistry of their violence.

He spent nights wondering if what he had seen was real, or if it was a film set – staged, framed in the cruel cut of a camera's lens, single moments that were the beginnings and the ends of an ongoing terror.

The rioting calmed after a few days. There were pieces to pick up.

In Bombay, bodies were burned, the evidence slowly interred. Life resumed its normal pulse, and the process of forgetting began immediately. Some people laughed, standing idly in the street, enjoying the midday sun.

In the new year, a fresh bloodletting began. The curfew was reinforced. The city was made up of locked doors and darkened windows. Reza lived with his widowed mother in her flat near Bombay Central, where the cries were close enough to hear, as though they would turn the corner and be upon him. Otherwise, the roads were deserted and no one dared leave home. It was understood, an unspoken truth, that if you were caught, there would be no one to save you. No guard, no police. No, today there was no power higher than your attacker – he ruled the city. Bombay was not your own, not now, perhaps not ever again, and from this day forth you would walk in the shadows.

But something was different. The rich and powerful were beginning to tremble as the mob attacked buildings in Breach Candy and Nariman Point, the long footpaths and shady streets, the regal homes where wealthy and beautiful people went when they left their leisure clubs and five-star hotels. Faceless and unnamed men moving in groups, flying their saffron flags and shouting their slogans, charging through the places where the women travelled only in chauffeur-driven cars and the windows always overlooked the sea.

It was the middle of the afternoon. Reza was taking pictures of the damage done to shops and homes, photographing families that had lost loved ones, widows and orphans. He didn't ask their permission; the living resembled the deceased, they took on the hues of their fallen kin. And one cannot speak to the dead.

He heard screams behind him, and a mob of men came running, waving sticks. Fearful, he hid behind a bus parked in front of a building. He tried to take pictures of the approaching mob, but his hands shook. Then he ran. He ran into the dark entrance of the building, up the stairs, hitting walls, knocking on doors as he went along.

A young woman was standing on the third floor, about to go inside her home. Reza was breathless, shaking.

'What's wrong?'

He could not tell her, could not speak, but she heard the men's voices in the stairwell. She pulled him in through the door, bolted it shut.

He heard the locks. One. Two. Three.

He didn't tell her he had seen locks like those before. He had seen them snap in half when a door was kicked in. He had seen them still intact when everything around them had burnt down. Instead, he clutched her arm and thanked her.

Then he looked around. Men, women and children looked back at him.

The girl's name was Rukhsana. The others were aunts, uncles, cousins. Her grandmother sat in a chair by the window, deaf and blind, oblivious to the scene below. Her young brothers were bent down on their knees and whispering to one another, their bodies coiled.

The family's last name was Shah. He stayed with them, slept beside them. Sometimes, at night, they sat together and listened to screams and gunshots. They peered out at the deserted streets below. Every day, they prayed that the phone would work and the power would return, but nothing changed.

Days and nights unhinged from dates and hours, and time was only recognizable by the passage of the moon in the sky.

When calamity is so near, one must never speak of it.

Reza felt a gratitude that anyone could have mistaken for love. The mob would have killed him if the Shahs hadn't taken him in. He ate their food, lived off their kindness. They were generous, but he knew there was mistrust in their eyes. Everything was different then. Each day felt like a lifetime. He wondered if he would ever leave that place alive. There was a danger in being locked up in a house like that. Rubbing shoulders shaved nerves down into delicate strands. A single pull and they would snap. The sound of Rukhsana's prayers made him want to sob.

So he married her.

Her family acted as witnesses.

They created a happy little world in that house.

There was little to eat and nothing to do. He thought it would be terrible, but they slowly learned to ignore the sounds from the outside, and everything became bearable. More than bearable. A pleasure. Some days were nothing less than a celebration.

When he finally came out, his mother was pleased he'd found a devout Muslim girl. She said everything happens for a reason.

*

'Where is Rukhsana now?'
    'She lives with my mother.'
    'And you?'
    'I move around.'

The questions began after he developed the film. Images of death and destruction were interspersed with quiet interior spaces, the smiles and awkward poses of a family. And the wedding portraits. They were austere and serious. Reza had taken them on a timer. He told his editor about his experience. Pogroms, death and destruction, but love still appeared in glimmers.

Mr Chaudhury, whom Reza reported to, said he wanted to meet this Rukhsana. She came to the office the following week but was too shy to look anyone in the face. She wasn't educated, and this room where words and images came together to tell a story of the day was mysterious to her. She nodded when the bespectacled man asked questions, and she corroborated what her new husband had said.

'It might have a very interesting human perspective,' Mr Chaudhury said, 'but we have to handle it in the right way.' He knew how to sell a paper.

Underneath her dupatta, Rukhsana had hair as curly as corkscrews. Not many people knew that secret. Some days, Reza wanted to tell someone, anyone, even a stranger on a crowded bus, so they might look at her, imagine her hair, but never know what it really was. Sometimes when he was with her, he realized his absolute authority. The pleasure this knowledge brought scared him.

Reza never wanted to be a human-interest story, packaged and sold. He was an auteur, a maker of images. The next day, he showed up at an art gallery in Colaba without an appointment, carrying a paper envelope full of negatives.

The gallerist asked him to repeat his name and said she wasn't interested in taking on new artists.

He persisted every day for twelve days. His job had always required stamina, standing in inhospitable weather and enduring long breaks in activity. If there was one quality he had in abundance, it was patience. After day five, he was not permitted to enter the gallery and he sat outside, borrowing a folding chair from a man who sold out-of-date magazines. He started chewing tobacco, a habit which lasted until the end of the week. He abruptly spat out his last mouthful when the gallerist swung open the door and crossed her arms.

'I only have ten minutes,' she said.

The show came together slowly. There was the political climate to consider. The gallerist didn't want to be a target. The concept for the exhibition also took time to reveal itself. The photographs, though powerful, felt incomplete, and Reza resorted to charcoal. He drew on large pieces of paper, and cut board into the shapes of furniture. The gallery became the Shahs' apartment, not as it was during that endless fortnight, but as Reza remembered it. Chairs were indicated only by their shadows on the ground. Windows were frames draped in fabric, obscuring the scene outside. It was a room not of objects but excesses, not of space but of claustrophobia. The photographs were interspersed throughout, and the opening was quiet but well attended.

Reza spoke to a group that gathered around him, reciting the order of events that led up to the show. There were questions and conversation when he finished, and Reza was confident about the beginnings of his career. He didn't read the reviews that came out in the paper – who read reviews anyway? – and was surprised to receive a folder from the gallery with some magazine cut-outs.

The show, the critics had agreed, was troubling to say the least, full of ethical problems that the artist had been unable to explain. The story, they said, of how the pictures were obtained was questionable, punctured with holes, and made the work immediately unappealing. He had invaded the space of a family, photographed them without explaining his intent and seized their identities for his own purposes. And then he had married one of their daughters so his foul appropriation could be sanctified. The violence against Rukhsana, in both image and person, was unacceptable. All this during one of the most heinous moments in the history of his city. One review called for the show to be taken down, asking, 'Haven't the Shahs been through enough already? Must their terror, suffering and ignorance be commodified and distributed by a man who lacks moral fibre?'

The gallerist took down the show ten days before schedule.

Reza collected his work three months later. Nothing had sold. The gallerist said this experience had damaged her reputation and was an utter disaster.

Reza shrugged. He told her he didn't understand what all the fuss was about.

Ma was holding his hand by the time Reza finished his story. Her other hand was on her breasts. Kali Mata breathed deeply, and I realized she had been moved as well. As for me, I wasn't sure I'd heard or understood the story in full. I vaguely recall a sense of discomfort, not with my surroundings but with what was inside of me. I had been taught for most of my life that the moment for living was yet to come, that the phase I was living in, a perpetual state of childhood, was a time for waiting. And so I waited, impatiently, resentfully, longing for this period of incapacitation to pass. And in that interim, I listened less than I should have, and felt no need to engage.

I believed that this want to be older meant that age would answer all my questions, that my desires would be fulfilled at a later date, but as the years pass and I wish for youth once more, the habit of waiting has already been instilled. It's deeply ingrained, something I can't seem to unlearn. I wonder if, when I'm old and frail and can see the shape of my end in front of me, I will still be waiting for the future to roll in.

1996

Reza moved into our flat. One morning, I found him sharing the bed with my mother. The pockmarks that covered his body were savage in the early light. I thought he looked repulsive and told him so.

'You're no beauty queen,' he said with a laugh.

I was told to keep quiet, but soon the neighbours caught on and whispered about it at the Club. Ma scolded me for telling her secret. 'How could you do this?' she said. Reza seemed less bothered. He poured some whisky into a glass and offered me a taste. I touched the surface of the liquid with my tongue. It recoiled of its own volition.

On the street below, cars were honking as they shuffled along. Our neighbours had gathered for a meeting in plain sight. Every so often they looked up at us, at me and Reza leaning over the edge of the balcony. He let some saliva drip out of his mouth and sucked it up again.

I laughed. Reza took a sip from his glass.

I noticed a scar near his temple, one that dipped down and cut through the hair.

'What's that?' I asked.

Reza touched his forehead. 'I got into a fight at school.'

'What kind of a fight?'

'The kind that makes you realize how many piss-heads there are in this world.'

Piss-heads. Piss-eds. Piss. Head. I wanted to ask him more about this word, ask him if it was one word or two, and if he could use it in a sentence again. I looked at the sharp angle of his jaw and the blue under his eyes. He touched the area around his crotch, reached into his pocket and took out a handmade paper boat. I held the little thing in my palms. It was made of smudged newspaper, crushed from being inside his clothes.

I thanked him, even though I thought it was a little bit stupid. He nodded. 'Don't put it in water.'

The neighbours were still below us. Mr Kamakhya, a plump and balding father of four, was glaring up at us with his hands crossed in front of his stomach.

Without a word, Reza released the glass in his hand. The neighbours scattered with Mr Kamakhya's warning. The glass fell two storeys, shattering on impact. Fragments flew in every direction like flecks of shimmering confetti.

My mother and Reza would go for walks when the sun was mellow. Sometimes they'd let me tag along. He carried paint and charcoal everywhere, and we would watch him mark up walls, the sides of buildings, private property. He would leave behind poems with simple alliteration. They were mostly senseless and sometimes funny. I rolled the words around on my tongue afterwards, and stored them away in the back of my mind.

He left his writing without a name. 'I'm not into being an author any more,' he said. Weeks later, on one of our walks, he returned to the places he had been before and covered the words he had written. He painted them over with white, and they dried like a spot of milk against the yellowed city. Sometimes he would kiss my mother as we walked, reach into her blouse to tug at her breasts. He would look at her while he did it, hold her gaze, and she always smiled and moved further into his hand.

Reza mapped corners of Pune in his mind. It was how he knew where he could belong one day. He hated the crowded thoroughfares, the shops and markets, the wealthy and the poor searching for space to stand side by side. Reza searched for crevices, the cracks that others had fallen through, that the city itself never knew of. They were points of rest, he told us as we walked, where everything stopped. In those places, the city was silent.

My mother told him he was self-indulgent. He seemed to like this and kissed her again. I walked a little behind. He was a dirty brute, but in some recess I recognized what he said. His words hit me powerfully, an old lesson learned again.

Reza wanted to wear Ma's clothes and suggested she wear his. She demurred at first, but later gave in. This was a common pattern for her in their time together. His jeans were salty, worn but stiff. His T-shirt was light. She said she felt naked in it.

'How do I look?' she asked me.

I laughed in spite of myself. She came to where I sat on the sofa and hugged me in his clothes. There was something comforting about the smell of him. I helped her tape the back of his jeans to keep them from falling.

He knew how to drape a dupatta and hold it easily on his shoulders. The pink fabric strained across his back. I covered my mouth at the sight of him. He grabbed me, mimicking a lady's voice, said I was his sweet little daughter, and pretended to put me to his breast to feed me. Ma and I laughed until our ribs ached. I imagined his hands would feel wet, but they were as dry as stone. From the balcony, I watched them walk through the gate. A small number of people glanced at them. Most did not notice anything at all. I stayed where I was until I couldn't see them any longer. My ribs still hurt from laughing, but I felt angry at the same time. They could be each other, but I was only myself.

Reza wanted to know what things felt like from the inside. Not because he cared about what I was feeling, but because he liked differentiating between me and himself. I felt the more I answered him, the more raw materials he had and the more difference he could manufacture.

I was fat and he was thin. I was dark and he was fair.

Food seemed to produce a drug-like ecstasy in me, whereas only illicit drugs could have that effect on him.

One day in my room, he found all my lists and didn't hide the fact that he had been snooping around. He wanted to know what they were for, and laid them out on the bed, pages and pages of them. Reza handled them with reverence, as though they were some kind of evidence, and I felt proud and strange when I saw this.

He asked me directly about certain entries, what the letters and numbers meant. I evaded where I could but tried not to be rude. The more he asked, the more certainty he seemed to draw that we were unlike each other in our thoughts and interests. We were different, he seemed to conclude, opposites even. This seemed to fortify him, as though understanding me made him sure of himself. I didn't feel the same, though I found the attention comforting at times.

It was pleasant to feel fascinating until I realized he was like a scientist taking notes, and each bullet point on his list punctured me a little, making me more porous every day.

'You don't want him to leave, do you?' Ma said, when I asked her how long Reza would be with us. She seemed to look sad, and I felt a sudden responsibility to keep him so we all could be happy.

If I tried to draw the balance between us, a kind of triangulation, I found myself unable. Ma and I both understood that there was something Reza shared with me that he didn't with her. Somehow it fell to me to make sure I kept it up, though I had not agreed to it.

'I love him, you know?' she said when we were alone. 'If I have ever loved anyone, it's him.'

We took the long road down to Goa once. I sat on the back of the bike. Reza knew the way. My mother sat between us. A satchel cut into my shoulder. I was fourteen and took up too much room. We passed eucalyptus forests, and the trees seemed to uproot themselves and fly away in the other direction. The view opened up into an endless stretch of farmland, with patches of gold and green, and browning hills in the distance.

The temperature dropped at the higher elevation. Like in Panchgani. Villages went by, and I looked for something familiar, but the trees were dense, with bulbous roots.

We didn't stop until we saw a sign for Candolim House, and walked for a while before we found the entrance of the hotel. The proprietress spoke with a soft sway. Her bottom seemed to move even when she was still.

A small boy was lying sideways on a single bed, his legs up in the air, leaning against the curved bars of iron that fitted together in a floral pattern over the window. I watched him from the front porch. He ignored us. I never understood why people liked children.

The print on the window dressing matched the hotel owner's dress. The lady rummaged through a bag of metal, digging further and further into the pouch. Squinting, biting her lip, apologizing.

From the bag she produced a key and handed it to Reza. Then she hugged me.

'My name is Pepper,' she said, 'and that's my boy. The room is just here.' She pointed to a door. 'And the toilet is out there.'

I turned at the sound of a low roar, but there was only darkness.

In the room, a dull yellow light appeared from an exposed bulb over the bed.

The air was wet, and salt and sand were on everything. It was a tiny box, with a small sink attached to a pipe in the wall. Just like in Nani's house. The ceiling slanted in the shape of the roof, and a rod hung down where the fan had once been.

We stayed up all night, the three of us on a vast bed. My mother remained in the middle, and in the morning we saw coconut trees and piles of plastic bottles. A dozen men wrapped cloth around the trunks and inched their way to the top. Fruit fell like bombs.

In the distance, between the dark gaggle of limbs, I saw the ocean.

For breakfast, Pepper made eggs and Goan sausages, and fried poi in butter on the stove. There was sour fish pickle with the bones gone soft and brittle. Beyond the bars of the window, the little boy fingered the trigger of a plastic gun while watching *Tom and Jerry* on a small television. He cheered every time Tom caught the mouse, and aimed his toy pistol at Jerry when he escaped. After firing, he brought the tip of the gun to his face and blew imaginary smoke away.

Pepper rushed in and out of the kitchen. Her brown nipples showed through the fabric of her dress. Her skin was smooth except for the round vaccination scar on her arm. I stuffed my mouth with red pork.

We took a bus up north and walked down a winding lane to the beach. My mother pressed me into the walls of magenta and purple shacks when scooters whizzed by. The sun was hot, but we followed the breeze, the smell of fish from the market, the voices of men and women.

The beach was long and empty, except for a single shack where hippies and locals sat under plastic umbrellas. The sand was golden and inviting, and we rushed in.

The grains between my toes felt foreign, almost painful.

A man from the shack asked us if we wanted to buy some water. Ma and Reza said maybe in a while and thanked him. He wore a T-shirt that was once imprinted with words.

He sat down and lit his pipe. He said his name was Herman. Herman's faded denim overalls were missing their metal closures, and he owned the only shack on Mandrem beach.

Reza removed his clothes. He left them in a pile, where they would fade a few hours later in the sun. My mother followed suit and told me to join them. I looked at the stretch marks on her stomach, the way her bottom had a layer of sagging skin.

'Oh, come on,' she said. 'What's the big deal?'

I watched them go into the water. Ma took an exaggerated breath and disappeared beneath the surface. I looked out at the sea, at the waves that kept coming in, the constant ebb and flow. It was hard to believe my mother was in there. I imagined her drowning, losing air.

When she finally came up, the sound and force of her bursting forth from the ocean made my heart lurch. 'Come on, Antara.' It was Reza this time. He floated on his back.

I stood up gingerly and pulled off my shorts. My T-shirt was next. I considered my underwear and decided it made little difference at that point. Using my hands to cover myself, I moved to the edge of the sea. Ma and Reza watched me. They seemed far away.

I turned back and looked at our belongings on the beach.

Herman's eyes moved from my body to my face. 'I'll watch everything,' he said. 'Don't worry.'

Herman took us to Old Goa, through the arches and stones, remnants of some other time and place. I scuffed my feet against the ground, hid from the sun in the shadows, and drank water so quickly my stomach expanded into a mound.

At the Basilica of Bom Jesus, we saw the holy remains of St Francis Xavier.

The body was in a glass coffin, desiccated beneath robes of gold and white. A portion of the cheek was missing, but otherwise the head had kept its form. Ma stared at the profile, the face of a man. It was a face of muffled details, the kind you saw just before your eyes fully adjusted to the dark.

'His arm is missing,' said Herman. 'The Catholic Church wanted him for Rome. But he belongs to us here. This was where his people were.'

'The Catholics were his people,' I said.

Herman shook his head. 'No, he didn't care about their baptism and their missions. People used to say he gave up Catholicism when he came here, that he started practising the local religion.'

'But he's a famous saint, the most famous in India.'

He looked at me. 'When he died, the Church wanted to take him, but the people here wouldn't let them. They wouldn't let him go. He was their saviour, not Jesus. Some people say that the locals tried to eat his body.'

I considered the shrivelled face, the nose that seemed like it had been nibbled down.

'That's how loved he was. Years later, Catholic priests came in the night and cut off his arm to send back to Rome. And even after all that time, the wound still bled,' Herman said. I imagined life pulsating beneath the brown parchment of skin.

'Hey, girl, you like fish?'

Herman was talking to me. I shrugged.

'Come for dinner. I'll make you some nice fish.'

That night, we went to Herman's shack with Pepper. He showed me how to pull the whole skeleton out of a pomfret. Then he presented the strange spine to me like a suitor with an offering. I ran my finger along the edge of bones, the skeleton that looked like a double-sided comb.

'I'm surprised you swam today,' Reza said.

I felt my face redden and was glad the sky was dark.

He smiled. 'Don't be shy. You're beautiful, like your mum.'

Reza drank beer and palm feni, and Herman told us of his plans to buy an old Portuguese house in the south and turn it into a spa. He teased Pepper, asking her to run it for him. She laughed like she was shy and he asked her to dance.

My mother smoked Herman's pipe, and we watched crabs scurrying across the beach in the dark. I pointed to each one as they ran sideways before disappearing into holes in the sand.

I sank into my mother's arms, feeling the skin around her stomach through her kurta.

'In my stomach,' Ma said, 'you were smaller than one of those grains of sand.'

I nodded. It was a day when I could believe it was true.

Cradled in a jute charpoy, Reza covered himself with my mother's shawl. It veiled his nose, and he inhaled its smell.

I knew what he could smell.

Reza watched me as I stood up and danced with Herman. In the shack owner's arms, I let my weight go. Slowly, slowly, slowly, Herman bent me and my head drifted back. When I looked up, Reza was there, upside down and unmistakeable, watching us. Above, the sky was milky with stars.

Sometimes my mother would come to my room at night, slip into the bed beside me and press her cold feet against mine. Then she would play with my hair and tell me what a lovely woman I was becoming.

On occasion, she asked to see my body parts. She would stare at them and compare them with her own; her breasts were bigger than mine, but my waist was smaller. She would comment on how my positive attributes were a symptom of age, declaring with certainty that my ugliness would surpass hers when I reached my forties.

It was a warning not to get too comfortable with myself.

Things were always changing, and I was only as good as my physical appeal, which would disappear, as hers had.

I had the distinct feeling that she was pleased to tell me these things, to know that I would suffer as she had – and her consolation came from seeing that the hurt would continue and I would not be spared.

When I look back on those days, I wonder did she ever see me as a child she wanted to protect? Did she always see me as a competitor or, rather, an enemy?

Those teenage years were the closest I came to hating her. I often wished she had never been born, knowing this would wipe me out as well – I understood how deeply connected we were, and how her destruction would irrevocably lead to my own.

When Reza disappeared one morning after nearly six years in our home, we assumed he had gone to get his camera fixed. He was anxious, overexcited, and said that it was time for him to go back in the field. In America, towers were falling. In India, the parliament building was under siege. Ma and I were dismayed whenever we turned on the news. We saw a world in shambles, but he saw a new beginning.

The world was changing, he had known it before anyone else – in the future, violence would be captured in its sharpest details. We were paralysed in our misapprehension, and he scoffed, called us stupid, and said we needed to understand this as an opportunity.

A few days later, he left, never to return.

Sometimes I think Ma started deteriorating after that day.

I always wondered what my mother loved so much about him, and why she continues to love him. Perhaps it's the feeling that stays, rather than the person. He made her happy for a time, and because she recalls only the larger drift of things, the minutiae no longer matter.

Reza Pine was never a mentor for me. He was sloppy, and never had the discipline required to make art.

In any event, I was who I am long before he made his appearance.

We decide that Nani and Ma should live together, at least for a little while. Both women agree, but I remain nervous.

I call Nani. Ma is managing as far as I can tell, but my grandmother is evasive when I ask questions. She tells me to focus on my life, that everything is fine. I believe her until I receive a call in the middle of the night from Ma's petrified maid. She reports that my mother has taken to wandering again, bewildered, unaware of who she is. Nani's house seems to be confusing her more.

'Where am I?' she often asks. 'And where is Antara?'

She looks for me and imagines she's forgotten to pick me up from school. She tries to dress herself and rushes out from the dark corridor into the empty street. There are only the few who make beds on flattened cardboard boxes, and they stretch and scratch and watch her as she disturbs the quiet. Where she goes, there is no distinction between day and night, and the logic of time and age has no sway over her fear.

Sometimes she cries out that she wants us back, she knows we are together and she wants us back, and when they ask who, instead of Dilip and me she speaks of Reza Pine.

The Governors give up their flat after news of the wife's affair becomes public in Pune. New neighbours move in, an English couple with a child and a Filipina nanny they bring with them from Singapore.

The wife introduces herself with a plastic container of madeleines that the nanny made. Her name is Elaine and her daughter is Lana, and they both have Cockney accents. The little girl has blue eyes – a blue I thought had only belonged to Kali Mata until now. A blue that makes me think of love, forests and the smell of rotting flesh. Elaine has dyed her hair the same colour as her daughter's but the top of her head shows four-centimetre roots of dark brown. She asks me within seconds if I am planning to have children.

I wobble my head a little.

She laughs and says she feels lucky that she has a daughter, daughters are amazing, girls are so good, except when they're teenagers, then they can be little bitches. She mouths the word 'bitches' so Lana can't hear, but Lana is watching her mother speak. I smile at Lana and wave, and she gives me a shy grin in return.

Elaine pats her daughter's head as though she is proud of her for that minor show of etiquette, and says she's cherishing her daughter now, while she can, because later everything changes, later it becomes all about men, prom dates, make-up and walking down the aisle, because the mother doesn't walk the daughter down the aisle, it just sounds wrong. It's always father and daughter, like a father–daughter dance where good old mom is missing, a milk-carton mom.

I nod while she speaks, and tell her I don't know too much about fathers since I didn't have one.

Dilip appears at the door just then with a pink rubber ball and hands it to Lana. I don't know where it has come from, and stare at him. Lana smiles at him widely. Elaine thanks us and says she'd love to have us over soon.

'You're always so intense,' Dilip says when they're gone. 'It's okay to keep it light sometimes.'

I begin to draw again, but it doesn't fill my days and I drift outdoors to escape the boredom. Sometimes I visit Elaine for lunch. Lana plays nearby, talking to herself at various volumes. Her mother smiles generously.

'Only children talk to themselves,' she says.

I watch them kiss and tickle each other and wonder what my own child would be like. I've always thought I would have a boy, even though the idea of a girl is more interesting. I sense my attachment to a daughter would be more profound, but maybe my feelings for her would pierce a little too sharply. I'm not sure if that particular pain would suit me.

Lana wears a pink hairband and socks with unicorns. She likes to pick her nose and taste what she finds there.

I visit my mother every day when Dilip is at work. I tell her things that no one else knows because I am sure she won't remember.

I tell her that I don't like the way Dilip puts the chocolate in the refrigerator.

Every night after dinner, he helps himself to a square piece.

He says he likes to change the taste in his mouth.

I asked him why he likes to store it in the fridge.

He had a ready list: 'It lasts longer. My mom kept it like that. And I like it cold. Don't you?'

He gave me the unfurled paper packaging. I looked down at it in my hand.

Soy lecithin. Nocciola.

I shrugged as though it didn't matter, but of course it does. Cold chocolate is harder to break. It makes a sound when it cracks in half. Cold chocolate takes longer to melt. It can never be eaten in stealth or in large quantities. I eat whole rows of chocolate straight out of the cupboard without anyone knowing. The bars in the fridge are not nearly as accommodating.

'That's obscene,' my mother says.

I tell her about how I packed a small handbag, took my passport and some jewellery, and left him one morning. How I sat in my car all day and bit my skin raw, only to return home in time for dinner. He never knew.

*

Dilip has been complaining of migraines, weakness and restless legs. His palms sweat whenever he drinks red wine. I make an appointment with a doctor and Dilip's blood reports are dismal. Anaemic, low vitamin D, B12 deficient. The doctor looks at me for an explanation.

I ask the doctor if these deficiencies are the reason for his symptoms. The doctor asks me where in Pune we live. I tell him. He says one of his nieces lives in that building, and that Dilip needs supplements.

I ask him about Dilip's sweaty palms. 'What about them? Will that also improve with supplements?'

The doctor rests his hands on the table and says I should get a second opinion if I want.

On the way home, we stop at the pharmacy. Bottles line the shelves with different colours and logos. I pick one up and look at the back.

'I wouldn't take that one,' the shop owner says.

'Why?' The picture on the front is of a rugged man with one leg on a log of wood. It seems like just what Dilip needs.

'That form of B12 isn't bioavailable.'

I stare blankly at him.

'It isn't methylated.'

Dilip rubs his eyes.

'Here,' the salesman says, pulling another bottle from the row. This one is purple with multicoloured DNA strands lined up like a field of flowers. 'This is a better choice.'

I ask him why any brand would sell a B12 supplement that isn't bioavailable. He says he doesn't know. He is looking around the shop, past Dilip and me. I sense he doesn't want to answer any more questions.

The following week, I realize I hate everything in our house.

I buy a new desk and chair without telling Dilip, and begin drawing again. The first day, I am sweating and my hands smudge the paper. Successive attempts are easier. I feel far away from the portrait but I am unsure of how to start something new. Drawing takes up only an hour of my day.

I look up other fanciful projects that I've listed in notebooks and spreadsheets, but they no longer make sense. Relevance dries out of ideas, leaving them brittle.

The small square space of my working life, distant from the world and other voices, feels oppressive today. I wish there was a way to carry my work out of this private room and into another place, where it can bang against other people's ideas and bodies.

I call Purvi. It's been some months since I've seen her and she is surprised to hear from me. She says she misses our walks at the Club. She's learning how to play bridge and mah-jong, and has made a lovely new group of friends in my absence.

I tell her I am not sure what to do, that maybe I've lost my imagination.

She says she never thought my work required much imagination, that it was copying an image over and over again.

I explain that I mean another kind of imagination, the kind that invents a world where my work matters. But the days seem endless and bright, so time doesn't seem to move.

I ask her if she thinks I should get a job. I hear the smile in her voice when she answers.

'I don't think it's so easy to get a job nowadays, and you haven't had a real job in years.'

'Yes, I know that,' I reply, but the realization moves through me like a tremor. If tomorrow I need one, I may not be able to get it. I will have no way of supporting myself if Dilip leaves me.

But why would he leave me?

But if he does leave me and I have to go back to my mother's house, how will I support myself? Nana is gone, and Nani isn't capable of taking care of me the way he would have. Where will I work?

Perhaps Purvi can ask her new friends if they have any leads.

I mentally run down a list of all the people I know and knock off the ones who don't look upon me kindly.

And then there's Ma. I will have to look after her as well. There is no telling what her medical bills may be as time goes on.

I rush to the small safe Dilip installed in the closet and punch in the code. The door swings open and I pull out a stack of velvet cases.

Some jewellery from my family, some from his. A watch his father bought him.

A silver rattle that was his as a child. Some American currency and gold coins.

How much would this be worth today? I consider getting it valued, but it is already three o'clock and Dilip could well be home by five thirty.

I think about every decision I've made until this point that has brought me here, and I wonder how much is because it was easy.

I call Purvi again and ask her for the number of her jeweller to estimate how much my things might be worth.

She tells me I sound bored. 'Maybe it's a good time to have a baby.'

A baby.

She laughs and I laugh in return, filling the silence with sound. A baby. A baby will take up time and space, a baby will fill the day. A baby will tie me irrevocably to Dilip, turn me from a wife to a mother. Maybe I'll be sacred then. He can never leave me once I have his child. He will never want to.

Relief bursts in me.

At night I come to bed without my clothes on, and while we have sex I whisper in his ear that he can come inside me because I'm expecting my period, even though I am not.

Through Elaine, I contact a life coach in the UK who specializes in helping caregivers of people with Alzheimer's and other forms of dementia. We fix a time to speak on the phone.

I tell her I didn't know that the field was so specialized. She says caregivers need care too. I see later that this is sprawled across the bottom of her website. I want to laugh when she says it, but her voice is deadly serious.

She believes I haven't started to fathom the danger I am in, how my own grasp on reality is being shredded.

I resist this idea at first, but soon find her words make sense. 'It is causing problems with my husband,' I admit. 'Sometimes I hate being married. Sometimes I think I am becoming my mother.'

'Reality is something that is co-authored,' the woman says. 'It makes sense that you would begin to find this disturbing. When someone says that something is not what you think of it as, it can cause slight tremors in the brain, variations in brain activity, and subconscious doubts begin to emerge. Why do you think people experience spiritual awakenings? It's because the people around us are engaged. The frenzy is a charge that's contagious.'

'Are you saying my mother is contagious?'

'No, I'm not. Though maybe I am, in a sense. We actively make memories, you know. And we make them together. We remake memories, too, in the image of what other people remember.'

'The doctor says my mother has become unreliable.'

'We are all unreliable. The past seems to have a vigour that the present does not.'

'Why do you suppose that is?' I ask, barely hearing her answer. We continue to say obvious things to each other, things I want her to say because I need to hear another person say them.

I know I am pregnant before my first missed period. I feel myself becoming fatter, stretching out fuller, wetter, a little more of everything. For a while I try to hold myself in, remembering from adolescence that to be large is to be feeble, a little out of control. I feel a familiar dread. I know I had planned this, but maybe it's a mistake. I mark a calendar with the last day I can safely have an abortion.

I watch the days go by until there is no turning back. Only then do I feel myself relax, coming to terms with the shift in dynamic, that there is something growing inside of me now that I cannot control and we are at the mercy of each other's decisions.

There's something else: I am beginning to smell different. By the end of the day, I have to bathe. My armpits are pungent and the discharge in my underwear gives off an odour. I fret at this discovery, washing myself several times a day, but that leads to yeast infections, courses of antibiotics and perpetual itching. I change the food I eat, from all fruit to no fruit, from gluten- and dairy-free to baby mash in glass bottles, from fasting to eating every two hours, but nothing seems to help. I suspect it is not me but the environment, that I am a cell in a hypotonic Petri dish, and the smells are being pulled from me in the interest of homeostasis. This is natural, I tell myself.

Dilip's boss takes us out for a Japanese meal. The restaurant is expensive, the only one of its kind in Pune, and our food is served in courses. The fish is raw, or sometimes warmed with a torch, before it is hand-moulded on to a cylinder of sticky rice. Each piece lies on the plate like a submissive tongue. Dilip eats a salad while I place the bite in my mouth and feel it melt. Starch, fat and salt. The flesh breaks apart and for a moment I can swear my mouth is dissolving. I wonder if the flavours are more profound because my tongue has come in contact with a mirror of itself, and if the experience is somewhere between consuming and kissing. Dilip watches me swallow, tapping the table restlessly with his free hand.

Sometimes I imagine different versions of the end of my mother's romance with my father. In my recent fantasies, I am the reason they are no longer together. Tara tells her husband that she is leaving him, that she has found her guru, that she is carrying his child, and my father looks down at her swollen belly and, for a moment, is torn. He wants her and yet she repulses him – the looming pregnancy, the illegitimate baby. He looks into my mother's beautiful face and he knows that the creature inside her makes it impossible for him to remain.

A psychotherapist I visited a few years ago at Dilip's insistence told me that my mother leaving my father, and my father letting us both go, has coloured my view of all relationships. I thought this was a little too easy and said so.

'And doesn't it make sense that people want to leave?' I asked.

The therapist jotted something down and asked me to elaborate.

I told her that staying doesn't have the appeal, the mystery, of escape. To stay is to be staid, to be resigned, to believe this is all there will ever be. Aren't we creatures made for searching, investigation, dominion? Aren't we built to believe there can always be something better?

'I don't blame my mother,' I told the therapist, though I know I do and always have.

'Did you worry as a child that she would abandon you? Do you worry you are like her now?'

I stopped seeing the therapist soon after that because she asked too many questions. Wasn't her job to sit and listen? In fact, worse than the thought of my parents' abandonment were all the unanswered questions she posed, the ones that continue to float around. Any time I come close to answering one, a whole series of other doubts assert themselves. I wonder at the terror physicists must have felt when the laws of Newton failed under a microscope. They poked a little too far. Many of them must have wished they could un-see what they had witnessed and go back to a simpler time. We dissolve with questions. Even question marks have always seemed strange to me, a hook from the hand of some nightmare.

2002

I became an artist the day I was accepted to art school. Never mind that I didn't attend. I finished my twelfth standard with less than stellar marks, but Bombay's J. J. School of Art saw merit in my drawings.

My mother tried to stop me from going. I asked Nani for the money to pay my fees.

Professor Karhade was a painter and would be my advisor. He was exasperated when I said I didn't paint.

'The course you have enrolled in is for painting and drawing.'

'I understand,' I said, 'but I won't be able to paint and draw. I'm very bad at multitasking.'

He didn't think this was an acceptable reason. The course was not flexible in that way. Besides, drawing and painting could be the same thing. I could learn to love one as I did the other. Painting could be the finished product, but drawing would always have a place. It was the preparations, the bones, the underpinning.

'Exactly,' I said. That was what I was interested in. Weren't the bones the part that was essential, timeless? Weren't the bones what future generations would dig up and marvel at?

'You won't know unless you dive in,' he said.

But I did know. I knew I would not resurface. I told him that I, like the course, was not flexible.

I left his office with my portfolio of drawings under my arm and meandered past Jehangir Art Gallery, where students peddled their work on the sidewalk. I knelt to look at a painting of a young man. It was accomplished, with thick, painterly strokes. The man looked bloated under the weight of the oils. Something about it felt grotesque, like mopping spilled blood on paper.

My load felt heavy, and I handed the folder of drawings to a group of children sitting on the stoop of Rhythm House. What I wanted to do didn't require a teacher.

I didn't tell Nana and Nani about my decision, but continued as a paying guest with an old woman who lived next to Colaba Fire Station. During the day, I read about modern and contemporary art, adding to and subtracting from the pictures in the books. I looked at old images, the ones Kali Mata had collected and bound into an album for me. I cut out the faces, the objects I couldn't remember, didn't want to remember, and turned them into black voids. I pasted the pictures on top of paper and redrew the empty parts as I would have wanted them to be.

In the evenings, I borrowed my landlady's cotton saris and attended openings and parties at art galleries around town. I spoke to some people. Mostly I sipped wine and drank in what filled the white spaces.

I learned that what I had done all my life had a name. Interventions. I had been making interventions for ten years. I distinguished, quickly, what I liked, what persisted in my mind. Painting was just an impression. Drawing, I saw, was the grid. Ground, walls, sky. All the things that were real and yet incomprehensible. The city was changing every day, bridges, skyscrapers, new hotels. Small Portuguese bungalows were being levelled to make way for malls.

Everyone wanted to build up. Only I had the urge to strip down.

That analysis seems laughable now. The truth is drawing was all I knew. It was automatic, something I did in my sleep. Even now my perception cannot completely fathom the wet complexity of colour. Wherever I look, I see lines.

We install Ma in my studio again. Kashta is to accompany her, sleeping on the floor beside the single bed, and is instructed to watch over her charge day and night. I clean out most of the studio contents and put them in boxes. Dilip asks where the baby will go.

'In our room,' I say.

'And my mother?' His mother is planning to come for the delivery. 'Where will she stay?'

I tell him we can switch one of our sofas for a pull-out bed. He seems put out by the suggestion, but doesn't argue.

I put Ma on a diet of various fats. A fat-burning brain is a clean brain, I have read. A sugar-burning one is mucky. I start her on a probiotic regime with occasional coffee enemas. I am strict and relentless – a tyrant over her plate. She eats imported avocados at every meal, and I dispose of all the sugar in the house.

In the morning, we check her ketone levels and record them in a book. If this can all be reduced to a metabolic problem, to some errant mitochondria, to a failure of apoptosis, then we will fix it. Together, we will find redemption.

I add a tincture of herbal extracts to her routine. Astragalus root and berberine. In only three days, her insulin-resistant brain seems more alert. She asks me how I am feeling, if the pregnancy is giving me any trouble.

I cry when she says this. I had told her about the baby before, but she'd always reacted like it was new information.

I tell her I think we should put her on a fast. She smiles.

I have calculated that she has enough fat stores to live on for two hundred days. That's plenty of time for her brain to get over its addled sugar dependence.

'You mean I won't eat anything? For two hundred days?'

I laugh. 'No, not so long. Don't worry, Ma. We'll do it together. You're with me now. I'll look after you.'

That night in bed, I take out my sketchbook for the first time in weeks. I start sketching the cloudy brain from the doctor's office last year. This builds into a dark sky. Below, I redraw the scene I presented to the doctor. This time, it is coherent. This time, he would not find anything wanting.

I begin with stick figures, filling them out with armour to mark their team, their army: leucocytes versus reactive oxygen species. On the ground are dead bodies, cells to be cleared away. The injured ones hold up white flags, signalling their wounded state, and are disposed of. The carnage calls forth an autophagic machine, emerging from a hole in the atmosphere, a mythical, many-limbed creature. In the background, the rest of the planet is at peace. Organs continue their functions, metabolism reigns benignly. The islets of Langerhans sit in the distant sea.

Autophagy, from the Greek, means to devour the self. I keep drawing, keep willing this to happen in her body, hopeful that I have been able to do what no one else has, that I have found a cure through my incessant research.

My stomach growls. Heat moves out from my chest but stops before reaching my limbs. I shiver.

In the morning, I wake up to the blinding sun. The room is sweltering.

Only then do I notice Ma is in the room. I turn to Dilip's side of the bed. There is a crumpled space where he slept. I'm sweating and my throat burns. I smell incense. My stomach roars, and I remember I haven't eaten since yesterday afternoon.

'Where's Dilip?' I say. My voice is raspy.

'Office,' she replies. She is fully dressed, in her walking shoes, as though she is about to step out. Turned away from me, she has her hands in the boxes that contain what was once my studio.

The careful order is being dismantled. Objects sit askew on the floor. Tinted glass bottles.

Coins from before Independence. Cuttings from newspapers and magazines.

I feel a surge of panic, swelling into dizziness when I try to stand. 'How did you get this?' she asks.

'What?' I say. I raise my neck, but can't see what's in her hand.

'This.' She turns. It's a three-by-five photograph.

I feel the blood rise to my face. Is it still the heat? I don't want to talk about the photograph now. Didn't I destroy it? I don't want to go into this.

'I don't know,' I say.

I can tell from her face that she doesn't believe me. She has a kind of lucidity in her that I haven't seen in some time. The food, the fasting, or maybe the photograph, has touched a memory.

Ma is coated in the knowledge that we are on the brink of something, that nothing after this will ever be the same.

'How did you get this?' she repeats. Her eyes are wide, and her hands close around the picture.

'I don't remember,' I say. 'Maybe I took the picture.'

She shakes her head slowly and places it on the bed. Reza's skin is the same colour as my bedding. He looks up at me from the photograph, newly creased by Ma's hand.

'You didn't take it, because I took it. It was the only time he let me touch his camera. His precious camera.' She points to the detail in the background, the garish movie poster, the Madras-check shirt he wore while fixing a cigarette behind his ear.

'Then maybe I found it. I found it in the house and I kept it.'

She sits down at the edge of the bed and smooths the sheet. 'It was still on his camera when he left. He hadn't developed the film yet.'

Ma flips the picture over. The text on the back reads 'J. Mehta & Sons, Mumbai'.

She runs her fingers over the words and looks at me. 'It was developed in Bombay.'

I inhale and exhale, but she speaks before I can.

'I knew that you were hiding something from me. I knew when I saw your show.'

2003

The wine has an acidic tang.

I top up my clear plastic cup with more liquid from the screw-top bottle.

Anthropofagio. The rambling curatorial essay stencilled on the wall defines it as cannibalism, which in the history of Brazilian art has long been an important concept. Incorporation and digestion lead to the production of something new. Something specific. The artist on show today has just returned from a residency in Belo Horizonte.

Another artist I am sharing a cigarette with outside calls the work derivative. I point out some grammatical errors in the text. We giggle and he pulls out a tightly rolled joint. I am obsessed with Paul Thek at the moment, attracted to the fact that he seemed to not exist. He appeared occasionally, as a side note or a phantom's hand, but never as the main event.

The other artist nods and goes on to tell me about his mentor in Cape Town. She was a semiotics teacher whose mouth was always painted a pomegranate red. She spoke fervently about how strange and distant our generation seemed to her, obsessed with television and oral sex, and insisted that blowjobs were culturally and temporally specific.

'Do you think for a second that your grandmothers would have ever thought of putting the genitalia of their husbands in their mouths?' she had laughed.

The rest of the artist's story is lost on me when a face I recognize appears close to mine. The face is smiling.

'Reza.'

'How are you? What are you doing here?' He wraps me in a long hug. I smell the whisky and sweat only as he moves away.

Later, I feel him watching me. We are in his one-bedroom apartment. We drank a little more wine at the opening before I agreed to leave with him.

He's standing by a dirty sink, full of dishes, and a pile of unwashed clothes. He says his maid hasn't come today. He makes no mention of his wife. I wonder if by 'maid' he means wife but don't ask because I am afraid to break whatever enchantment the alcohol has woven.

The whole house feels like decay. It bothers me, but it feels good to be bothered by Reza again, a familiar itch.

He asks me if I want to go out.

'Where?'

He says to meet his friends. I nod, and realize my mother never met any of his friends. It feels good to do things she has never done.

His friends are nothing special but I want to be impressed. There is Namita, with a ring that passes through the middle of her nose. She can touch the hoop with her tongue, wiggle it back and forth. She's older than me, but not by much. Her boyfriend, Karan, comes as well. He never leaves home without music and drugs. He scratches his beard often and purses his lips when deep in thought.

We go to a secret party out of town, in a jungle beyond the suburbs of Bombay. It takes two hours to get there. The locations are always unknown until the last moment, and we drive in borrowed cars through the night, looking for handmade signs to point us along. Electricity is a problem, but Karan attaches the music system to the car's battery. They mix powder and sugar cubes in bottles of water before passing them around. Reza warns me to take small sips.

The music shakes the ground. I resist the urge to cover my ears. I feel like a bore, like a freak, like all the things I've been called before.

Namita dances by herself in the distance. Her piercing glints and her hair swings behind her. She whips around, an undulating reed, encased in light, encased in honey, sticky like the origins of the world. She dances, coating the trees and ground with every step.

The men watch her, closing around the circle she has made. Marching, stomping, they're like soldiers waiting for commands. She pulls them both closer, disappearing between their bodies. A sliver of red, a sliver of pink. I squint. I've lost sight of her. Namita is nothing more than empty space, a ghost dreamt into being.

I have seen this before. I have been here before.

The song changes or seems to change and I feel a tunnel in my ears open up. The night turns brighter and the glow unfurls on the ground around me. The grass sways. Tiny specks of life tremble on each blade, drops of dew, water and resin. Flowers grow amid the frightened verdure, amid the stone. Each bud is a revolving thing. I watch them turn, spinning like propellers, until they pop off into the sky like tops from when I was a child.

The moon is full, a mercury pool teeming with life, and little heads poke out to watch the dancers, calling down in their own language before diving headfirst into the grey.

Arms pass over me, as black as spider legs, knotting up my shirt, creeping over my stomach. Reza whispers something in my ear, but all I can see are his hands. Black hands, half human, half insect.

'Drink water,' he says.

I turn to look at his fangs and spindly arms. The jungle is lush, and soon the music changes, the sky turns darker. I see a snake slithering nearby. We watch each other. I want to speak but the words don't come. I've lost language. The snake moves towards me, fully grown, waving its head, gnashing its teeth. It passes under the ground, and above, making its way between my legs, and for a moment I wonder if I am birthing it. I find my feet, stand, and follow it between the dancers. The snake weaves in and out in rings, growing longer. Soon, we are all caught, bound within. The snake keeps circling, round and round. It stops to look at me before disappearing, before turning into a moat filled with glistening liquid.

'Antara, drink some water.'

I don't remember how we leave or where we go, but I wake up lying beside him. The sounds are still on the surface of my skin. We are alone, but the room feels full. He lights candles and kerosene lamps, and we watch as thousands of creatures come in from the night.

The insects bang against the broken windows until they find the cracks. They circle the lamps, swarming around, drawing neon maps with their flight – moths and beetles. Their lacy skeletons tap the windowpanes. Glass is a cruel invention. It makes for a heartless prison.

In the morning, bodies are strewn around. They found their way in, the millions of moths, and perished in the warm room. The air is thick and heavy, and my heart sounds loud. I pick creatures out of my hair and from between the damp sheets. They lie around me, on their backs, their legs up in the air, ugly and dead in the light of day. Some are buried in the candles, preserved like fossils. I memorize the faint outlines of their bodies, deep within the waxy fog. They were alive when the wax hardened, as their world turned permanently white.

Reza looks at the insects. 'It must be like suffocating,' he says.

I realize he is naked.

I try to turn away but he kisses me, and his mouth, like a fishhook, drags me back, barely breathing.

We arrive at an opening holding hands. This provokes glances from those who are in the know about his past scandal and my future pretensions.

I was invited to be in this show but declined the offer. The curator in question likes to collect hungry unknowns around him – when they make it big, he demands they give him a work for discovering them. He also has a reputation for getting drunk and calling women cunts.

Reza stops in front of a large painting. Pasted on to the canvas are pages of books that have been taken apart. The frame is made of binding. The text is illegible but he lingers over it, leaning in, trying to read passages. They are pages from Márquez, an anthology of short stories, translated into French, Portuguese and Dutch.

The space doesn't do the show justice. Overall, it feels sprawling, ill hung. The project lost steam at the end, the artists lost interest — they gave him old works from other commissions, tried to make it fit into the confines of his curatorial bind.

The curator is already into his third whisky. He slurs a bit when I congratulate him. His breath rouses some fear in my subconscious mind.

I remembered when he invited me to be part of the show. I received an envelope in the mail — a prompt from the curator, a point of entry — written out in his hand on a piece of paper torn from a notebook. It was a passage from *One Hundred Years of Solitude*, a book I had never heard of, much less read: a man is losing his words, and he endeavours to remember them the only way he knows how — he labels everything he owns, covering his world incessantly in a mantle of language, protecting himself from the danger of the blank slate. He persists, until the futility of his project settles on him, that his work will be worthless when the value assigned to each letter eventually evaporates from his mind.

When I return to the apartment where I am a paying guest, the land-lady hands over a piece of paper on which she has written down the phone calls I have missed, the names listed in order. Each letter tilts perilously backwards, as though it is gazing up at the sky, and I wonder how long it took her to train her right hand to do what the left should have been doing. Kali Mata's name is the only one there. She has called me four times in the past few days.

I crumple the piece of paper in my hand. Back in my room, I begin to tear it into smaller and smaller pieces.

I hate Kali Mata. I don't know why, but I do.

I hate the questions she asks me on the phone. If I am eating well. If I have enough money. I hate talking about my art, trying to put it all into words for her, when at the end she only comes back with more questions.

I hate hearing about Pune. I left so I would never have to hear about it again.

I hate that her name is following me around, written on scraps of paper every day, again and again, sometimes Kali Mata, sometimes Aunty Eve, while my mother is forever absent. It would be easier if I could just kill her off, in story at least – tell everyone that Ma is dead.

So I do. I start spreading the lie, slowly at first until it catches like wild fire. I receive sympathy and condolences. Reza stares at me for a long time when he overhears me telling the news to his friends. My stomach bubbles inside. I have prepared a more elaborate version for him. But he never asks. He just looks back to the book he is reading. In another breath he is reabsorbed into that world, and I am relieved by his nonchalance but confused about why it has also caused me a little pain.

Reza has several fake library cards. He takes out books and doesn't read them. Instead, he opens to random pages and blacks out words and sentences. Then he leaves the books around the city, on street corners and in the hands of beggars.

I steal things every time I leave his apartment. The library cards. The insects. A single photograph, a three-by-five, a little bent, of his face. The only photograph of him that I can find in his collection besides the wedding portraits.

'Are you in love with anyone?'

We lie on his bed in the afternoon. The summer is high, and I drift in and out of sleep.

'No,' I say. 'You?'

'Many people.'

I have grown to like the craters on his body. I try to picture him in love, but I have never experienced it myself, and the image I conjure is deprived of detail and colour.

He breathes through his mouth when he naps, and mumbles occasionally. I wrap my arms around his chest and bury my face in his clavicle. His saliva wets my hair as I fall asleep.

When I wake up, I am still in the dark pit of his skin. There is stubble at his throat. He is awake, I can tell by his shallow breaths. The sun is still high in the sky and blazing through the windows, turning the backs of my eyelids into kaleidoscopes.

It's hot. I struggle to fill my lungs.

I count the distance between us with my fingers. Through his shirt, I see pockets of hair, a paunch from the whisky he sips throughout the day. He watches as I inch forward to close the gap. There is no coercion between us. Nothing is done to fill the silences. I know I am somewhere between desire and doubt.

I lift my leg and bring it around his hips.

He wipes something away from the inside of my eye and kisses me. His saliva is always brassy. I scratch the dark creases around his elbows. His skin is tough as hide.

Reza and I have been sleeping together for several months now. We never speak of it, but it happens regularly. Reza doesn't care much for foreplay. It always hurts when he pushes himself into me. We kiss a little to cover the croaking sound in my throat.

I remembered being surprised when Reza left us, surprised by how deeply we had soaked him up and how completely he then evaporated. Had he been there at all? Had we imagined it? Was it possible for a person to be a part of every moment and yet not leave behind any trace?

I looked for footprints, but there were none. Was it possible we didn't have a single photograph? Ma and I were not the types to indulge in picture-taking, but there were images of us. I realized, then, that he had always been behind the camera, capturing what he saw in his eyes, but we had never captured him.

When he disappears a second time, in Bombay, four years after we had run into each other in the gallery, I am not surprised.

Only a fool would be surprised.

The dull sadness that I carry for a little while remains a private one.

I return to Pune without the degree I had left for, making a strange kind of art that concerns my family. I spend my first year back working on a sculpture of dried mango skins preserved in formaldehyde, which I use as a base to print hundred-rupee notes. A video of me cutting and eating all the mangoes in one sitting is recorded to accompany the work. The project fails due to errors in mixing the chemical solvents. I develop a rash on my arms that takes two months to fully heal.

When I finish, Ma crosses her arms around her body as though she is covering a wound. I feel better somehow, lighter. My stomach yawns and rumbles. 'Is that everything?' she says. 'I'm warning you, I want to know everything, or I'm going to tell Dilip what kind of person you are and what kind of art you make. I always knew having you would ruin my life.'

Inside my chest I can feel an alarm going off, my heart shuddering in its cage. But the movement remains trapped there – everywhere else I am frozen still. Ma's breathing is rapid. A bead of sweat appears at her hairline and rushes down the side of her face. The room is unbearably warm.

'Say something, you bitch,' she says. 'Are you deaf and dumb?' Her voice falters into a mewl. Before I can react, she is crying into her hands.

I behold my mother – how did she come in? Don't I usually lock the door? I wish I had, or I wish Dilip had locked me in. I wish I wasn't such a hoarder, with objects and people.

Why did I invite her here when all I want to do is expel her? Why didn't I tell Dilip everything when I had the chance? Why didn't I destroy the picture? I thought I had – I was sure I had done that already. Did I look at it and wrap it back up in the butter paper? Was the thought of parting with it for ever too difficult?

So what if he knows? We are about to have a child together. I am safe. I must be safe. Motherhood is the safest place I have ever known. Our little family is my fortress.

But relationships are fragile. I think of Dilip, sitting across the table from me every night, watching me eat meat in a mirror, disappointed.

Dilip, knowing that every day I gaze into the face of another man, a man whom I loved, even though he'd loved my mother first. He would have no choice.

She could try to be a little forgiving. A little forgiving of the daughter who has suffered at her hands and has been there for her regardless. I have told her, isn't that enough, I have come clean and shared what I never shared with anyone, and still she threatens me. She threatens my marriage in my own house. While I sit in my marital bed. In the presence of my unborn baby.

I look down at my hands. They're trembling.

A drill outside switches on and the sound rises up into the room like an angry swarm of bees. I have an urge to close the window or escape through it. I sit back into the moment and everything, even the sound, begins to slow. If I go out of the window, I'll lose everything. My self, my baby. And Ma, she is still crying. What if I push her out?

I open my mouth and suck in air. I am safe. 'How could you?' she whispers, heaving.

'Okay,' I say. I stand up slowly and steady myself. The volume of blood in my body has increased, and sudden movements make me see stars. I must be safe. I have no choice.

Ma looks startled and stands up too. 'Okay?' she sniffles.

'Okay, I'll tell you whatever else you want to know.' I pick up my phone from the table and dial our driver. 'But first, we have to have breakfast. I'm pregnant, remember?'

She looks at my stomach and nods, and leads me out into the living room.

I set the table with biscuits, bread and jam. I send the maid to ask the neighbours for some sugar. Within twenty minutes, the driver rings the doorbell. He hands Ila a familiar red box.

'Give it to me,' I say. She hands it to me obediently.

I cut the ribbon and pull away the cover. Below a sheet of butter paper sit two-dozen Mazorin biscuits. I push the box towards Ma. She glances inside. Then she picks out two that are stuck together. Placing them into her mouth, she sighs.

Her descent into the abyss is fast. I spoon sugar into her afternoon tea and stir. Dilip has a conference call with the US office and comes home after dinner. Ma doesn't notice him walk through the door. She is smiling, staring at the empty space in front of her.

The watchman is watering plants below. Decomposing leaves release their tannins; the puddles are dark as tea.

I clutch the ledge of the balcony. The inside of my body tears apart.

I've already prepared my bag. Dilip is shouting from the door. Kashta kneels beside me, coaxing my chappals on to my feet, but my toes are swollen and don't fit inside the leather rings.

Ma smiles at me, my happy goldfish. She stands by the window and paces a little back and forth. I have a passing thought that she won't be safe alone. I call Nani and tell her to come over.

Our driver is nowhere to be seen. Dilip hails a rickshaw. The rickshaw-wallah has dark grooves around his eyes and tattoos marking his arms. He raises his hand in salutation. The watchman turns and water sprays from his hose, catching the edge of my clothes. Cold water trickles down the warm, tight skin of my ankles.

On my lap, I can see the mound that is my stomach moving. It already doesn't belong to me, this creature. It already has a mind of its own. I try to imagine myself without the mound. I can't remember that person. I wonder what my body will look like now. Will there be a hole at the centre? Will I be a fleshy doughnut? The thought makes me feel nauseated. Or maybe it is the return of the pain. Suddenly, I don't want to let it go. It should stay with me, inside me, for ever. I watch it for a moment, before turning my face out of the rickshaw and vomiting.

*

Afterwards, they tell me it's a girl. Rather, I hear them say it to each other. The doctor to the nurses, the nurses to Dilip.

'A girl,' they whisper.

They speak to each other as though I am not there. In hushed tones, so I am not disturbed. Then I realize the baby is in the room. It occurs to me that they are whispering for her now. I can't tell from Dilip's face if he is happy or alarmed.

They watch my face as I hold the baby for the first time. The child has the sweet smell of amniotic fluids on her face. She looks serene – she has passed through something dark and come into the light. The light is halogen, and moths knock against the bulbs.

I don't feel anything much as I hold her, but when they take her away I know something is missing.

They all wait for me to say something. I know I should express joy, that if I don't they will think I'm disappointed to have a daughter. A bigot. The scum of the earth.

I want to assure them I'm not disappointed, but I can't show delight either. Maybe I'm too tired. Maybe it is the continuing urge to stuff the little bundle back inside of me, like meat into a sausage skin.

I'm hungry.

I stare at the girl's little face because I don't know where to look. Her head is round. She looks like no one, but when her eyes are closed she could be a sleeping cat. I don't much care for cats. Or for people who resemble animals.

I try to smile, but all I can muster are the blank eyes of relief. Relief that the pain has stopped. Everything that comes now is just an aftershock.

The baby has trouble latching on to my nipples. No one mentioned that this could be a problem. I begin to think I am the first woman in the world to have substandard nipples. A nurse tries to help. She tucks some tissues into her pocket and goes to work on me. She is plump with dark skin and wears a white dress with blue buttons. Her hair is captured in a braid but the curls rebel. She handles the dead weight of my breasts.

I can't decide what is more difficult, the labour or the feeding. Of course, the pain of contractions has no earthly comparison – but it ends, eventually. Now, the hours of feeding stretch before me.

This is only day one.

My breasts are double what they once were. My vagina is a crime scene.

Did this happen overnight, or have I always been slightly misshapen? Lines like silver thread appear. Or were they always there? Maybe I just could not see them. The nipples darken and become as large as saucers. The skin cracks and bleeds. At night, I place strainers over them to avoid chafing.

The next day, the baby sleeps in a bassinet near my bed. Her hair is black, and her skin is yellow due to a mild case of jaundice. I wonder if she is sickly, but don't have the courage to ask. What if the answer is yes? I will be to blame. When the baby yawns, her mouth opens wide and I see the edge of her pink gums.

Purvi comes with gifts that day. She brings toys for boys and girls. She says she wanted to be prepared for any outcome. Clothes, too, in metallic wrapping, the sizes on the labels ranging from six months to one year.

'The baby will grow into them,' Purvi says.

Dilip makes a joke about whether she will survive that long. No one laughs. In fact, I feel offended. I'd forgotten about my husband until now. He is the only one who has remained unscathed through all of this. The baby and I are bruised and battered. He looks smug, proud of himself or his family. I have the urge to ask him what he's done for any of us.

A frown mars the baby's forehead. It mirrors the one on mine. At least I think I am frowning. I touch my forehead. Yes, there are creases. I wonder if she felt my irritation. Or was she the one to frown first?

I wonder if she is dreaming, and what she is dreaming of. In her sleep, she draws her mouth in like an old woman. She looks a little like Ma, like Nani. The beginning of life so closely resembles the end. I can see it there, in that wise face, the plan to live to a ripe old age.

My mother-in-law arrives the following day. She has already called the astrologer with the baby's date and time of birth. Letters are revealed, ones that will be auspicious when choosing a name.

'The letters are *a* and *va*,' she says. 'The same as yours were, Antara.'

I shake my head. Those were not my letters. My mother named me to be her foil. My daughter should have different letters from her mother.

My mother laughs. I had forgotten about her standing behind my shoulder. 'Antara,' she says. 'I'll call my baby Antara.'

Everyone is silent. I turn and smile at her. 'I'm right here, Ma.' I stare at her face. It is illuminated. I wonder where she is right now, and when she will decide to return to us, inhabit the body that she only loosely resides in.

'There are many good names,' my mother-in-law continues, as though nothing is out of the ordinary. 'Anjali, Ambika, Anisha.'

'No. None of those.'

'We can't just call her Baby for ever.'

Baby. Baby was just fine. It was easy, meaningless, belonging to every child in the world. I wish Kali Mata were here. She would have known exactly what to call her. She named many of the sanyasis all those years, fashioning something from Sanskrit, joining a series of sounds together that would call them to their destinies.

I wish Kali Mata were here. She would love this baby. She would know exactly what to do. With the baby. With me. With Ma.

The nurse with blue buttons comes into my room.

'You should rest for some time,' she says. The side of her nose looks raw. She must have a cold. I don't want her to touch me. I definitely don't want her to touch the baby.

I try to close my eyes but cannot turn away from the window. The sky is pale fire. It's not so late, there are still colours to be found. The light makes its way inside. In the distance, the speaking streets and plumes of smog are incandescent.

Kali Mata was dead in her apartment for four days before someone found her. She was nearing seventy. The servant who was supposed to sweep her house daily had not been going. We refused to give him the last month's salary. After Baba died, Kali Mata didn't have much to do with the ashram, but I hear they buried her black clothes beneath the old banyan tree near the meditation hall.

A year ago, Dilip and I finally made a trip to Pushkar to scatter Kali Mata's ashes. When I looked in the box, I was amazed that such a large woman could fit into that small space. The dust looked clean and I had an urge to put some on my skin.

Dilip shook his head. How could I even think of that? I didn't know. I could not explain to him how much I wanted her as a part of me.

The city of Pushkar was cold that winter, and I shared a chillum with an elderly mendicant roaming the alleyways near the Brahma temple.

Dilip didn't approve. 'That's disgusting. Did you see his teeth?' The temple was orange like the setting sun, and as the day got darker it looked bloody. I was stoned and followed a single white cow that walked with a delicate sway. The animal had never known the weight of a yoke and freely trawled the streets. Through the narrow corridors of the old city, where the doors were barricaded shut and the havelis were inhabited by monkeys and men, the crowds dispersed to let me and the animal pass.

Was this real, or had it been staged just for us?

The chillum was strong. Kali Mata must have walked this way, through the same alleys, a young widow, a childless mother. The walls of the city looked blue at midday, and the colour reflected off the cow, turning the animal iridescent, somewhere between sky and water. I tried to take pictures of it, but the colour couldn't be captured. The cow sat at the edge of the ghats and we followed her there, sitting a couple of steps away. I wanted more of the chillum but settled for the smoky air.

A musician plucked at his santoor. His wife was dressed in a ghagra choli, soiled at the hem, and a buttoned waistcoat. She covered her head with the edge of her dupatta and sang solemn notes in accompaniment. Their sleeping child awoke, rising from his father's wooden wheelbarrow. The child glanced at my impervious cow and turned to his mother. The mother squatted as she sang, her bottom hovering off the ground. The boy pulled up her blouse and exposed her dark breasts. I could see her nipples. They looked like bruises. He stood before her and drank, and she pulled him in, her voice faltering as she held his head.

The boy turned and looked at us, smiling to show his sharp teeth. Then he turned back to his mother's breast and bit her. She cried out in pain but continued singing, pushing the boy away and smacking him on the cheek. I touched my face. The boy went back into hiding.

I am tired of this baby.

She demands too much, always hungering for more.

I have become an assembly line. Each part is incidental, only important if it can do its job. Milk drips when my daughter cries, staining my clothes. In the mirror, I see my stomach, dark and shrivelled as a date. I try to cover it with my hands when Dilip enters the room.

I can't imagine what he thinks when he looks at me, and I try to never be alone with him anywhere. He is thrilled with the baby, and cannot bear the sound of her cries.

There is never enough time for sleep. I wish I had rested all the years of my life. I wish I had done so many things. Instead, I did all the things I am doing now. Sitting in the house. Staring at the walls.

I've never been a stickler for manners, but this baby doesn't stand on ceremony. She's a rude little bitch if I ever met one. There are no polite pauses.

I wonder how long it takes for children to grow up, and in my mind I mark the milestones, still so far away. When the baby will walk, when the baby will eat by herself, bathe by herself. When the baby will have her own life, go off into the world.

There are other days when I feel I'll never let her go.

The baby looks so small at times. Dilip was right – it is a wonder we haven't killed her yet. She exists from one day to the next; her life is forceful but tenuous. I always assumed children came into the worlds of their parents, but maybe the opposite is true. I can see myself in my daughter. It's as though, through this birth, I have been twinned.

Sometimes, I resent others helping me – when Kashta or my mother-in-law gives the baby a bath, or if Dilip rocks her when she cries. I hate that no one lets Ma hold her, that my blood should be prohibited from caring for her. I insist that they let my mother look after her. All arguments to the contrary meet with my ire.

When she nearly slips out of Ma's arms, I concede. My mother-in-law glances at Dilip with consternation.

If I let my mind go back far enough, I resent that the cord was cut without my permission. No one tells you the full story, no one informs you of your rights as a mother. I would have kept the cord for longer. I've read that there are health benefits for the baby in maintaining the connection as long as possible.

The baby scratches her own face, and I gather the courage to trim her nails. My hands shake the first time I hold the small, curved scissors. I break a sweat. The child sleeps. At the end, I collect the trimmings. A mound of little white slivers sits on my palm. I keep them by my bedside until my mother-in-law throws them away.

'Hoarding this garbage will make you madder than you are,' she says.

That night, I think of ways of butchering Dilip's mother. A week later, I collect the next batch of nail clippings and wrap them in a handkerchief in my cupboard.

This is madness. I feel it – I inch towards it daily. But it's a necessary madness, without which the species might never propagate.

Weeks pass.

In the day, nothing can be hidden. Not dangers or fears. Not the smell of putrefying milk, or the green veins below my eyes. I can see my hair thinning in the early light. Specks of dandruff gather along my parting. Entire days pass before I can wash my face. I run my tongue across my teeth and feel the film.

A loud crashing sound rouses me one morning.

The baby has fallen off the bed. She is crying bloody murder.

Dilip rushes in. He finds me and the child both in tears. 'I dropped her, she fell down,' I say.

He nods. His eyes move over the floor to find the guilty tile. 'I don't know if I can do this,' I hear myself say. I am rocking back and forth. I wipe my nose with the baby's sleeve, clutching her close.

'I don't know if I want to do this,' I think to myself. I realize from Dilip's face that I have said this out loud.

'Okay, okay. Shh-shh.' My mother-in-law is in the room. I didn't see her enter. She takes the child into her solid arms. The baby settles into a roll of fat.

'You know,' my mother-in-law says, 'I didn't have a maid when I was your age, and I had to do everything by myself in the whole house. All alone, in the US. Cutting the vegetables, cooking all the food, doing the washing – you know babies give a lot of washing.

And don't forget, I have a demanding husband. Hot food on the table, three times a day. But I managed, no? Look at Dilip, he's still alive, isn't he? I didn't go here and there and let him fall off the bed. And I had an easy situation. Only two. What about people with six children? Can you imagine?'

She continues talking about how difficult things were. These tales have been passed down from mothers to daughters since women had mouths and stories could be told. They contain some moral message, some rites of passage. But they also transfer that feeling all mothers know before their time is done. Guilt.

My mother-in-law tries to control what I eat. This makes me hate her more. She adds ghee to my rice and gives me tinctures to 'remove the gas' from my milk. I feel they make me gassier. I pass wind through the night. Dilip pretends not to notice.

I imagine this is a ruse she has concocted to take my husband and child away from me. I want her gone, until one morning I find the baby's white nappy stained blood red. I scream, rousing the household.

'You ate beetroot last night, didn't you? I told you not to,' my mother-in-law says. 'What do you expect poor baby to do?'

Afterwards, I eat only what my mother-in-law puts on my plate. Every morning, I swallow a thick paste of fenugreek seeds with my breakfast. My perspiration grows more pungent and I am forced to wash my armpits in the sink throughout the day.

Purvi arrives on some days, unannounced, bringing sweets and gifts. She holds the baby until she gets bored, then spreads herself out on the bed. Purvi complains of exhaustion, of a kind of homesickness, though she knows she is at home.

My mother-in-law shakes her head. 'Your husband's home will never be the same as your mother's home.'

The baby turns her head away from my breast to look at Purvi.

She smiles, showing her toothless gums.

'She likes you,' I say. 'You should have one soon.'

'Maybe. For now, this one is enough for both of us.'

Purvi turns on to her side and gives in to the natural slump of her body, curving her back until her chest disappears. Sometimes she crosses her bony legs around themselves twice. Dilip doesn't like it. He finds it creepy. I wonder if Purvi's husband knows about her double-jointed thumbs, or the way she can crack her knees after sitting for too long.

'She looks like you,' Purvi says.

I look down at the baby. Milky white spit drips from the side of her mouth. It pools around her neck, wetting the collar of her undershirt. I look back at my friend and know what she's thinking. Nothing is quite the same. The baby reaches once more for my breast. Purvi watches. I feel exposed. Suddenly I don't like having Purvi here, don't want her in the house. She reminds me of too many things we have done together. I don't want her around my daughter.

At night, we eat in silence until cries sound from my bedroom.

The baby is awake, trying to escape the swaddle I have imprisoned her in. My food is half eaten. I lift her with my clean hand. The other is stained, wet with spit. This act of juggling seems normal now.

'Shall I take her for some time?' my mother-in-law says. I am about to nod, but my mother stands up.

'Let me hold baby Antara,' she says.

'No, Ma,' I say. 'You have your food. I am not hungry.'

In the room, my stomach rumbles, but I ignore it and bring out my breast. The baby suckles, her throat moving up and down. Food has already dried on my fingers. They are pruned and yellowed.

When I look at the window, I can almost feel myself going out of it, drifting, smelling the air beyond this still room, just beyond the wall, jumping down, faltering a little, maybe even falling the rest of the way, brushing off the dirt and dead insects from my palms and knees and running to the end of the lane to find a rickshaw-wallah smoking a bidi who might be willing to take me as far as Purvi's house for half the rate.

Or not.

Why go to Purvi's?

I can go anywhere, there's nothing stopping me. Maybe back to the train station late at night, and convince a chai-wallah to give me a cup for half the going rate, maybe something free for a girl alone, and there I can wait. There, I can be cleansed of all this. Of the dirty hands, the same food every day, my mother who thinks I am my daughter, my mother-in-law who is slowly taking over this house. Even Dilip. I cannot remember the last time we had a real conversation.

I open the window and the warm air comes in, touching my face. It feels wet, the air. I wish it would stop. I wish it would still again.

The baby's head is covered in dark hair. A faint, dark fuzz covers her shoulders. She sucks her lips in her sleep.

The window is open, and a small body can fall quickly, soundlessly. By morning, it can be gone. Isn't that why the window is still open? And if not now, if not quietly in the dark of night, then when?

I should close the window. The baby will get sick. The air inside is thick and still, but outside the dampness blows back and forth. This is not the kind of night for a baby or a mother. This night is for everyone else.

The window is still open. Again, she begins to cry. I wish she would stop. I have heard babies' cries before, but hers are worse. She is louder, so insistent. I can never seem to make her stop. My mother-in-law manages. I should have given the baby to her – I should give the baby to her. Maybe she can take the baby back to the States, raise her in the same way she raised Dilip. Dilip can go too. I can stay here alone, with Ma, with Nani. I can stay here alone and have some quiet.

What does a dead child look like? Not so different from a doll. Kali Mata would know the answer. She had seen her child alive and then dead.

The baby is crying. My arms tighten at the sound. My hands follow. She wails and I look out the window again. Patting the child's back with heavy hands, I look down at the long pipes that drain into the ground, at the tops of balconies, at the hanging clothes and silent birds. The watchman is down below, concealed in the shadows, sleeping on duty.

It must be quiet down there. Not too far, but so much quieter.

In the morning, my mother-in-law opens the door without knocking and gasps.

The baby sleeps on a pile of blankets on the floor. The bed is stripped down to nothing but a mattress. I am sitting at the edge of the bed, still looking out the window.

I rub my face. I can feel the red spreading across my eyeballs. 'What happened?' she asks. Smudged spectacles cut across her eyes, and her pupils dart up and down like two fish bobbing in water. She has seen her son sleeping on the sofa, kicked out of his own bedroom, denied access to his California King. She is angry, disapproving of how I have managed sleeping conditions for both of her babies last night.

'She couldn't sleep on the bed. She was happier on the floor.'

'Have you slept at all?'

'No, not really. I needed to think.'

'About what?'

'Names. I've been thinking about names for her.'

She comes to stand closer to the bed. I am a little less disgusting to her for a moment. Her mouth is almost trembling.

'I've decided that you should choose. You and Dilip.'

Her entire face opens up. She cannot contain her happiness. 'Do you mean that?'

'Why would I say it if I didn't mean it?'

'I mean,' she says, recovering, 'is that what you really want?'

'Of course.' The window is closed now. I don't know when I finally

209

resolved to do it. The light makes pastel streaks in the scratched glass. Do I deserve to name her after last night?

My mother has a beautiful name. Tara. It means star, another name for the goddess Durga. Like Kali Mata.

She named me Antara, intimacy, not because she loved the name but because she hated herself. She wanted her child's life to be as different from hers as it could be. Antara was really Un-Tara – Antara would be unlike her mother. But in the process of separating us, we were pitted against each other.

Maybe we would have been better off if I had never been designated as her undoing. How do I stop myself from making the same mistake? How do I protect this little girl from the same burden? Maybe that's impossible. Maybe this is all wishful thinking.

The baby is finally asleep. She exhales deeply, heavily. Air thrusts in and out of her lungs, expanding her abdomen. I put my hand near her nose. For a moment, my daughter is breathing fire, and I decide to call her Kali when no one is around.

If feeding is a form of love, eating is a kind of submission. Meals are conversations, and what we don't say is left over in the food. In scientific studies, mice on a calorie-restricted diet begin to eat each other.

In laboratory settings, rats enclosed with a square foot of flame-retardant fabric drop dead in a week.

There are some other variables to consider, but the message is clear. I throw open the windows and fill the tables with food.

Dilip and I are never alone. We don't speak much, and conjugal rights are a thing of the past. We just want to stay afloat.

On the nights that I sleep, I dream so vividly that the mornings are as dry as cotton balls, a hazy waking moment with a plangent drone coming from the mosque at the end of the road.

My mother-in-law is fulsome, calling me beautiful, her own precious angel. She must have read up that the way to win a girl over, the girl who has stolen your son, is to make her believe that she has surpassed him in your heart. Kill her with kindness.

I dream about killing them all sometimes. Not me, but some version of me, a masculine me, a muscular me. Their bodies are left to rot. They bleed different colours, and Anikka is happy that they are dead and knows they're more beautiful this way. We burn them together and are untouched by soot and flint.

Anikka. They named my daughter Anikka. It's a sound that mating birds make. Her name is unfinished, new age, pointless. When I asked them what the name means, they could not tell me, but my mother-in-law said people could call her Annie for short when she goes to study abroad. My grandmother says it's a name for the goddess Durga, which appeases me, but I am angry again when I search for the name and the first entry that appears is the biography of an American porn star.

Overwhelmed by my questions, Dilip asks, 'If you didn't want me to choose, why did you give over your power?'

All I know is that a certain kind of madness comes over you when you are locked within walls with so many women. A certain madness erects itself when the way you tell the time of day is by the water levels in a vase of flowers.

I hug Anikka to me tightly every day and synchronize the activity to a timer so she will remember the abundance of love and physical affection she received as a child. Some imprint of the sensation, being compressed, the restriction of blood flow, the warmth of another body, should stay with her. Babies like to be straitjacketed, to feel cloistered – anything that reminds them of the womb. After a day of this, the baby doesn't like the attention. She makes it known. She doesn't understand how lucky she is, and she protests.

I begin to question whether she is lucky – and whether I am mistaken. Doesn't she want to be swaddled by my body? Is the sensation of receiving a kiss less pleasurable than that of giving it? I have heard that babies find adults terrifying and ugly, that our textured skin and large bodies are repulsive to them. I can almost remember having these feelings as a child – that even the most beautiful adult was dirty and wretched. Maybe, later in life, she will flee this home. Maybe she will run from me. Maybe our mothers always create a lack in us, and our children continue to fulfil the prophecy.

*

My mother watches me and I cannot recognize the expression in her eyes. Sometimes I think she is aware of what is going on, that she is trying to communicate something to me. She hasn't mentioned anything to Dilip, has said nothing about my relationship with Reza.

Dilip still believes that the photo is something I found but never truly owned, something that is absurd and unrelated to me. So much of the art he has seen is absurd, why should he look for meaning in any of it? He would never imagine that this man who was my mother's lover would subsequently become mine.

He would never imagine that I had kept this a secret from everyone. To Dilip, Reza is a name that was only ever uttered by Ma – the hallucinations of a demented woman, whose past of promiscuity was well known.

I feed Ma sugar daily, and she consumes it like an addict. She becomes more like another sofa every day. No one notices this is the reason – no one makes the connection. They don't believe in science unless it comes from the mouth of a doctor and in the form of a tablet. They don't go to the studies, to the source. Rats. Rats and mice are the key to understanding who we are as humans. What happens to a rat in ten days may happen to us in ten months or ten years, but it will happen.

The people I live with don't think about diet, about insulin, gut bacteria, the whole solar system that is contained in a single molecule of our bodies. Dilip and his mother believe that I am looking after my mother, indulging her because she is unwell, and sweets and rich cakes will make her feel good.

The difference between murder and manslaughter is intention. Or is it premeditation? But intent can only be proven if you inhabit the brain of another. Motive would also be difficult to discern. Who would argue with the fact that my mother is my only true parent, and as a loving daughter I want to give her pleasure while I still can?

It is clear to me that my mother is a child – emotionally, she has never progressed past being a teenager. She is still at the mercy of hormones. She still thinks in terms of freedom and passion.

And love.

She is obsessed with love, and the idea of the love she had with Reza. Did he even love her? Did he ever say it to her?

He left her one day without a thought about how she would feel. Is that the kind of man she should be pining for well into her fifties? Doesn't she have anything better to do than threaten her only offspring because of a man who had no lasting interest in either of them?

Sometimes, when we are too many in the house, I wish she would die, at least for a little while, and then come back in any form I saw fit. Maybe a dog who would follow me around.

Even as these thoughts enter my head, I can't believe I am thinking them. I love her, my mother. I love her to death. I don't know where I would be without her. I don't know who I would be. If she would only stop being such a terrible cunt, I would get her back on track.

And this won't actually kill her, it is calming her down. Life without sugar makes her sharp and erratic and, in truth, unhappy – like she was when she came into my room and went through my things.

At least I don't think this can kill her.

I don't want her to die. Sometimes I think that, when she goes, I will just float away. Sometimes in the chaos, I forget that she is there. We all forget. We forget to speak to her or acknowledge her presence.

The rest watch me give her a blue pill at the appropriate time, with no grasp of how useless it is. I leave the prescription out as proof of my good care. Can it really be so simple – to fill her with biscuits and bread every day and poison her in plain sight? Sometimes I think I am doing this just to see if I can get away with it.

I begin administering a sleeping pill her doctor suggests to help with the insomnia. This seems to work for a few days, until she begins to wake up in the middle of the night, groggy and doddering, to use the toilet. I tell the doctor this worries me. What if she falls? What if she breaks her hip while the rest of us are sleeping? He advises me to try an increased dose and see how she does with it. I give Ma two at bedtime, and she sleeps through the night, sometimes well into the following day.

My father calls. My mother-in-law answers and doesn't know who it is. She hangs up on him the first time. He calls back and clarifies his relationship to me. My mother-in-law is sheepish when she tells me who is on the phone. My father clears his throat when I say hello. I am pleased that they are both embarrassed, but try not to show it.

My father says he has heard about a baby and would like to meet her.

I pause at his choice of words before telling him that I have not been taking her out of the house much, only for vaccines and when I have to take Ma to the doctor. He says that's no problem, he would be happy to come and see us.

'How is your mother keeping?' he asks.

'Not well.'

He is silent, and I imagine he is nodding. 'Well, I should come to see her too.'

I tell Ma that my father will come over the weekend to see us.

Dilip smiles at this news. 'I'm looking forward to meeting him.'

My mother nods, and looks at my mother-in-law. 'My husband,' she says. 'My husband and his mother are very difficult. Mothers-in-law are always trouble. Don't get married if you can avoid it.'

'He isn't your husband any more. And his mother is dead.'

She nods, seems to think over this information, before her attention returns to her plate.

'You don't seem to be taking an interest in helping her,' Dilip says. We are in our bedroom. I am snapping the removable fabric of my new bra. My breast looks like it is in a harness. Anikka nuzzles it, smelling for milk, before she finds the nipple.

I censor my thoughts around Dilip now. How do I explain that we are all refugees in this place, constantly redrawing the borders?

Nothing is certain. Yesterday, when I called Nani to speak with her about hiring a nurse, she burst into tears. 'I don't want to know,' was her only response. She repeated this phrase again and again. The natural order has been upended. Nani is an old woman now, she is supposed to grow old before her daughter. But Ma is the one who is senile. We lose her a little bit every day.

I feel a touch of guilt when I think about this, but I parcel it for now. Tension suppresses my milk flow.

The next morning, Dilip brings my mother a ballpoint pen and a notebook. I watch him settling her at the dining table.

'Write it down,' he says.

'What?' She looks up at him.

'Whatever it is.' His voice is kind and patient. 'If it's written down, you will always have it with you.'

She takes the pen and looks at it, then stares down at the yellow pages lined with dark blue. Running her fingers over the first page, she flips through the pad and giggles to herself, amazed by how many pages there are.

'Write about your first day at school. Can you remember that?'

Ma wobbles her head back and forth and looks at him with a wide smile. He pats her arm.

'What are you doing?' I ask when he comes to sit next to me on the sofa.

'We should be making her remember. She needs rehearsal.'

'I have been doing that. There were stories from the past all over her apartment and it didn't help at all.'

'We don't need to exercise your memory, Antara. We need to exercise hers.' His voice has risen louder than I have ever heard it. My arms contract. The baby cries.

'You used to make me feel so bad,' Ma says.

'Me?'

'Yes. At the ashram. You would talk about your father all the time.

You used to cry for him day and night, not eat, not drink. Papa, Papa, Papa. He was the only one you wanted. Even when you were born. You said Papa much before Ma. You waited for him to come from the office like a little dog.'

I feel my forehead crinkling. Her eyes are bright and she seems sure. 'I don't remember doing that.'

'Yes,' she says. She nods wildly and laughs. 'You used to make me feel like shit.'

My father hugs me by putting his arm around my shoulder and bumping the side of my body against the side of his. He takes the baby from my arms without asking, without washing the outside world off his hands. His knuckles are dark and hairy against her pale face. The mirrors in our living room show me the back of my father's head. He has combed the thin hairs down to cover their scarcity. The new wife stands back, watching, hugging her son with one arm. She has a smile on her face that is worn too tightly.

My mother-in-law offers the new wife a cup of tea. They fall into conversation, and I wonder if they are both grateful for the appearance of another, possibly less liked, outsider. I shake my head a little to lift out of my stupor and give the maids orders to bring some food. My brain is still full of cotton wool since the birth.

My mother-in-law dashes around efficiently. She has become lady of the house.

She has suggested on multiple occasions that Dilip start applying for positions in America. 'Somewhere closer to home,' she says. They bring this topic up when they think I am sleeping or out of hearing range. They do not realize that I have the ears of an owl now, that my aural reach can pick up the movement of my daughter's breath across the city. This is what it means to be a mother. My claws are ready. I am always hunting.

I ease into the sofa while everyone else still stands. My buttocks spread against the leather cushion. I glimpse myself in the mirror before looking away. The swelling on my jowls is still visible. The skin is dark around my neck. Stripes of scalp show through my thinning hair.

My father's son sits down across from me. We smile at each other without showing teeth. In the mirror, I see that his hair is long and curly and he has tied it into a ponytail. It reminds me of what mine used to be.

'Are you still painting?' he asks.

I don't correct him. 'I've stopped for the moment.'

The new wife laughs and she melts down beside her son. Together, they fit on a single chair. 'With children, there is less time for hobbies.' Her gums recede further as her smile expands. I don't correct her either. She touches her son's hair, as though she knew I was looking at it. 'Children today have their own style,' she says.

Dilip pours my father a peg of eighteen-year-old Scotch he brought back from a work trip. My father gives Anikka back to me and puts his nose into the glass. Dilip is jovial. Father is at ease.

My mother-in-law brings a tray of tea out of the kitchen and the air takes on the smell of hot oil. Samosas and pakoras sizzle inside.

The doorbell rings and we all jump. The baby squirms against me, rubs her face on my cotton T-shirt. She can smell the milk that has dried there, her own vomit too, the smells that even laundry detergent cannot wash away. I always smell like milk now. Like milk, shit and vomit. I can never shower it off.

Nani enters but lingers by the door. She looks at everyone's feet and stoops to remove her shoes. They have buckles at the back and she bends down to undo them, her weight tilting to one side and the other, her balance feeble. She reaches out for Dilip to take her hand while she struggles with the last strap.

'Oh, Nani,' Dilip says belatedly. 'That's okay, you don't have to take them off.'

She pats his face, then looks at my father, her gaze grazing below his ankles before she turns away. There is something regal in her disdain of my father's feet, still in shoes. She nods to my half-brother and the new wife, and brings her hands up in greeting to my mother-in-law. On me and Anikka, she releases the full force of her affection and smiles. As she comes towards me, I realize I look more like her than I do Ma. My ankles and wrists have expanded and haven't gone back to what they were before. I am an old woman before my time.

Fried food is placed on the table. Plates and napkins are passed around. Dollops of chutney – green, garlic, coconut, tamarind – colour the rim of everyone's dish.

Nani opens a box of sweets she has brought from the store. She helps herself to a taste before offering it around. Her eyes roll back in ghee-filled glee. She passes the box to my mother-in-law.

There are too many people in the room. I tell Ila to open the windows.

'Good to meet you,' my mother-in-law says to my father. She holds the box out to him and he breaks a trapezoid sweet with one hand. 'We didn't know Antara had a father at first, so we are happy to know you.'

The room is silent. Dilip avoids my eyes and his mother's. The new wife looks perplexed for a moment but recovers when the box is offered to her. She takes the rest of the triangle her husband mutilated and offers it to her son. He has a bite of pakora in his mouth and turns his face away. She holds her hand there, waiting for him to accept the taste of sweet.

Everyone is smiling and quiet. The baby makes a sound and the adults all sigh and laugh and look at me, relieved that she has woken up. They begin talking softly among themselves, Dilip and my father to my mother-in-law. The new wife to her son.

The gathering is mostly a success. They all are enjoying themselves. Or they are pretending to. They all have reasons to pretend. The new wife and her son are pretending for my father. My father is pretending for himself, and perhaps even for Anikka and me. Dilip has the same interests, and his mother pretends for him. Nani will not pretend. She has left the room, perhaps to check on her daughter. She is not interested in being polite to anyone.

I have not had to pretend, at least not yet. I am still, almost invisible in the room. The only reason they look at me is to glance at the baby.

I feel like I am not here.

Dilip says something and my father chuckles, his shoulders moving up and down. I wonder how long they can continue this act. How long will it take for them to grow tired, for the masks to fall away so the true essence of their feelings can show through? Though if they repeat it long enough, if the act is internalized – would it be an act any more? Can a performance of pleasure, even love, turn into a true experience if one becomes fluent enough in it? When does the performance become reality?

The doorbell rings again. We are not expecting anyone else. My mouth drops open a little as Purvi and her husband walk in. He is carrying a bag of toys. From the few I can see peeking out of the bag, they are too big, too dangerous for Anikka.

Purvi's husband stops when he sees my father and they embrace in a hug. They know each other from the Club, my father says. Purvi sits down next to my father's new wife. They are on the same bridge team, Purvi explains.

Dilip comes to where I am on the sofa. He takes Anikka out of my arms.

'They wanted to come and see the baby,' Dilip says, reading my expression.

Nani's voice calls our attention. She has Ma on her arm and is walking her into the room. Nani smiles widely at Ma, who looks around at the gathering. The sight is dissonant. Who is the elderly mother and who is the middle-aged daughter?

Tears sting my eyes and, like a sneeze, I have to turn away to hold them back. How have we reached this place?

Through trays of Mazorin biscuits.

Purvi runs forward to embrace my mother. Ma lifts her hands and runs them down Purvi's back, stopping at the protrusion above the waist of her jeans.

Purvi's husband leans towards Dilip. 'The reason that a child wants to touch their ass and balls all day is because of parasites, did you know that? Parasites are what really control the brain.'

Dilip bounces the baby and looks at me, before turning towards my mother.

'How are you feeling today, Mom?' he asks her. 'Did you do your journal?'

Ma smiles vaguely and allows herself to be seated in a chair next to the new wife and her son. She nods at them before reaching into the box of sweets.

The arrival of Purvi and her husband, and maybe even my mother, has somehow broken the ice. A bisexual, a power-monger and a demented lady walk into a bar. We are eleven people in the room, but the reflections make us almost seventy – some of the group are hidden behind furniture, like my father's son, who is only another head on his mother's body. My little Anikka shouldn't count at all, she is nothing more than a bundle of white cotton in her father's arms. But I count her. My eyes follow her as she's passed around the room. There are too many bodies. The space feels compressed. I turn to look at the windows. They're open but the air feels warm. I'm having trouble breathing. My forehead feels heavy. The levels of carbon dioxide must be rising. My father laughs and coughs at something my mother-in-law tells him. He is breathing greedily, sucking up the air. I wish he had washed his hands before touching Anikka. Purvi's nostrils are flared as she bends forward to greet Nani. I watch her pull the remaining oxygen into those great big cavities.

Dilip pours more whisky for the men, and asks the women if they would like some wine. They are coy at first, shrinking from the question, looking to the others in the room.

'I don't mind,' Nani says, breaking the silence. The others smile and nod at her.

'I don't mind giving Aunty company,' my mother-in-law says. A number of long-stemmed wine glasses are brought from the kitchen. Dilip begins to screw the top off a bottle of red when my grandmother complains she only likes white. Offering to open one of each, he receives shy smiles from his mother and the new wife.

Everyone has a drink in their hand except my mother and me. Even the son takes a sip from my father's glass. I have barely said a word to my father since he has arrived. He holds his glass of Scotch close to my child and is emphatic about what Purvi's husband is sharing.

'The next time you are in China, let me know,' my father says, scratching the top of his head. 'My good friend Kaushal is settled there with his family.'

'Your good friend Kaushal is a creep,' I say.

The room goes silent so quickly that I feel a funnelling in my ears. The new wife's hand trembles as she taps her son's back.

My father looks at me and blinks. The curve of his mouth straightens into a line. His lips disappear. 'What is that?' he says.

I sit back against the sofa. I don't know what else to say. I didn't have anything planned.

The silence carries on a little longer. I begin to count the seconds. By the time I get to seven, my mother-in-law calls out to Ila to bring more coconut chutney into the room.

We all turn to look at her and everyone begins speaking at the same time. Only Dilip remains still and quiet. He is frowning as he moves Anikka into his other arm. My mother is also silent. She looks at me. I see the sugary glaze on her eyeballs.

How can they all sit here, eating and drinking, when I just made this announcement? I jump to my feet, feel an ache in my knees and move back towards the window.

Maybe they think I am unstable, like my mother. That I can't be trusted.

Why did I say it? What was I expecting? Some relief? Who in this room could give that to me? I look through the window, down at the ground, and wonder at the distance. I had considered throwing Anikka down there. The thought is repulsive to me now. Perhaps I should have done it to myself.

I turn back and see the reflections of my guests. I notice their profiles. It's something I haven't studied before. Nani has a small hook in her nose that Ma and I do not. My father and Purvi's husband have remarkably similar faces from this angle.

Ma's eyes move around the room from time to time but quickly return to the floor. I wonder if she can take in all that she is seeing in front of her. The conversations must be moving too fast. Does she get the tone that people are speaking in? Can she catch all the words?

I wonder if she recognizes my father. She hasn't said a word to him. Does she know that woolly woman is his wife, and that the boy is their three-ply son? I want to tell her, but there is no point.

I stand beside my mother's chair and put my hand on her shoulder. She starts a little, but doesn't look back at me. Maybe she doesn't really feel it because she doesn't know where she is. Or perhaps she knows it's me, knows just from the weight of my hand.

'Antara,' Ma says.

'Yes, Ma,' I reply.

'Antara.'

'Yes, I'm here.' I bend down beside her chair.

'Antara.' She puts her hand up and points at Dilip. 'I want Antara.'

Dilip smiles at her. 'Mom, this is Anikka. Antara is next to you.'

'Antara.' She stands up and moves across the room. Purvi's husband and my father stand back. Ma claps and smiles. She looks up at Dilip for a moment, before returning her gaze to the baby.

Purvi looks at me and touches her chest. So sweet, she mouths to me.

'Give me Antara,' Ma says. Dilip gives her the baby and hovers close by. Ma brings the bundle to her face and kisses her. She looks at my father and smiles. 'Antara,' she repeats. 'This is my baby.'

Father smiles and nods at her. 'Yes, very good,' he says. 'You have a beautiful baby.'

My mother-in-law comes out of the kitchen. In her hand is a bottle. She tests the liquid on the sensitive part of her wrist. 'Should I feed Antara now?' she asks. She turns to wink at me.

Mother-in-law reaches out to take Anikka from Ma, and Ma screams, clutching the baby to her chest. 'No, it's my baby. Antara is my baby.'

My mother-in-law puts her hands up, still holding the bottle. Nani rushes to one side of Ma and kisses her forehead. Ma allows herself to be consoled. She leans against Dilip.

'Antara is our baby,' Ma says. She looks up at Dilip and smiles. 'My husband and my baby.'

The new wife puts her hand to her mouth. She is standing behind her husband, holding her son's hand. Fascination and disgust mingle in her eyes.

Anikka begins to struggle. She cries a little bit and Ma rocks her.

'Okay, Tara,' my mother-in-law says. 'Why don't you feed Antara?'

Ma takes the bottle and places it against Anikka's lips. The baby starts sucking and immediately calms down. Ma rests against Dilip and smiles at Nani by her side. I try to imagine where she is in her mind, where she imagines this place is. Is this a figment of her imagination? Or is it a happy memory from the past she wants to relive?

She rubs her face into Dilip's shoulder. He smiles, not seeming to mind. 'Do you love Antara?' she asks.

Dilip laughs. 'Yes. I love Antara.'

Ma smiles and looks down at the baby. 'And me?' she asks. 'Do you love me?'

Dilip nods again. 'Yes,' he says. 'Yes, I love you.' My mother-in-law giggles. 'We all love you.'

They are crowding around her, smiling at Ma and Anikka, on one side of the room. I see my mother swaying against Dilip.

'Okay,' I interrupt. 'Okay, Ma. I'm Antara, and that is Anikka —'

Purvi stops me with her hand. 'Enough now. She doesn't remember, poor thing.' She rushes over to my mother. 'Tara, should we all sing a song to Antara?'

Purvi starts clapping and singing the words of a song. I smile, before realizing I don't know the words. The tune seems familiar but I cannot place where I have heard it before. They continue on to a second verse, and I realize the language isn't one I recognize. It isn't Marathi, that's for sure. Maybe Gujarati. But how would Nani know it so well? A Bengali tune? Something by Tagore? Everyone is singing along. Ma remembers the words. My eyes stop on Dilip and I sink to the floor. He is singing and clapping.

My husband, who can barely speak Hindi, is singing the lullaby.

The verses continue, they seem endless. Songs, when they are unfamiliar, seem unnecessarily lengthy. It finishes abruptly and everyone claps. They look at Ma and Anikka. Their backs are to me, and I can barely find my daughter between them any more.

I come to my feet and see Ma is holding Dilip in an embrace. Anikka is in her other arm. Purvi and the new wife have joined hands.

Once again I feel invisible, until I notice Ma looking at me.

Her eyes are wide and she is not blinking.

The room is warm, and I reach for my neckline. Ma has not taken her arms away from my husband or my child. She watches me, continues to watch me. Her eyes are clear and sharp.

We both watch each other. Ma is quiet. I am quiet.

Everyone laughs and smiles. They still hum the tune of the song I do not know, still playing along with the charade. They let her do what she wants because she is sick.

Unless she is not sick at all.

Is she trying to write a story without me? Is she trying to erase me? Even as I think this, I feel myself evaporating.

The doctor never found anything. No plaque, no formations.

They begin the song again, still gathered around my mother and Dilip. Anikka looks like nothing more than wrapped laundry in her arms. The song is maddening, the language is strange. They repeat it twice and begin a third round. No one turns to look at me, to even acknowledge I am there. Are they avoiding eye contact with me so as not to upset my mother? They don't want to break the spell.

Everyone cheers for Tara and little baby Antara. They repeat the song once more. How many times must a performance be repeated before it becomes reality? If a falsehood is enacted enough, does it begin to sound factual? Is a pathway created for lies to become true in the brain?

I stand up and shout at them to stop.

No one can hear me, their voices together are too loud. I am drowned out. Or is my voice sticking to the insides of my throat? I feel the interior of my larynx when I speak, as rough as Velcro.

No one is looking at me any more, not even Ma, and the air in the room has been replaced with something noxious. This must be what drowning feels like. I cough and begin to retch. No one notices.

I don't want to die. Not here. Not with this song filling the air. I can't breathe and I have to get out. I must get out.

On the other side of the door, I am gasping. Bent forward, I let my head hang by my knees. The sciatica that comes and goes since Anikka was born climbs up my leg. I cover my mouth with my hand to muffle a low scream and the voice that comes out is someone else's. I touch my face. The sudden urge to look at my reflection, to make sure it's still there, is overwhelming.

I push the call button for the lift furiously. The tension leaves my body as the doors slide open. The inside of this moving cage feels like home in a way I never noticed before and I see myself in every surface — the walls, the ceiling, the floor. The lift goes down gently. I notice the front of my T-shirt is wet, and think of my breast pump and my child, contemplating how much of Anikka's sustenance is being wasted. My little baby. My little Kali. The only person in the world.

I take a single cigarette from the paanwala beyond the building gate. He stares at the patches around my breasts but says nothing. I mumble that I will pay him later and he nods.

The pavement looks like ancient ruins, and I realize I am shoeless only when I step on wet ground. The urine of beast or man, I'm sure. A girl in shorts is giggling into her mobile phone. Her feet move slowly, in rhythm with her words, and she stops in response to what she hears, some delightful secret to make her chuckle. She runs her hand against the concrete wall, spreading her fingers out, making contact with the rough surface fearlessly. I think I recognize her from the building, but she's older than I remember, at least fourteen, almost a woman, loitering without direction, untroubled in her own skin. She smiles when she sees me watching her, opening her mouth wide, and I look away, look down at my clothes and turn belatedly to hide my mess. I walk down the street, barefoot and quickly, unsure of where I am going yet, but I continue to think of her, of what it takes to preserve that smile.

I wonder if they have noticed I am gone yet. The new wife and mother-in-law must be relieved that the worst inconvenience of their lives has vanished. Maybe they will take the opportunity to flee while they can, my mother-in-law with Dilip and Annika, and the new wife with her husband and son. If I turn back now, will they be gone by the time I return? I imagine them laughing and dancing ecstatically around the room, calling to their secret gods, undressing and bathing in the wine, all together, in some orgiastic ritual they have been waiting to perform once I am gone. Fear and longing mingle in me. I feel a slicing pain in the sole of my foot, but I don't stop walking.

The street is raucous. I look around and I don't know where I am. Has the city transformed so much since my internment? Was this the plan all along, to come together and watch me dissolve into nothing? Maybe this is the point of a pregnancy, of motherhood itself. A child to undo the woman who bears it, to pull her safely apart.

What came before now? I can't recollect the shape of my life. But I see the future of it. There are hill stations I want to visit, places I want to sleep – treetops, woodsheds, charpoys in forgotten farmlands. There are men I want to fuck. I know there were other uses for my body once, when my stomach was unmarked, my nipples uncracked.

And there is the endless stack of Reza Pine's face alight, finishing the work my mother started, and a blank sheet of paper where I will immortalize myself instead of him.

My legs seem to move of their own accord, taking me further and further away. I collide with other bodies without seeing them. Someone calls to me and I move faster, stumbling a little and running across the street. Panting, I hear the call again. Tara.

My own mother. The more deranged she becomes, the greater her clarity of purpose, like a picture with minimum aperture – the background dims as the singularity of the focus intensifies. Dilip didn't stop her, and why would he? If he can love me, he can love her. We are interchangeable, after all.

I will never be free of her. She's in my marrow and I'll never be immune. What would Purvi's husband say about a parasite so advanced that it makes a host of its own offspring? There is something resourceful in consuming what clings to you.

From above, my feet look fine but beneath I know they are battered. The pavement is wet again, inexplicably. I look around and the man who sold me the cigarette is watching me. Beyond him, the girl in shorts leans against the compound wall, looking intently at the screen of her phone.

I am outside my building.

I never left this place.

The bright day blinds me as I enter the darkened hallway. My legs are heavy. I push the button for the lift and go inside. In the mirror, I see the milk on my clothes has dried and yellowed.

Ma is there in my face. I nod and she nods back.

Standing at the door of the flat, I can still hear their voices inside. I ring the bell twice and lean against the wall, waiting to be let back in.

ACKNOWLEDGEMENTS

Everyone who supported earlier drafts of this book at Tibor Jones and the University of East Anglia, especially Neel Mukherjee, Martin Pick and Andrew Cowan. Madelyn Kent, because sometimes it's obvious, and sometimes it's elusive. Kanishka Gupta, for going beyond the call of duty. Rahul Soni, for the wonderful work he did on the Indian edition. Udayan Mitra and everyone at HarperCollins India.

Hermione Thompson, who surpasses her reputation for brilliance and kindness. Simon Prosser and the entire team at Hamish Hamilton for believing in this story. Chloe Davies for the tremendous work she did to promote the novel.

Tracy Carns, Maya Bradford, Kim Lew, Mamie VanLangen, Jessica Wiener, Andrew Gibeley and everyone at Overlook.

Maria Cardona Serra, for her tireless support every step of the way. Anna Soler-Pont and the whole team at Pontas.

My friends and family for their encouragement. Neha Samtani, Sharlene Teo, Kate Gwynne and Manali Doshi in particular.

Nani, for her grace.

Bodhi and Lila, for changing everything.

My husband, for knowing my voice on any page.

My parents, for all that I am.